THEN HE WAS GONE

THEN HE WAS GONE

A NOVEL

ISABEL BOOTH

NEW YORK

Published in the United States by Crooked Lane Books, an imprint of The Quick Brown Fox & Company LLC.

Library of Congress Catalog-in-Publication data available upon request.

ISBN (hardcover): 979-8-89242-468-4
ISBN (paperback): 979-8-89242-469-1
ISBN (ebook): 979-8-89242-470-7

Cover design by Danna Steele

Printed in the United States.

www.crookedlanebooks.com

Crooked Lane Books
34 West 27th St., 10th Floor
New York, NY 10001

First Edition: February 2026

The authorized representative in the EU for product safety and compliance is eucomply OÜPärnu mnt 139b-14, 11317 Tallinn, Estonia, hello@eucompliancepartner.com, +33757690241

10 9 8 7 6 5 4 3 2 1

For Zach and Gabe
And for David, always

C H A P T E R

1

Nick

I HAVE A PICTURE of my little brother, Henry, that my dad took that day. He was six years old.

It was the longest hike we took in Rocky Mountain National Park. All the other hikes were warm-ups, my mom said, to get used to the altitude and get our climbing legs. It was still dark when we left our cabin that morning. It was misty and quiet and all I could hear was the wipers on the Jeep flapping back and forth, and I wrote my name across the window with my finger. Henry was half-asleep in the back seat with me. He kept falling over on my side, which was pretty annoying.

There weren't a lot of cars in the parking lot at the trailhead at Glacier Gorge Junction, which is why my mom said we wanted to get there early. We got out and Mom handed out all our stuff. Fanny packs and water bottles for Henry and me. A backpack for my mom and dad with peanut butter sandwiches, bags of trail mix, ponchos, sunscreen, wildlife books. Stuff like that. The first thing we did was we looked at the map at the trailhead. We were hiking to The Loch, then up Timberline Falls to Lake of Glass, then to Sky Pond. About nine miles round trip.

"Are you crazy?" Henry said. "This is reedickallus." That's really how he said it. *Reedickallus.*

Some people would say my parents were crazy to take a six-year-old kid on a hike that long that went that high up. But they don't know that kid. In June he caught his finger in a gate at the Little League field and had to have four stitches. It took three grown-ups to hold him down for a shot to numb the finger. We let Henry and Mom go first, and Henry complained for like a mile. His head hurt, his stomach hurt, his knee hurt, and he couldn't go one more step. I walked up behind him and whispered in his ear.

"You walk like a girl. Let me take the lead."

That made him so mad. He called me penis breath, only he said it so Mom wouldn't hear, and he pushed me when I tried to go around him. He didn't slow down again.

I love the mountains. One time on a hike when we stopped to rest we could see the whole entire valley. The town of Estes Park and Lake Estes looked so tiny so far away, and I said, "This is the best day of my whole entire life."

We took off our hiking boots when we got to the top and ate lunch on the rocks at Sky Pond. Henry took off everything but his shorts, the neon-yellow ones he wore all the time that hung down and showed his belly button. My mom made a crown from shrub branches and set it on his head. He had the best head, kind of a perfect shape, and a buzz cut for the summer. The water was freezing cold but Henry was dancing in and out of it at the edge of the lake. His skinny little arms were in the air and he was shaking his butt and singing. "I . . . just want . . . to . . . fly." Mom and Dad and me watched and laughed, and I finally stood up and we were dancing and singing. "Put your arms around me, baby, put your arms around me, baby. I . . . just want . . . to . . . fly." And there was no place else in the whole entire world that I wanted to be.

We were almost back to the trailhead when it started to rain. The mountains were like that—a storm could blow in anytime. Henry and me ran most of the last mile. Our ponchos were flapping like Superman capes, and we were screaming and laughing because the rain was like ice on our legs. I think my dad yelled something like, "Be careful, the rocks are slippery." I got to the Jeep first. Henry stopped running when he saw me win and called me a cheater. The Jeep was locked, so we crawled under it to get out of the rain.

We were on our backs staring up at the engine and stuff and our teeth were chattering and we had mud and goosebumps all down our legs. Henry rolled over and rested his head on my chest, and we listened to the rain and the thunder like that until Henry raised his leg and let loose a fart.

"Geez, Henry." I pushed him away and he was laughing and trying to hang on to me.

"It smells like rotten peanut butter," he said.

"It's way more disgusting than that."

Henry was into farting. My mom came home in July after two months in trial in Alaska, and on the drive home after we picked her up at the airport, Henry listened to her and my dad talking for like ten seconds before he interrupted.

"If you were on a date with a girl for the first time and you farted, do you think she would ever go out with you again?"

I almost choked. "Mom's been gone for two months, and the first thing you want to talk about is farting on a date?"

My dad laughed, but my mom turned around in her seat, looking serious and like she was really interested in talking about farts.

"I think it would depend on the circumstances, Henry. How well you know the girl, how interested she is in you, whether you handle the situation maturely. You would certainly want to apologize and not give the girl the impression that you engage unthinkingly in such behavior."

Henry thought about that for a minute.

"But what if you farted a lot of times? Not just once? You just kept farting."

"That would suggest to me that you are ill and should bring the evening to a close. If you're not feeling well before a date, even if it's one you've been looking forward to, the better course would be to postpone it. If the girl is worthy of your attention, I'm sure she would understand."

My mom really talked like that. Henry could say the dumbest thing and she would act like it was something we should take seriously.

The fart smell was trapped under the Jeep. I waved my arms, but it was no use.

"I have to poop," Henry said.

"There's a toilet at the end of the parking lot."

"Those things are nasty."

Well, duh. There was no water and no real toilet, just a seat that kind of looked like a toilet. You could hear your pee and poop splash at the bottom, and I told Henry when we used the toilets at other places in the park that it was probably like a fifty- or sixty-foot drop.

Henry scooched on his elbows army style to the back of the Jeep and stuck his head out a little. He motioned to me. *Geez.* I rolled onto my stomach and pushed myself up beside him, saying, "Dammit, dammit" because my knees were scraping on the pavement. All around the parking lot were these tall dark pine trees and they were kind of spooky-looking, all wet and the branches like droopy arms. The toilets were far off at the other end of the lot.

"Where are Mom and Dad?" Henry said.

"I don't know. They'll be here soon."

He scooched forward some more.

"I can't see anything. I think it's nighttime."

"It's kind of late, but I don't think it's night yet. It's just dark from the storm." I reached in my fanny pack. "Here. Take my flashlight."

Henry took the flashlight. Clicked it on, clicked it off. Clicked it on, clicked it off. On and off. On and off. I grabbed for it, but he stuck it under his stomach and held tight with both hands.

"Come with me, Nick."

"No way. You always act like you're so tough. But you won't even go to the bathroom by yourself."

That did it.

He took a big breath, then another one and another one like he was in the Olympics getting ready to do the high jump or something. He crawled out from under the Jeep waving the flashlight around like a sword and screaming, "Ahoy, mates, ahoy." Then he ran off into the rain.

* * *

I waited like forever. Mom and Dad didn't come, and Henry didn't come, and I was starting to get mad and maybe a little scared lying under the Jeep alone. I heard an engine start, then tires scrunching. A truck came toward me from the end of the parking lot where the toilets were, driving slow, and I thought they should turn the headlights on because it's not safe to drive in the dark. And it was kind of creeping me out because I didn't notice any other cars in the parking lot when we were running to the Jeep, and what if this was some kind of *Christine* thing. The truck rolled past me and my heart was beating like crazy and I was afraid the truck was going to stop. Then the driver hit the lights and turned onto the highway.

"Oh, wow."

Me and Henry were playing the license plate game ever since we got to Estes Park. We got Florida, Alabama, South Dakota, and Maine. New York, Michigan, Illinois, Wisconsin, and Tennessee. Lots of Texas and Colorado and I can't remember where else. I was ahead by five. And I couldn't wait for Henry to get back from the toilet so I could tell him. Game on, buddy. Game on. I just got Alaska.

CHAPTER

2

Elizabeth

I WAS NEARLY INSANE by the end of the trial in Anchorage. Two years of traveling back and forth between there and Houston, culminating in eight weeks of fourteen-hour days, mind-numbingly boring testimony from expert after expert detailing construction flaws, project delays, and damages based on the declining price of oil. I missed Nick and Henry terribly, called home every night and wept alone in my hotel room after Henry described his kindergarten graduation and the award he'd gotten for running the most laps in PE over the course of the school year. The jury came back with a fifty-million-dollar verdict in our client's favor, and I could barely sit through the celebration dinner. All I wanted was to be on the first plane home in the morning.

My father built the cabin in Estes Park where we spent our summers on nine acres overlooking Longs Peak and the Front Range. My brother, Sam, and I inherited it when Dad died, but Sam sold his half to me not long after and moved to Oslo with his Norwegian wife.

We flew from Houston to Denver in early August, our vacation cut short because of the trial. We arranged for shuttle service from the airport to Estes Park, the old Jeep and an even older Ford pickup kept at the cabin year-round along with clothes, camping supplies, and almost everything we needed besides groceries. We cheered when we rounded the curve on Highway 36 and looked down into the valley for our first glimpse of the town. Elk grazed on the side of the highway by Safeway and when we rolled down the windows to drink in the pine-scented mountain air, I felt myself starting to relax.

The boys knew the hike to Sky Pond would be long and strenuous, but I didn't give them all the details. They were exhausted when Timberline Falls came into view, and when Nick realized we had to climb the nearly vertical black granite wall to the right of the falls to reach Lake of Glass, he shook his head and said, "No, no, no, no, no." But we made it, and then on to Sky Pond—desolate and magnificent, the wind across the high alpine lake nearly constant but the sun fierce enough to make us drowsy. We ate lunch and the boys danced as if they had conquered the mountains and were on top of the world. I was ecstatic in that moment but didn't feel victorious as I took in the jagged spires and chilling wind. The cliffs that guard Sky Pond are beautiful but menacing, a reminder that it is still untamed wilderness and we were only visitors there.

We stayed longer at Sky Pond than we'd planned, but the hike back was easy, the panoramic views breathtaking. I watched Nick fall in love with the mountains that summer as I had years ago, the aspen leaves trembling with the slightest breeze, purple and yellow wildflowers, whispery ferns, black moss, and cold, clear streams. Nick and Henry walked ahead of us on the way down, fanny packs swaying on their hips, hiking boots clunking on the rocks, bills of their baseball caps pointing backward. They talked constantly. An occasional shriek or giggle floated back to us, but we couldn't hear what they were saying. Nick was ten, a prepubescent pear shape, and seemed twice the size of Henry, whose wiry little legs made his oversized boots almost comical.

"You look better today," Paul said. "Starting to feel human again?"

"Definitely getting there. Every day in the mountains helps."

"Yeah. It was hard on all of us."

It was a familiar refrain.

Paul is a poet. He'd quit his teaching job the year before to write, and in a few days would start his studies for an MFA, hopefully a PhD, in creative writing at the University of Houston. It was an incredible honor, a longtime dream of his to be accepted into the program, and I was thrilled for him. For years he had endured the thinly disguised condescension of my male law partners and their feigned interest in a high school English teacher and then stay-at-home dad with poems published in magazines they'd never heard of. But that was about to change, the prestige of the program already having given his ego a noticeable boost.

I was reluctant when Paul first told me he wanted to quit his job to write. I wasn't convinced that poetry could fill that many hours in a day, but he assured me that his creativity needed the space and that he would be more available to help with the boys and around the house. I suppose his acceptance at U of H proved the first point, although I hadn't seen any evidence of a significant volume of poems produced over the past year. As to the second, suffice it to say that the services of Jimena, our full-time housekeeper, were still required. If anything, his frustration with the demands of my work schedule and my absences from home grew. He seemed to think I could strike a perfect balance of professional and personal life by simply setting limits on the cases I took, refusing to work nights and weekends—a strategy destined to send my career to the graveyard. And, in the meantime, I didn't notice poetry paying any of the bills.

"I know," I said. "I'm sorry."

A gust of wind hit us, and the sky quickly darkened. I stopped in the middle of the trail and shrugged off my backpack.

"Boys," I called. "Come get your ponchos."

Nick and Henry turned back to us as it started to rain. They grabbed their ponchos, pulling them on as they ran.

"Be careful," Paul yelled. "The rocks are slippery."

I handed Paul his jacket then put mine on and tightened the hood around my visor.

"You think I should hustle after them?" Paul said.

I adjusted the backpack. "You can if you want. But they'll be fine."

"We should have started back sooner," he said. "Gotten ahead of the rain."

We hadn't gone far when Paul drew up.

"Shit. I have a rock in my shoe."

He leaned against a boulder on the side of the trail and unlaced his boot, pulled it off and shook out a few granules, then bent down to lace it up again. He repeated the process with his other boot. I waited, hands in the pockets of my jacket, rain dripping from my visor. It was getting colder.

"You want me to carry the backpack?" he said.

"No. I'm fine."

We set off down the trail again.

"I'm getting excited about graduate school," he said.

"Me, too."

"They accepted eight people this year—out of hundreds of applications."

"I know. You're so talented, Paul."

"It'll be a shitload of work. But we're in this together, right?"

I held up a hand for a fist bump. "You and me, babe."

The roar of Alberta Falls was audible over the rain, and when it came into sight we stopped for a moment, picking our way carefully over the boulders for a better view. I don't know how many times I've seen the falls, dozens probably, but the power of the water is mesmerizing—foaming as it careens against the walls of the passage it carved for itself, the granite chute still too constricting for the river that flows through the narrow canyon. Paul tugged at my sleeve, drawing me out of my reverie and back to the trail.

"We need to sit down in the next couple of days and talk about our schedules, what you've got coming up," he said.

"I'll have a short trip to Anchorage for a hearing on posttrial motions. But other than that, I don't have any out-of-town trips on the horizon, thank God."

"Great." He paused, shot a glance in my direction. "So you can take the boys to school?"

The terrain was fairly level the last quarter mile and we picked up our pace.

"I should be able to on most days."

Paul's a night owl, reading or surfing the internet, writing sometimes, I suppose, until after midnight, and on most mornings drags himself out of bed just in time to kiss Nick and Henry goodbye. I didn't push him to make the morning school trek—Jimena picks up the boys in the afternoons—because he's on duty when I'm out of town. But mostly because I love those twenty to thirty minutes in the car with the boys, the quiet companionship in an enclosed space, their time as captives conducive to offering up confessions and reflections and sometimes highly useful information.

We crossed the final hundred yards and the bridge to the parking lot.

"I'm going to the privy before we hit the road," Paul said.

I nodded and turned toward the Jeep. The boys were nowhere to be seen—hiding, no doubt, and planning their surprise. I expected them to jump out from somewhere around the vehicle as I approached and prepared myself for the shouts of "Boo!" and the required assurances that they had scared me half to death. I unlocked the tailgate and pulled it open. I tossed the backpack in and bent over to unlace my boot, just as a hand inched out from under the bumper and grabbed my shin. I gasped, squealed, "Help!" and backed away as Nick giggled.

"You crazy boys." I squatted down, peered under the Jeep. "Come on out."

Nick rolled toward me and pushed himself up.

"Where's Henry?"

"Pooping." Nick opened a rear door and climbed into the back seat.

"Where were you?" he said. "What took you so long?"

"Not that long, Nick. Maybe thirty minutes, max."

"More like an hour."

I heard the tremor in his voice, went to the open rear door and gave him a hug.

"I'm freezing, Mom."

I shut his door and got in the driver's seat, started the Jeep and cranked the heat to high. I saw Paul walking toward us from the privy, rolled down the window and called to him.

"Where's Henry?"

Paul came to my window. "Isn't he in the car?"

"He went to the toilet," Nick said.

Paul shook his head. "He's not there."

I got out of the Jeep, started toward the privy.

"Henry," I called. "No more games. We're all tired and wet, and it's time to go home."

No response. I reached the end of the parking lot, opened one privy door, then the other. Empty.

"Henry?" I circled the privy, then went around again, peering into the trees and brush in every direction. The rain had slowed to a drizzle. I crossed the parking lot to Bear Lake Road, looked up and down the deserted highway. I heard Paul calling to Henry, then Nick echoing his calls. There was no response. The forest was deathly silent. My heart began to pound, my stomach turned. I started to run.

Henry was gone.

CHAPTER

3

Paul

NICK AND HENRY suffered those two months Elizabeth was away. They wouldn't say it to her, upbeat most of the time on their telephone calls, asking if the good guys—her clients were always the good guys—were winning the trial. "It's up and down," she'd tell them. "One day you're winning, the next day you're losing, and you can never be sure until the jury comes back with the verdict."

"It's all good days on the home front," we'd say. Then we'd hang up the phone and Nick would disappear into his room for a while. Henry usually crawled into my lap and laid his head on my shoulder.

Texas was hit by a drought that summer and the heat in Houston was unbearable by mid-June. I told the boys we could take off for Colorado whenever they were ready, but they didn't want to go without Elizabeth. Which was fine with me. I like the mountains, but I'm not inclined to hike or fish without Elizabeth, and the tourist scene in Estes Park gets old pretty quick—putt-putt golf and go-karts and crowds. At least in Houston I could keep Nick and Henry occupied. They went swimming and played video games, stayed up late watching movies, slept until noon and spent the days with friends.

Elizabeth took charge the moment she arrived home, even though she was plainly exhausted. She cleaned out the end-of-school mess of notebooks, papers, and art supplies still strewn about the mudroom. She checked what progress had been made on the boys' required summer reading lists (none) and reestablished reasonable bedtimes. She took them to the dentist and for their annual physicals, all appointments she'd made before leaving for Alaska, went through the information packets we'd gotten for the coming school year, and bought uniforms for the fall. She was a woman possessed, getting her family back to normal.

I found that attractive about her when we were younger—her confidence and determination, her sheer physical and mental strength. Now, sometimes, I hate her for it.

Like the fucking hike to Sky Pond.

It was a lot to expect from all of us, but especially from Henry. He's like his mother, a ferocious kid, but still, he'd just turned six. The hike up took longer than we expected, we were wiped out when we got to the top and stayed longer than we should have, risking the afternoon rains that park visitors are advised to avoid. I considered that possibility before we left, suggested we find an alternative, but Elizabeth wouldn't hear of it. She'd grown up hiking, camping overnight in the backcountry, had climbed Longs Peak God knows how many times. I supposed she'd spring that on us next.

When the rain hit that afternoon, I realized that only ten days into it, I was ready for the vacation to end. The backs of my legs were sunburned, my feet hurt like hell, and now I was freezing. The cabin was comfortable and large, a house, really, after all the work we'd done on it, but at Elizabeth's insistence there was no television or internet, and I wasn't looking forward to another game of Monopoly or Hearts. I couldn't wait for my classes to start.

Taking a year off to write had been good for me, although with family responsibilities and Elizabeth's trial schedule, I hadn't gotten as much work done as I'd hoped. Her schedule always took priority, and if she couldn't cover an appointment or make it to a basketball or soccer game, that was my job. I showed her a few of the poems I'd written most recently, and she said they were beautiful and insightful, but I wasn't convinced she liked them or even understood them. Elizabeth is a voracious reader when she has the time, but I've never seen her browse through or even pick up one of the hundred or so books of poetry I've collected over the years. I was anxious to meet my fellow graduate students, be part of a community that understands the value of art and writing and knows the amount of work and discipline required to create it.

We reached the end of the trail, and I veered off to the privy. There was no one around and I thought about just pissing on the side of the parking lot, but I'd catch hell from Elizabeth if she saw me. I stepped inside to the dark and the smell, unzipped and let go with a sigh of relief.

My hands were cold, my hair soaked under my baseball cap. Water dripped from my jacket down my shins, joined the puddle of mud and whatever else I was standing in. I decided then and there that I would go back to Houston. Elizabeth could stay in Colorado with the boys, and I would have some time to myself before school began. She'd be okay with that—we'd given each other space before—and she could hardly argue after having been gone for two months. But she was tired after the hike. I'd raise the subject in the morning, after breakfast and a good night's sleep.

I finished, pushed open the privy door and slammed it shut, crossed the parking lot to the Jeep. Elizabeth rolled down the window. She was in the driver's seat. Nick was in the back. Henry was nowhere to be found.

C H A P T E R

4

Monroe

THE 911 CALL came in near the end of my shift. Dispatch said the woman was frantic, could hardly speak, she'd driven halfway to the park entrance to get a cell signal. A six-year-old boy was missing up at Glacier Gorge trailhead. I radioed Mike Hernandez to get a hasty team together and meet me there.

We don't get a lot of crime in Rocky Mountain National Park—traffic violations for the most part, occasionally some idiot trying to feed the wildlife, a few cars broken into at trailhead parking lots. Nothing like what I saw in my years as a sheriff in Montana. But people do get lost in national parks. Kids can disappear in a minute. They wander twenty-five feet off the trail and become disoriented, head in the wrong direction. Sometimes they're never found.

I took the job four years ago, not long after my wife, Maggie, died. I wasn't sure how I'd feel about being a law enforcement park ranger. But I like it fine. I bought a little place near Lyons, on the North Saint Vrain River. My daughter lives in Denver, and I see her and her two kids pretty regular.

I turned on my flashing lights, hit the gas then slowed to pass a long line of cars and RVs stopped on both sides of the road, people crossing the pavement, not watching for traffic, taking pictures of a herd of elk grazing in the tall grass. Millions of visitors to the park every year and most of them never get off the highway. That's the closest they come to a wilderness experience.

The rain stopped and the sun came out for a few minutes as I rounded Moraine Park. The first time I looked across that valley and the high peaks west of it along the Continental Divide, long shafts of light piercing through the clouds at sunset like the fingers of God, it nearly took my breath away. Maggie would have liked it here.

I drove on up Bear Lake Road, turned off into the Glacier Gorge parking lot, and pulled up next to a Jeep, the only vehicle in the lot. The parents and a boy who looked to be about nine or ten huddled around me as I got out of my truck.

They were Paul and Elizabeth English and their son Nick.

"Hollis Monroe," I said.

They told me they'd hiked up to Sky Pond, stayed longer than they should have, that on the trek down the boys had run ahead when it started to rain. Henry went off to the toilet while he and his brother waited for their mom and dad. He hadn't come back.

"We've got the call out for search and rescue," I said. "Our people will start arriving shortly. I'll have a look around while we wait."

I didn't find anything. Not that I'd expected to. No evidence of a struggle, no signs of an animal attack. Mountain lion attacks are rare, but there had recently been an increase in sightings in the park.

"Nick didn't hear anything." Paul English had followed me. "No scream, no call for help."

Not likely that he would if it was a big cat. Mountain lions are built for ambush. They stalk through the trees and attack when they reach striking distance, leaping on the victim's back with a neck bite. A six-year-old boy would be dead before he knew what hit him, then dragged off into the brush.

I didn't tell the father that. I wanted to tell him that he and his wife were stupid for letting their boys run ahead, but what good would that do.

"Henry's a smart boy," English said. "He has a lot of common sense. He wouldn't just wander off."

"That's good to know. But he is just six."

Three SUVs pulled into the parking lot. Hernandez, one of our climbing rangers, got out of the lead vehicle; two rangers had come with him and more were on the way. I went to meet them, and after a quick huddle the three of them set off toward the trail, calling Henry's name and blowing air horns and whistles. I told Hernandez I would secure the trailheads when more help arrived, to contain the exit points in case Henry popped out.

I walked back to the Jeep. The tailgate was open, Nick English sitting in the wayback with legs crossed, head in his hands and elbows resting on his thighs. His mother sat next to him, an arm around his shoulders, bent toward him and speaking softly. Paul English stood by the side of the Jeep, staring at nothing.

"How you doing, Nick?" I said.

He looked up at me.

"I don't feel so good."

"You've had a long day. I know you're tired, and you're worried about your little brother. But I need you to take me through everything that happened when you and Henry got to the parking lot after your hike, in as much detail as you can remember. Can you do that for me?"

He nodded.

He and Henry had raced the last quarter mile, Nick winning of course, then lay under the Jeep to get out of the rain. Then Henry was farting and said he had to poop. Henry ran off to the toilet, yelling, "Ahoy, mates." That was the last Nick saw of him.

"Had the rain stopped by then?"

"No. It was still really dark and raining pretty hard."

"You didn't go with him to the privy?"

"No."

"Didn't go looking for him before your mom and dad got back?"

"No."

Paul English shook his head, blew out a deep breath. "Stay together. That's the rule. When Mom and I aren't with you, the two of you always stay together."

He might as well have punched the kid in the gut. Nick uncrossed his legs, jumped down from the Jeep and took only a few steps before bending over to vomit.

"For God's sake, Paul," Elizabeth said.

She started toward Nick. I waved her back. He heaved a few more times then wiped his mouth on the sleeve of his sweatshirt. I handed him my handkerchief and he started to cry.

"I gave him my flashlight."

"That's good." I turned to the parents. "How about Nick and I take a little walk? Would that be all right with you?"

"I think it would be best if I came with you," Elizabeth said.

"Oh, for God's sake, Elizabeth," Paul said. "Would you stop acting like a fucking lawyer? The man just wants to talk to Nick."

Her face went tight. "Fine."

I pointed in the direction of the trail. "Let's walk that way, Nick. We won't go far."

We walked along in silence for a while, then stopped and sat on a rock outcropping on the side of the trail, looking down at the creek below.

"So, you a Texans fan?" After his parents' contribution to the conversation, I was afraid Nick would clam up on me. Anything to get him talking again. He nodded but didn't say anything.

"Pretty exciting for Houston to have a football team again."

He nodded.

"How about Henry? Does he like football?"

I thought I might have to continue this line of questioning for a while, but Nick finally spoke.

"He likes just about every sport. He reads the sports section of the newspaper every morning."

"No kidding? And he's just going into first grade?"

"Yeah. Crazy, huh? I mean, he doesn't get every word, but he gets a lot. And he really loves basketball."

"Ah. Rockets fan."

"Yeah. But he likes college basketball the best. He goes nuts over the Final Four. He wants to play for Coach K someday."

"I bet he will."

Nick's face clouded over, and I was afraid I'd lose him.

"So, your mom's a lawyer?"

He nodded.

"What does your dad do?"

"He's a poet. He taught high school for a while, but he quit about a year ago."

"What's he been doing since he quit?"

He shrugged. "I don't know. Writing poems, I think. He's taking classes at the University of Houston this fall."

"Back to school, huh? What's he going to study?"

"I'm not sure." He bent down, picked up a rock and threw it toward the creek. "Maybe how to write better poems?"

I smiled at that. "Your parents must be smart people. I know I could never be a lawyer or a poet."

"Me neither. I read a couple of my dad's poems. They were pretty weird. And being a lawyer really sucks."

"Sucks?"

"Yeah. It's nothing like on TV. I went to my mom's office for Take Your Kid to Work Day. All she did was sit at her computer, writing something to send to a judge."

"That does sound pretty boring."

"Yeah. She says being in trial is a lot of fun, but most days she just has to sit at her desk and work."

I picked up a handful of rocks and passed half of them to Nick.

"So things are good at home? With you and your parents?"

"Yeah. My parents are awesome."

"How about you and your brother? You get along okay?"

"Yeah, sure. I mean, he's a pain in the butt sometimes." He stole a quick glance at me.

"Well, he wouldn't be a little brother if he wasn't a pain in the butt, right?"

The wind picked up and Nick shivered. It was getting dark.

"When you and Henry got to the parking lot after your hike, did you see anyone?"

He shook his head. "I didn't see anyone. It was raining, and we were running."

"Any other cars?"

"Not at first. But I saw a truck later."

Jesus. I looked at him. He hadn't said anything about the truck in his first telling of Henry's disappearance. I stood up.

"Let's walk back while you tell me about the truck."

He chucked his handful of rocks far out over the creek and joined me on the trail.

"Where was the truck, Nick?"

"At the end of the parking lot."

"Which end?"

"Down by the toilet."

"When did you first see it?"

"I don't know, maybe five or ten minutes after Henry went to the toilet. It seemed like a long time. I heard it start, and then it came toward me really slow."

Shit. I picked up the pace.

"Could you see who was driving?"

"No."

"Or anyone else in the truck?"

"No."

"Do you know what kind of truck it was?"

"Maybe a Ford? Or a Chevy?" He was huffing, struggling to keep up. I slowed down a bit.

"Did you see what color it was?"

"Black, I think. It was hard to tell. The driver didn't turn his lights on until he got to the road."

Shit, shit, shit. "Did you happen to notice anything about the license plates?"

"Yeah. It was an Alaska plate."

We were back to the trailhead.

"Which is so crazy," he said.

"Why so crazy?"

"Because my mom just got back from a trial in Alaska."

The parents saw us coming, met us halfway in the parking lot, and followed me to my vehicle. I called in a BOLO on a black or dark-colored pickup, Alaska plates, last seen approximately six PM at Glacier Gorge trailhead, of interest in the disappearance of a six-year-old boy. I turned to Nick.

"Did you see any numbers or letters on the license plate?"

He shook his head.

"That's all we have at present," I said to the dispatcher.

"I don't understand," Elizabeth said. "What pickup?"

"Nick saw a truck," I said. "He didn't notice it at first. It was at the end of the parking lot. It took off five or ten minutes after Henry went to the privy."

"Jesus, Nick," Paul said.

I took a step in Paul's direction, gave him a look that he correctly understood as shut the hell up.

"Maybe the driver saw Henry," Nick said. "Or saw something that will help us find him."

"Maybe so," I said. The kid wasn't stupid. But it's hard for an adult, much less a ten-year-old, to start wrapping his head around the possibilities when a child goes missing.

"Monroe."

It was Hernandez, coming toward us, holding something between his latex-gloved thumb and fingers.

"We found this not far from the privy."

It was a flashlight.

"That's mine," Nick said.

"You sure?" I said.

He pointed to his initials scratched onto the side of the flashlight in a shaky child's hand. "N.E."

"Oh my God," Elizabeth said.

Nick looked at his mother, stricken, then at his father, and when his parents didn't make a move, I put my arms around him and pulled him close as he began to cry again. His words were muffled, halting, as he struggled between sobs to speak.

"I told him to take my flashlight. So he can see in the dark."

The sobs turned into a wail. "How will Henry find his way back now?"

CHAPTER

5

Elizabeth

IT WAS GETTING dark. The park ranger, Monroe, had taken Nick for a walk. I'd wanted to go along, but Paul was furious that I would, in his words, act like a fucking lawyer. I suppose he thought it was a sign of cold rationality when the situation called for—what? I wasn't falling apart. Not yet. I kept thinking that any minute Henry would appear, that this was somehow a mistake, a misunderstanding, that he'd taken a wrong turn and would make his way back in a short while. Or one of the searchers would step out of the trees with Henry in tow, holding his hand, silly grins on both their faces, saying, "Here he is! He got a little lost, but he's fine!"

But during that brief period of time until Henry returned and everything was straightened out and back to normal, an outsider, law enforcement, might consider the possibility that Nick had something to do with Henry's disappearance. The notion was beyond preposterous, the boys loved each other, but Monroe wouldn't be doing his job if he didn't follow that line of inquiry. A ten-year-old boy, no matter how brilliant, would be no match for a skilled interrogator.

I closed the tailgate, leaned against the back of the Jeep, and listened to the searchers calling. Monroe had said more were on the way; why weren't they there yet? Paul paced the perimeter of the parking lot. When he circled back to the Jeep, he stopped, then came and stood silently in front of me for a few moments. He took my hand, pulled me to him and rested his chin on top of my head. We put our arms around each other.

"They'll find him," he said.

"Of course they will. He can't have gone far."

I saw Monroe and Nick at the trailhead. We went to meet them and followed Monroe to his truck. Then the instruction to the dispatcher, be on the lookout for a black or dark-colored pickup, Alaska plates, of interest in the disappearance of a six-year-old boy. Nick's flashlight, the one Henry had carried, found near the privy. Monroe holding Nick and looking at me, his eyes sad and compassionate and too full of the horrible weight of experience.

It was in those few moments that I came to know the meaning of terror.

I couldn't move. It was as if I were in deep water, the sights and sounds around me distorted, fading in and out in waves. Paul and Monroe looking at Paul's camera, then Paul leading Nick in slow motion to the Jeep, telling him to lie down in the back seat and settling him in. Monroe saying something to Hernandez then to me, his lips moving but the words guttural and unintelligible. The *whump, whump, whump* of lights on park vehicles slicing the parking lot. Monroe speaking to me again, and I shake my head no, no, no, even though I don't know what he's saying, and he puts his arm around me, tries to walk me to his truck, but I can't move and then I start to fall. He bends down, lifts me up and carries me, sets me in his passenger seat, pulls a blanket from a storage compartment and wraps it around me. I pull it over my head and put my head between my knees so I won't faint, but I think I fainted anyway.

"Mrs. English?"

Monroe was seated next to me in the driver's seat.

"Mrs. English?"

I pushed the blanket away from my face and sat up. Monroe had rolled down the windows and I took a deep breath of mountain air. He poured water from a thermos and handed the cup to me.

"I have coffee if you'd prefer," he said.

"No, thank you. Water's fine." I took a sip then drained the cup and handed it back to him. The night wind whistled through the trees, rocking the truck slightly.

"It's cold outside," I said. "Henry will be so cold."

Monroe didn't respond.

"You don't think he's cold, do you?" I said.

He rested his left elbow out the open window, rubbed his right hand on his thigh.

"I hope Henry's not cold," he said.

"You don't think he's cold." I nodded toward the trees. "You don't think he's out there."

"We don't know where he is. We'll have people posted at exit points on the nearby trails through the night in case he walks out. We'll do a hasty, then start a massive search when the sun comes up."

More rangers arrived, gathering in a circle a few yards from us, discussing the trailheads they'd cover, outlining their strategy for the night. Paul was with them. After a while some of them went to their vehicles, drove them to various points in the parking lot, facing outward, and left them running with the lights on and emergency lights flashing. They pulled on gloves and backpacks and scattered.

"We're shining the lights so Henry will see them and come to us," Monroe said.

I saw movement at the other end of the parking lot, a ranger pacing, something in his hand. Yellow tape.

"You didn't park them at the trailhead or the privy."

"No. For now, we have to treat that area as a possible crime scene."

I leaned back against the headrest and groaned. "A truck. There was a truck."

"Every law enforcement agency in the area is on the lookout for that truck. We've asked for an Amber Alert. And we've got rangers going to all the campgrounds looking for it."

An Amber Alert. In my mind, I saw messages scrolling on electronic billboards towering beside the freeways in Houston, lost child, six years old, buzz haircut, missing two front teeth, wearing yellow nylon shorts and hiking boots, last seen. . . .

"It had Alaska plates?" I said.

"Yes. I want to ask you about that."

"Why? I didn't see it."

"Nick told me you just got back from a long trial in Anchorage."

I looked at Monroe, bewildered. "You think that could have some connection to a truck with Alaska plates that shows up in Colorado?"

He shook his head. "I don't think anything yet, Mrs. English. I'm just getting started."

"Well, that's pretty farfetched. It has to be a coincidence."

"It probably is. But most abductions are by family members or someone with a connection to the family. We'll talk more about it tomorrow. In the meantime, I'd appreciate it if you could think whether there's any reason someone from Alaska would come looking for you or your family—even if it's some farfetched notion or just a hunch."

"Of course." I couldn't imagine such a thing.

"Another question. When you and your husband got back to the trailhead, you split up. He went to the privy, and you went back to the Jeep."

"Yes."

"How long was he at the privy?"

"I don't know. A few minutes."

"And you didn't hear anything from that direction while he was gone? No shouts, no unusual noises?"

I rubbed the back of my neck. Every part of my body ached. "Paul's a poet, Mr. Monroe. And a gentle father. He loves Henry with every fiber of his being. He could never hurt him."

"Okay." He put on his hat. "I've got to get back to my team here, and you should go home and get some sleep."

"I'm staying. I want to be here when Henry is found."

He was quiet for a few moments. "It'll likely be a long day tomorrow, Mrs. English. Nick needs some supper and his mother. Mr. English has already said that he'll take you home then come back."

"I'll talk to Paul." I reached for the door handle, then stopped. "You'll need a picture of Henry."

Monroe patted his shirt pocket. "Mr. English gave me his camera. Lots of shots of Henry. Even a little video—it's the darndest thing what you can do on these digital cameras."

I held out my hand. "May I see?"

He pulled the camera from his pocket, clicked it on and held it so we both could see the screen. It was a video of Henry at Sky Pond, stripped down to nothing but neon-yellow nylon shorts that hung below his belly button to a few inches above his knees. I had woven a garland from shrub branches and rested it like a crown on his perfectly shaped head, shaved almost bald in a buzz cut for the summer. Henry danced slowly in and out of the ankle-deep freezing water at the edge of the lake, arms in the air and hips moving side to side, singing through the gap left by his missing front teeth. "I . . . just want . . . to . . . fly." Then Nick got up and joined him and they danced, singing and laughing, for a few seconds before the video stopped.

CHAPTER

6

Paul

I LISTENED TO THE search team's reports and strategizing for a while, watched one of the rangers cordon off part of the area with yellow tape, then went to Monroe's truck. He and Elizabeth were looking at my camera. He glanced up, saw me standing outside his window, then got out. Elizabeth came around from the other side.

"I know you're all professionals," I said, "and presumably you know how to do your job. But there doesn't seem to be a real sense of urgency here about finding my son."

Monroe looked me up and down, then said in a quiet voice, "There are different ways of expressing things, Mr. English. As a poet, I'm sure you understand that. The way we express urgency in this situation is to do everything our training and experience tell us to do, with a high priority on the safety of our searchers. We may not be running around and waving our arms, but I assure you that every person here is focused on finding Henry."

If that was intended to make me feel better, it didn't. How much training and experience did these people actually have?

"What about Henry's safety? How about putting a high priority on that?"

He put his hands on his hips and blew out a long breath.

"Take Nick and your wife home. When you get back, if there's any particular suggestion you have, we can talk about it. And do me a favor."

"What's that?"

"Bring me Henry's sheets and pillowcase. We'll need them for the dogs."

He turned to Elizabeth. "Good night, Mrs. English. We'll see you in the morning."

Elizabeth was wrapped in a blanket. She pulled it off her shoulders, but Monroe stopped her.

"Keep it for the ride home."

Nick was stretched out in the back seat of the Jeep, asleep. I drove slowly down the mountain, on the lookout for deer or elk darting into the headlights. I almost hit a buck a few nights before and that was the last thing we needed at that moment.

"What time is it?" Elizabeth said.

"Close to midnight."

She pressed her forehead against the passenger window.

"Monroe told me they'll have people there through the night," she said. "And more in the morning."

"I think you should call Bob Simon as soon as you get up tomorrow." Simon was the managing partner of Elizabeth's law firm.

"I guess he should know."

"Not just know. He needs to get on the phone with the governor, senators, whoever the hell else he can call to get backup on this. FBI, National Guard, U.S. fucking Marines."

Elizabeth was silent.

"You've worked your ass off for Bob Simon. He owes you."

"Bob Simon doesn't think he owes anyone anything."

"Goddamn it!" I pounded my fist on the steering wheel. "What's the point of being a partner in a high-powered firm if you don't use it to get what you want?"

"All I want is Henry back. Getting Bob Simon in the middle of this is not the best way to go about it. Let Monroe do his job."

"Who the hell is Hollis Monroe?" I said. "Hey, I know! Our son's missing! Let's call Smokey the Bear!"

"Would you stop cursing? I don't appreciate your foul language, especially in front of Nick."

I drove, fuming, through Estes Park, the town dark and quiet, turned left past the Stanley Hotel and up Devil's Gulch Road to the turnoff for the cabin. I pulled off the road and stopped. Elizabeth jumped out to open the gate across the gravel lane that led to our place, waited until I had driven through then closed it again and got back in the Jeep.

"Did you lock it?"

"No."

We usually didn't.

"Would you lock it when you leave?" she said.

I nodded.

I drove the quarter mile to the cabin and parked in front. Elizabeth woke Nick and we went inside, turning on lights in the hall and the living room. Elizabeth asked Nick if he wanted anything to eat.

He shook his head. "I just want to go to bed."

I pulled him to me, rubbed the top of his head.

"I'll see you later, man. I'm going back to the park."

"Okay."

Elizabeth followed him to his bedroom, and I went to the kitchen. I laid out bread, ham, and mustard. Elizabeth came in a few minutes later, carrying the sheets she'd stripped off Henry's bed. She hung them over the back of a bar stool, then lifted the top sheet and started to fold.

"How's he doing?"

"I don't know. He didn't say anything. Just used the bathroom, pulled off his clothes, and went to bed in his underwear. I think he's already asleep."

"Want a sandwich?"

She shook her head. I slapped two sandwiches together, put them in an empty bread bag, and got a bottle of Gatorade from the refrigerator.

"I'm gone," I said.

I took the sheets from Elizabeth and grabbed a heavy fleece jacket from the coat rack. She walked with me to the front porch.

"Paul."

"Yeah?"

"It won't help the search effort if you get crossways with the park rangers."

I looked up at her. Did she really think I needed to hear that? I opened the driver's door, tossed the sandwiches and Gatorade on the passenger seat.

"I won't get crossways with anybody. I'll call you if there's any news."

CHAPTER 7

Elizabeth

I watched the Jeep stop at the gate and again on the other side, then turn onto Devil's Gulch Road. I went back inside, locked the front door behind me and turned off the lights in the living room and kitchen, looked in on Nick, sound asleep. I went down the hall to the master bedroom, pulled off my clothes in the bathroom and kicked them to a pile in the corner, then stepped in the shower. I let it run over me until the hot water was gone, toweled off, and slipped into a nightgown and got into bed. The windows were open, the room cold the way I liked it. I didn't think I would sleep, but I closed my eyes and was gone.

A long, mournful cry woke me an hour later. *Aaaaaaaahhhhh.*

"Henry?" I whispered, my heart pounding.

Aaaaaaaaarrrrrhhhhhh. The sound rose and fell, up and down a minor scale, and then a chorus of yelps. Coyotes. Running in a pack close by, their calls and answers eerily human at times.

I got out of bed and closed the windows, pulled on fur-lined moccasins, flannel pants, and a sweatshirt. I went to the kitchen and made a cup of hot chocolate, took it to the living room and lit a fire.

The original cabin my father built now serves as the common area of the house. Paul and I tore down the bedroom walls to open up more space for the living room, and added a master bedroom suite on one side, a children's and guest wing on the other, and a garage. We'd kept the wood floors, the loft area for a study, the weathered bookshelves crammed with yellowed volumes of Hemingway, Trollope, and Chekhov. A stuffed buck gazed mutely at me from his eternal perch over the log mantle of the stone fireplace. My mother died only a few years after the cabin was built, but there were reminders of her everywhere: an antique checkerboard, chintz-covered chairs, a Corning Ware percolator, and cast-iron skillets for frying trout and eggs.

I finished the hot chocolate, covered myself with an afghan, and lay on the sofa staring at the fire.

"Henry," I whispered. "Henry. Where are you?"

I closed my eyes, pushed away the thoughts of what we should and shouldn't have done on the hike to Sky Pond and back, and concentrated on an image of Henry's face.

"Henry. Tell me where you are."

The firewood popping as it burned was the only sound. I got up and went down the dark hallway that led to Henry's room. There were toys on the floor, pajamas tossed hurriedly aside to get dressed for the early morning hike. A wave of dread hit me when I took in the stripped bed, the bare pillow, the comforter hanging from the footboard. I drew the comforter across the mattress, smoothed it, and put the pillow back in place. The windows were open, and I closed them. Henry was afraid of coyotes howling at night.

I checked on Nick on the way back to the living room. Retrieved my worn canvas field jacket from the coat rack, wrapped myself in the afghan, and stepped out onto the front porch to wait for sunrise.

Our property has 360-degree views of Longs Peak, Twin Sisters, Lumpy Ridge, the Front Range, Twin Owls, and the Continental Divide. I'd lost count of how many offers we'd had for it over the years. The first blush of morning light was on the horizon when the door opened behind me.

"Mom?"

"Hey, darling."

Nick stepped outside in a T-shirt and bare feet.

"I looked everywhere. I thought you were gone."

"I'm just watching the sunrise. I'll come inside."

"No, it's okay. I'll sit out here with you."

"Good. Put on some warm clothes and I'll wait for you."

He went back inside, came out a few minutes later bundled up, a quilt from his bed around his shoulders. He pushed a chair close to mine, sat down and hugged his knees to his chest.

"Did they find Henry?"

"I haven't heard anything yet. But they'll have a lot more people looking for him this morning."

"Do you think they'll find him?"

I took his hand as he started to cry, kissed his palm, and laced my fingers through his.

"They'll find him. I believe with all my heart. They'll find him."

He wiped his nose with the back of his free hand.

"I want to go up there," he said. "I want to help."

"Okay." I stood up. "Let's eat breakfast, and then we'll go."

* * *

Nick helped me load the old pickup with a cooler of sandwiches and drinks and a couple of folding camp chairs. We had binoculars and a cell phone charger and Nick's detailed terrain map of Rocky Mountain National Park.

"Can you think of anything else we might need?" I said.

He thought for a moment, shook his head as he surveyed the shelves of camping equipment in the garage. “Maybe some warm clothes for Henry?”

“Great idea.”

I blinked back tears, holding it together until I made it to Henry’s room. Then I sat on his bed, put my hands over my face, and wept.

“Mom, let’s go!” Nick yelled from the garage.

I wiped my eyes and called that I was coming. I found Henry’s Rockets backpack and filled it with jeans, a sweatshirt, socks, and underwear, muttering, “Get it under control, Elizabeth. Get it under control.”

Nick was in the truck, waiting for me.

“Ready,” I said. I tossed Henry’s backpack on the seat between us, backed the truck out of the garage, and we headed for the park. I told Nick to call his dad. Paul didn’t answer, and Nick left a voice mail letting him know we were on the way.

There was a long line of cars at the Beaver Meadows Entrance Station. When we finally rolled up to the entrance, the park ranger glanced at my season pass and welcomed us back.

“If you’re planning a trip up Bear Lake Road, it’s closed just past Bierstadt Lake trailhead,” she said.

“But we have to get to Glacier Gorge.”

“Sorry. There’s a search and rescue operation underway. Only emergency and park personnel are allowed past the barriers. You should be able to get there tomorrow, maybe even later today. They won’t close the road for long.”

“They’re looking for my son. Henry English. He’s six years old.”

The ranger looked at Nick, then back at me.

“May I see your driver’s license, please?”

She checked my license, then made a short phone call.

“Ranger Monroe is at the command post at the Ranger Operations Center. He said you should go there.” She waved over another ranger and explained to him who we were.

"Would you escort Mrs. English to the command post?"

He pointed me to his vehicle. I pulled in behind him then followed as he U-turned and headed in the direction we had come. We drove slowly, slightly under the speed limit, and Nick grew antsier by the minute.

"Why doesn't he turn on his siren and let it rip?"

"I'm sure he doesn't want me speeding. If I had an accident or hit an animal, he'd have a hard time explaining it to his boss."

We drove past the Beaver Meadows Visitors Center and I saw for the first time that there were news vans parked in front, cameramen and reporters milling around.

"Wow," Nick said. "Are they here for Henry? Are they gonna put this on TV?"

I suddenly felt sick. I hadn't thought about the press coverage, photos of Henry in the newspapers and on television, brief glimpses of the anxious family captured by the cameras. Would we be expected to make a statement, an appeal for Henry's safe return? How many times had I watched that scene play out over the years, in fiction and in real life, always thinking that parents can't give up hope, it's what you do as a parent, you always hope, but the rest of the world knows what the likely outcome will be. Never imagining that the nightmare would be mine someday. *Please God,* I thought. *Let them find Henry.* Curled up in the forest somewhere, frightened and hungry, but nowhere near a pickup with Alaska plates.

We turned, then drove behind the Visitors Center and parked. The ranger showed us in and led us to a small room with workstations and phones and a huge map of Rocky Mountain National Park on the wall. Monroe and Paul were inside, with a third man who rose and extended his hand when we entered.

"Detective Dennis Carpenter," he said. "Estes Park police."

I shook his hand. He was tall and lanky and looked to be in his midthirties. I knew he must be there in connection with the possible kidnapping, but I didn't want to discuss it in front of Nick. I turned to Paul.

He looked exhausted, eyes bloodshot and hair flattened against his scalp, the clothes he'd worn on the hike even worse for the wear. Monroe looked to be in a little better shape, but not by much.

"Any news?"

Paul shook his head. "No."

"We have over a hundred people out," Monroe said. "Helicopters, search dogs. There are teams at The Loch and Mills Lake, working their way down. Same with Emerald Lake and Bear Lake. We've got people covering Prospect Canyon, generally all over the area."

"Why send people to search higher up the mountains?" I said. "It doesn't make sense that Henry would walk uphill."

"Happens all the time," Monroe said. "Henry could have decided he would head up the trail to meet you—maybe take a shortcut through the trees. He drops the flashlight and can't find it, maybe gets disoriented in the dark. He might have thought the trail to Bear Lake was the trail to Alberta Falls."

"Or he could have fallen in the creek and been swept downstream," Paul said.

Monroe looked at Nick, then back at me. "There are any number of possibilities."

"What about the dogs?" I said.

"They're not getting any indications outside the privy. But that could be because of the rain."

I knew it also could be because of the truck with Alaska plates. But Nick didn't need to hear that.

"Paul," Monroe said. "Maybe you and Nick should get a little fresh air."

Paul rubbed his eyes and put on his cap.

"Yeah, sure. Come on, buddy. Let's take a walk."

"I want to help with the search," Nick said.

"I appreciate that," Monroe said. "But I'll be honest with you, Nick. It's not a good idea. Those hundred people out there—they have years of experience looking for people in the wilderness. You get off trail, it's easy to lose your bearings and not be able to find your way back. That's why we don't want even your parents out there—because if any of you got lost, we'd have to look for you when we should be looking for Henry."

Nick was somewhat mollified, but not ready to give up.

"I'm a Webelo Scout. I've been hiking and camping a lot."

"That's good. When you turn eighteen, come see me. I'll give you a job here in the park. We're always happy to find men like you."

Nick nodded.

"There are news trucks out front," I said.

"We sent out a press release early this morning. The more coverage we can get, the better."

"We'll stay out of sight," Paul said. He and Nick left the room together.

"Have a seat, Mrs. English."

"Call me Elizabeth."

"I will do that. Just don't call me Hollis."

Detective Carpenter snickered.

"Why?"

"The only person who calls me Hollis is my mother. Everyone else calls me Monroe—even my wife."

He noticed I was looking at his left hand. He didn't wear a wedding ring.

"My wife used to call me Monroe. I lost her four years ago. Cancer."

"I'm sorry."

"Well. Let's get to finding Henry." He pointed to the map, but Carpenter interrupted.

"I'd like to talk to you and your son at some point today. And I've already discussed with your husband that I'll need access to your home."

"Monroe has talked to all of us at length," I said. "And why do you need to come to my house? Henry wasn't anywhere near there when he disappeared."

"It's standard procedure. We'll want to collect a few books and toys that might have his fingerprints. Toothbrush, hairbrush, hat, anything that might have his DNA. I'll come by in a couple of hours if that's all right."

I hesitated a moment. "Sure. Okay."

"Thank you. We'll do everything we can to find your boy." He nodded at Monroe. "I'll touch base with you later today."

Monroe turned back to the map when Carpenter was gone. "All our searchers have GPS set on tracking mode to lay down track as they go. At the end of the day, we lay the GPS tracks on the map so we can see where we've been and decide where we're going the next day. I've been over all this with your husband, but I can show you where every team is, if you want. What our search strategy is."

I shook my head. "I assume you're in constant communication with all of them—that you'll hear the minute they find anything."

He nodded.

"Are they all park personnel?"

"No, no. We've got help from Larimer County Search and Rescue, Rocky Mountain Rescue Group. If we need more resources, we'll get them."

"What about the truck?"

"Carpenter's working on that. He's talked to the Larimer County Sheriff's office and Colorado State Patrol. We have hot sheets of vehicles stolen in Alaska over the past year, and info on stolen plates. The limited description we have doesn't give us much to go on."

The room was getting warm. I took off my jacket. Monroe propped the door open.

"I want to talk about Alaska," he said. "Everything you can tell me about your case up there, the people involved."

"Ugh. It's not very exciting—a dispute over a production platform. My client has oil and gas leases on a field in Cook Inlet. They contracted with a German company to build and install an offshore platform. There were problems with construction, then problems with the installation, and significant delays in the project."

"While oil prices continue to drop."

"Exactly. We sued for delay damages and cost of repairs. The Germans pointed the finger at my client, arguing that they made a number of unreasonable decisions and changes along the way that were the cause of the problems. It was a long, technical trial and I have to hand it to the jury for staying awake."

"Did you win?"

"Yes. Roughly fifty million dollars in damages. And attorneys' fees on top of that."

"That's real money."

"It's real money. It made the papers."

"Did you piss off anyone in particular on your opponents' side?"

"I pissed off a lot of people, Monroe."

"Yeah, I'm sure. But I mean would there be anyone associated with the case that really came to despise you, that might want to do you harm."

I hesitated. Early in our marriage when I was recounting the details of one of my first victories, Paul had accused me of being cavalier with people's lives. I don't think I am, but it is a fact of litigation that of the people involved—and it's always about the people, not a faceless corporation—some are vindicated, some rewarded, some disappointed, some vilified.

"It's likely that a few managers and engineers lost their jobs as soon as the trial was over. But vicious enough to harm me or my family? No."

"What about the lawyers on the other side?"

"A prominent New York firm and a small firm in Anchorage as their local counsel. We had some difficult moments, but in general the relationship was cordial and professional."

He laced his fingers behind his head and looked up at the ceiling.

"This is crazy," I said. "Henry gone, and the idea that someone would have driven here from Alaska—would even know that I'm here with my family—watched and waited while we went on a hike. . . . It's insane."

"It is insane. The other possibility is that it was a crime of opportunity. Someone happened to see Henry alone and took him. And just happened to have a car with Alaska plates. That's even more unlikely."

My head started to pound. I closed my eyes.

"What about hangers-on at the courthouse?" he said. "Someone with no connection to the case that you saw more than once, maybe you wondered what they were doing there?"

"No."

"Where did you stay in Anchorage?"

"The Marriott downtown."

"She stays at all the swanky places," Paul said. He and Nick were at the door.

"Right," I said. "Like the week I spent at the Days Inn in Lufkin." I stood up, gave Nick a hug.

"Nick and I decided we'll go back to the cabin for a while," Paul said. "I could use a shower and a nap, and I can be there to show Carpenter around."

I walked outside with them. Nick wrapped his arms around my waist, then Paul joined him and the three of us held each other tight for a moment. I kissed them both and watched as they drove away, then went back to the command post.

"At the Marriott," Monroe said. "Any problems with anyone at the hotel?"

"No. The staff were very courteous. We were long-term guests, and they were anxious to accommodate whatever we needed."

"What about other people staying at the hotel? Rude, friendly, chatty, anything that stood out?"

I looked at the map behind Monroe's head, the lines of the search grid that blurred and swam before my eyes. The room had gone from being warm to unbearably stuffy. I pulled a tissue from my pocket and wiped my forehead, then turned back to Monroe.

"No. No one stands out at all."

CHAPTER

8

Monroe

SHE WAS HIDING something. Or someone.

So far, I liked Elizabeth English more than her husband, although I'd come to think that my first impression of Paul as a complete asshole was off the mark. He was a man under a lot of stress, from his boy missing, sure, but even before that. We'd talked through the night about Elizabeth, his kids, his writing. No question they had a good life and he was proud of his family, but living in his wife's shadow was taking a toll on the man. He didn't say as much, but I could tell.

And no wonder. If the two of them walked into a room together, she'd be the one to get your attention. Tall and slender, light brown hair that she'd pulled into a ponytail, and hazel eyes. Not beautiful, but pretty even with no makeup. It was the intelligence that made her shine, the open and honest look about her.

So I thought. But she'd just shut down. I saw it plain as day.

She stood in the doorway. I was thinking to myself, *let's try this again*, but Hernandez appeared behind her.

"Superintendent's meeting with the press in about twenty minutes, Monroe," he said. "She wants you there."

"I don't have to talk to the press, do I?" Elizabeth said.

"Not today." I didn't tell her that if this dragged on, if we didn't find Henry soon, there would be no escaping the press. She'd face questions from reporters about the circumstances of Henry's disappearance, make a plea for his safe return. The scrutiny would be intense, a public airing of their pain at the point when it would be sinking in that they might never see Henry again.

"You taking over while I'm gone?" I said to Hernandez.

"Yep." He motioned to Elizabeth. "Have a seat, ma'am. Monroe won't be long."

* * *

I did more press conferences than I could count during my years as sheriff. I don't care for them much. I don't have a problem with reporters, they have an important job. I'd just rather be doing something else. The first time I saw myself on camera, I said, "I look like crap on TV," and one of my deputies said, "Nah, Monroe, TV's got nothing to do with it. You always look like crap." And every once in a while someone asks a question that makes you want to hit him with his microphone.

The superintendent, though, she's good. A thirty-year veteran of the National Park Service, and she knows how to handle the public.

There were reporters from Denver, Boulder, and Colorado Springs. We explained that Henry English, age six from Houston, Texas, had gone missing the night before while hiking with his family. A massive search inside Rocky was underway. Also of interest, a dark-colored pickup truck with Alaska license plates that was seen in the vicinity around the time Henry disappeared. We'd be working with the Estes Park police department, and any information viewers had should be directed to the office of the superintendent or to the police, telephone numbers provided.

"Are you saying Henry English might have been kidnapped?" a Channel 9 reporter asked.

"We have drawn no conclusions at this time," I said. "The search and the investigation are ongoing."

"Where are the parents?" This from Channel 7.

"They are staying in the vicinity and, of course, are assisting us in every way possible."

"Can you tell us where they are staying?"

"No."

Back to Channel 9 lady. "Does Henry have brothers and sisters?"

"One older brother."

"Was he with Henry when Henry disappeared?" Channel 7 guy, not to be outdone.

I looked at the superintendent.

"Thank you," she said. "We have no further information for you at this time."

I walked the superintendent to her vehicle, filled her in on the status of the search.

"Keep me informed," she said.

I gave her a salute and went back to the command post. Elizabeth was outside, sitting in her truck, looking a little more shell-shocked than when I'd left her. I propped my elbows on the open driver's window.

"How are you doing?"

She pursed her lips, shook her head slightly. A tear rolled down her cheek, then another.

"I had to get out of there. Every time someone walks into the room, I expect them to say they've found him." She wiped one cheek with the palm of her hand, then the other. "But they haven't." Her chest began to heave. I didn't say anything, just let her cry. After a while she reached into the glove compartment for a box of tissues and blew her nose.

"I don't know what to do," she said. "I feel like I should be doing something, but I don't know what to do."

"There's not much you can do at this moment." I looked at my watch. It was after two o'clock. "Let's go have some lunch."

"Nick and I packed sandwiches. They're in a cooler in the back."

"No, let's get out of here for a while."

"Not a restaurant. I can't stand the thought of sitting in a crowded restaurant, listening to people chatter about stupid things that don't matter at all."

Yeah, and not only that, the news was out, and she didn't need to be seen in public with me.

"Please don't take this in any way as suggesting something inappropriate—I'd be happy for you to come to my place. I made a pot of chili last night. 'Monroe's killer cowboy chili,' my daughter calls it. I'm not sure she means it as a compliment."

She didn't exactly jump at the opportunity. She wiped her nose with a crumpled tissue and gave a little nod.

"It sounds delicious."

* * *

I left the park vehicle in the lot and we took my Bronco. I found an old hat under the seat and Elizabeth put it on. The news vans were still parked in front and I didn't think they would see us leave, but no reason to be conspicuous. Her cell phone rang as we pulled out on the highway and she let it go to voice mail. She put it on silent, and I heard it buzz nonstop on our way through town.

My cabin is a little over fifteen miles from the park, about four miles from Lyons. I turned on CR 80, onto Longmont Dam Road and then into what the realtor called a private drive—more like a wide gravel trail—leading to the house.

The cabin was built in 1950. It's one room, 580 square feet inside, with exposed logs, a big stone fireplace, and partitioned-off bedroom and bathroom. I put in bamboo floors and a new septic system when I bought it. The covered front porch is another couple hundred square feet and looks out over the river. I didn't need much furniture—I'd brought a couch, a few chairs, and a bed from Montana and given the rest of my furniture away. I bought a little dinette set for inside, a hammock and wicker chairs and a bigger table for the porch.

"This is charming," Elizabeth said.

"I like it."

I put a pan of chili on the stove to heat.

"Can I help?"

"This is a one-man kitchen." That was no exaggeration; it was just big enough for me to maneuver.

"I have beer, water, and coffee," I said.

"Water."

I filled two glasses from the tap, put them and bowls on a tray, and handed it to her. "We'll eat on the porch."

She went outside. When the chili was hot, I carried the pan and a couple sleeves of saltines out and set them on the table. Elizabeth served herself, swallowed a spoonful of chili, and coughed. She took a long drink of water and coughed again.

"That's not a good sign," I said.

It was the first time I heard her laugh. It was a nice sound.

"It's very flavorful. And very spicy."

"Too spicy, you think?"

"Maybe a little. I like spicy. But I can't make anything spicy at home. Nick and Henry won't eat it."

Her face clouded up, and we ate the rest of our meal in silence.

"More?" I said when we'd finished.

She shook her head. I took the pan and bowls inside and refilled our glasses, got a package of cookies from the cabinet, and went back to the porch.

"Dessert," I said.

"Fig Newtons," she said. "I love Fig Newtons."

We chewed on the cookies.

"It's so quiet here," she said. "All I hear is the river and the birds."

"That's about all you'll ever hear. Coyotes every now and then."

"Coyotes woke me last night. I thought it was Henry crying."

She stood up and went to the porch railing, leaned over it, and gazed out over the river.

I gave her a few minutes. Then said, "I want to go back to the subject of Alaska."

She didn't respond.

"In my experience," I said, "there's a lot of give and take in a marriage. Forgiveness when you least expect it, love when you think it might be gone. The loss of a child, though—it's hard for a marriage to survive the loss of a child."

"Are you saying you think Henry's dead?"

"No. I'm saying that something happened in Alaska that you don't want to talk about. But you have to. Whatever it is, even if there's only the smallest chance that it will help us find Henry, I need to know."

"If I thought it had the slightest bearing on Henry missing, I would have told you already."

"I don't doubt that, Elizabeth. But let me be the judge."

She turned to face me, jammed her hands in the back pockets of her jeans, and began.

* * *

"The Alaska case was big for me. A high-profile client, huge dollar amount at stake, and I landed the business. They came to me."

"Impressive."

She shrugged. "Then as things go in big firms, over the course of the case and on more than one occasion, male partners more senior than me tried to worm their way in and replace me as lead counsel."

"How does that even happen?"

"Easier than you'd think. Taking client executives out to lunch, just to be sure they're happy with how the case is going. Insinuating to the managing partner that I was in over my head, that the case would be better handled by someone with more experience. Hoping that he would step in and move me to second chair."

"Would he do that?"

"He does it all the time when it suits his purposes—whatever those might be at any given moment. And it's much easier to do when the target is a woman."

"It sounds pretty cutthroat."

"It's brutal." She came back to the table and sat down.

"Anyway, I managed to survive. I had a great team—a partner a few years junior to me, a couple of associates, the two best legal assistants in the litigation section. Experts that killed it in their analysis and on the witness stand. Just one problem."

"What was that?"

"Bob Simon—my managing partner—suggested that I hire a trial consultant. A guy named Bradford Riegle."

"Let me guess. It was a suggestion you had to take."

"Oh, yes. Riegle's a friend of Bob Simon, and he's done a lot of work with our firm. Not that Simon's really trying cases anymore, but for a long time you wouldn't see him at trial without Riegle attached at the hip."

"So you hired Riegle. What was his job?"

"He wanted to run the case. He thought I needed his help on everything—case themes and strategy, witness prep, graphic design, jury selection, writing my opening statement and closing argument. All at great expense to the client, of course."

"Did you let him?"

"No. He was good at analyzing jurors, reading people's faces and their reactions. But I consistently found him to be dead wrong on just about every other piece of advice he gave me. I'm convinced that if I'd done the things at trial that he suggested, we would have lost the case. So I ignored him."

"I'm guessing that didn't sit well with Mr. Riegle."

"It did not." She ate another Fig Newton, washed it down with a drink of water.

"Just to give you an idea of what he's like—a few months before trial, we did some work with mock juries. We hired about fifty average citizens and paid them two hundred dollars each to listen to our arguments and summaries of what the case was about, got their reactions and comments on what they thought was good, what the problems were. We did that for two days. It was helpful. It also was the source of a Riegle quote that was repeated more than once by the other members of our team."

"What was that?"

"When the mock jurors were signed in and assembled, he went to the front of the room to give them instructions on how the two days would go. His first words were, 'I'm Bradford Riegle. I'm in charge.' And he was dead serious. 'I'm Bradford Riegle. I'm in charge.' They couldn't get a drink or go to the bathroom without his permission. By the end of the first day, they all hated him. I don't think any of them would have come back the second day if they didn't have to stick it out to the bitter end to get paid."

"Sounds like a real jerk."

"He is. But it's not just that. He has anger issues—particularly with women. He was in the military, carries a gun in his briefcase. He's been divorced twice, and his latest girlfriend left him a few weeks before we went to Alaska. From what we heard, she packed up all her stuff one night when he was out of town, and he has no idea where she went."

"Problems with women, he's angry at you. Probably hates it when a woman's in control. Did he ever threaten you?"

She put her elbows on the table, wrapped her fingers around her empty glass. Stared blankly toward the river then looked at me.

"Could I have some more water?"

* * *

She was standing at the edge of the porch again when I came back outside. I handed her the glass, then leaned against the railing next to her. I waited. She pulled at her ponytail, twisting the end through her fingers.

"Paul and I met when we were students at the University of Texas. He moved to Houston after he got his degree, and I stayed in Austin for law school. The next three years were hard. We saw each other when we could, broke up too many times to count, then got married the summer after I graduated. I started work at the firm, he was teaching high school English and writing. Things were good."

She drained her glass, went to the table and set it down. Came back.

"I don't know if it was the pressure of beginning a career, or being a newlywed, or just blowing off steam after the stress of law school. I started to drink. Heavily. I'd go out with other lawyers from the firm after work and get drunk. I'd miss dinner with Paul, come home late. On the weekends, there was always a party somewhere and I'd drag Paul along. He hated it, couldn't think of anything more insufferable than a roomful of lawyers, especially when they were loud and wasted."

"Can't say I blame him there."

"No. Anyway, we'd been married two years when I started to think about getting pregnant. I didn't want to wait seven or eight years until I'd made partner—assuming I did. So one morning while I was getting ready for work, I told Paul I thought we should have a baby. He looked up very calmly from his cup of coffee and said he didn't want to have children with me. That he didn't think he wanted to be married to me anymore."

"Out of the blue?"

"I suppose. But it wasn't like I'd been paying attention. I said, 'What are you talking about?' And he said, 'Go look in the mirror.' He said he was tired of going to bed with me drunk, and tired of looking at my hangover in the morning."

"Well, you're still married, and you've got two boys. It must have been the kick in the ass that you needed."

"It was. I got sober."

"Twelve steps?"

"No. I just quit. Cold turkey. And I stayed sober. Until Alaska."

Her cell phone buzzed. She pulled it from her front shirt pocket.

"It's Paul."

She answered it, told him there was no news. She'd had a late lunch with me, would come home in a while. Listened, said okay, love you, and hung up.

"He thinks it's important that one of us be at the command post—that we're there when Henry is found."

She put her cell phone back in her pocket.

"Could we finish this on the way back?"

"Sure."

* * *

I put the pan and bowls in the sink to soak while she went to the bathroom. I closed the door behind us, and we got in my Bronco.

"You don't lock your doors?" she said.

"I don't have anything worth stealing. I've never had any trouble, but I figure if someone comes out here while I'm gone, I'd rather they go in and have a look around without breaking a window or kicking in the door."

I turned onto 36 West and headed toward Estes Park.

"You took a drink in Alaska. The first time in how many years?"

"Thirteen. And I didn't just take a drink. I got wasted on the weekends. We all did—the lawyers, the clients, the experts."

"And Riegle," I said.

"And Riegle."

She stuck her head out the open window, ponytail whipping around her face, breathed in the cool air. Clouds were forming over the mountains. She pulled her head back inside and took a deep breath.

"I don't know if I can tell you this."

"You can tell me. I've got a pretty good idea already."

"You have to understand being in trial."

"I seriously doubt that will ever happen."

"It gets to be like you're living in a different reality. It's all-consuming and so much work. I thought about Nick and Henry, of course, and I missed them terribly. But otherwise, you kind of lose track of the outside world."

She fidgeted with her ponytail, then rested her elbow outside the window.

"So, Riegle. He's not a nice person and I wouldn't hire him again, but he was part of the team. He was there. And he is one hell of a good-looking man. As one of my closest girlfriends said, he's fucking gorgeous."

This is when I'm reminded again that I am hopelessly old-fashioned—I find it jarring to hear her say the f-word. I recall a few *damns* out of Maggie over the years, well-justified and of which I was usually the cause, but never anything stronger.

"A little over halfway through trial, he started coming on to me when we were out on the weekends. And because I was drunk, I started kind of flirting with him. All of a sudden, there was this . . . attraction."

"Even though he's such a jerk?"

She shrugged. "Yeah. Well. He's different from Paul."

I got it. A little more dangerous than the stay-at-home poet.

"So. One Saturday night not long before the end of trial, Riegle and I were the only ones at dinner. The team was pretty sick of spending every moment together and people went their separate ways."

She paused as we approached the Ranger Operations Center.

"After dinner, we rode up together in the elevator. He got off on my floor and followed me to my room. I let him come in."

"Then one thing led to another," I said.

She pulled at her ponytail again.

"Yes. One thing led to another."

I parked but didn't get out. I wanted to finish this conversation while she was willing to talk about it.

"Are you still having an affair?"

She winced. "An affair. It was only one night. Does that count as an affair?"

"I'm not an expert on that." I wasn't sure I believed her, either. "Only one?"

She hugged herself and gazed out the window.

"Paul and the boys called early the next morning. They were making Sunday pancakes and put me on speaker phone. So I could have breakfast with them."

"I'm guessing that was rough."

"You have no idea. Riegle was still there."

Jesus. We sat quiet for a while.

"Is that all?" I finally said.

"No. When I hung up the phone Riegle wanted . . . he tried. . . ."

I didn't need to hear every little detail. "And you said no."

"I said no, and . . . and he got angry. He pushed me down on the bed and I kicked and hit him. I told him I was going to scream and that wouldn't work out well for either of us. He stopped. He called me a lot of things as he was leaving. But he left. It didn't happen again."

"Have you seen him since Alaska?"

She shook her head. "We weren't on the same flight back to Houston. I went to the office a few times before we came to Colorado but didn't hear anything from him. And I certainly didn't try to contact him."

"Did he know you were coming to Colorado with your family?"

"Yes, we talked about taking vacations, what we planned to do as soon as trial was over. Everyone on the team was envious of my house in Estes Park."

"Okay. I want to talk to Riegle. You have his contact information with you?"

"Yes, I'll give it to you. He has a lot of issues, but I don't think he would do anything to Henry. Or to me. If he wanted to hurt me, he could have done it in Alaska."

"You're probably right." I opened my door. "Then again, he's had some time to think about it."

CHAPTER

9

Nick

IT SUCKED THAT they wouldn't let me help with the search for Henry. I kind of understood why, but I know first aid and how to mark a trail and how to send a distress signal. I wished it was me that was lost instead of Henry. I'd know what to do. Ranger Monroe said come see him when I'm eighteen and he'll give me a job. Yeah, right. Like that's supposed to make me feel better. He was just treating me like a kid.

Dad was really tired. When we got back to the cabin he went to take a shower, and when he didn't come out after a while, I peeked into him and Mom's bedroom and he was sleeping on the bed in his underwear. I thought maybe he'd get cold like that, so I put a blanket over him and turned off the light and closed the door.

The sandwiches Mom and me made were in the cooler in the truck, and I was wishing we'd remembered to bring some of them home. I went to the kitchen and looked in the refrigerator. A bunch of healthy stuff. Thanks to Dad, though, we had three kinds of ice cream. I got a big scoop of each and took the bowl to the couch in the living room. I ate a couple spoons of ice cream then pulled out my phone. I got it for my birthday. It was just a flip phone, not a Blackberry like my mom's, but it was cool to finally have one. I had a text from Ashley. She's been one of my best friends since preschool.

Her: OMG. R u ok? Heard abt Henry it's on the news.
Me: Idk. No, prolly not.
Her: Y?
Me: Cuz it's all my fault.
Her: ???????

All of a sudden I didn't want to talk to Ashley anymore. I didn't want to talk to anyone.

Me: Call u later. Gotta go.
Her: When?
Me: Idk. Later.

I finished my ice cream and set the bowl on the floor. The cabin was really quiet. I thought Dad had been asleep a long time then I looked at my phone and saw it was maybe only half an hour. I told Mom last summer that we really needed a TV in the cabin. She asked me why and I told her there were times it would be nice to have one. She said like when, and I said like when we can't think of anything else to do. And she said we'd never have a problem thinking of something to do in Colorado. I was wishing Mom was there because I'd say see, this is what I was talking about. This is one of those times it would be nice to have a TV.

I went to my room and got my Nerf gun, then came back out to the living room and blasted a round of darts at the deer above the fireplace. The darts bounced all over the place after they hit the deer. I picked them up and reloaded and shot again. The deer just stared. Shooting at Henry was a lot more fun. He'd take cover behind the couch, then poke his head over and shoot back before making a break for it, sliding in his sock feet and diving under the dining room table, which was dumb because he was trapped under there. I'd move in, circle the table if he tried to get out the other side, and blast him at close range. He'd laugh until he peed his pants, then get mad and call me a fucking fucker. And that would be it for the guns for a while because Mom would take them away. I must have told him like a hundred times, "You can't say this word around Mom."

I dropped the Nerf gun on the floor. Henry's room was at the end of the hall, past mine. I wanted to go have a look around in his room, but I was kind of scared. Then I thought, *That's stupid, there's nobody in there.* I kicked off my shoes and took a few steps down the hall. I stopped and went back and picked up my Nerf gun, reloaded it, and held it ready as I tiptoed to Henry's door. The door was open, but I pushed it open even more with my gun and took a quick look behind it. I turned on the light and went in.

There was a pile of Transformers and Teenage Mutant Ninja Turtles on the floor under a poster of Hakeem Olajuwon. It was a life-size poster, like seven feet tall. Henry liked to stand next to Hakeem, and I'd say, "You're like as tall as his balls." His baseball stuff and his basketball were in a crate by the closet door. I took a look in the closet—just clothes and sneakers and more toys, stuff like that. *Frog and Toad* books on the table by his bed. That's about it. I thought about looking under the bed, but that made me kind of scared again. I picked up the basketball, went back to the living room and put on my shoes, then went outside to shoot hoops.

The part of the driveway by the house is cement, not gravel, so we can play basketball. The goal's at the edge of the cement. It's one of those that you can move up and down. It was set at six feet for Henry, and I liked it there because I could dunk when it was that low. I dunked a couple of times, slammed the ball against the garage door, caught it, and dribbled in for the dunk again. "Bam! That's what I'm talking about."

"Hey, buddy."

It was Dad, coming out the front door. He'd put on jeans and a T-shirt, but he was barefoot and his hair was kind of sticking up from sleeping on it wet. He still looked tired.

"Hey, Dad. Did I wake you up?"

"No. My cell phone woke me up. Everyone we know is calling. I'm letting most of the calls go to voice mail."

"Did you tell Grandma?"

"Yeah. I called her before I got in the shower. I talked to Aunt Kathleen early this morning, and she's calling the rest of the family."

I took a shot about ten feet from the basket. It went in, all net.

"You want me to raise the basket?" Dad said.

"No, it's okay. Henry may want to shoot some hoops when he gets home."

Dad didn't say anything, just watched me shoot for a while. Then he went in to get a cup of coffee, and when he came back out, he sat on the front porch. I took a few more shots, moving closer to Dad and farther from the basket, until my last shot was from the front porch. It hit the backboard but not the rim and bounced off into the grass. I sat down beside Dad.

"Don't leave Henry's ball out in the grass."

I got the ball and came back to the porch.

"Detective Carpenter should be here in a little bit," Dad said. "Like we talked about on the way home, he'll want to ask you a few questions about Henry."

I bounced the basketball between my knees, hard and fast.

"Would you mind not doing that, honey? My head hurts a little."

I held the basketball on my lap. And I tried really, really hard not to, but I started to cry. It's like I was crying all the time when I don't really cry that much most of the time. Dad put down his coffee cup, took the basketball and set it on the porch, and pulled me on his lap.

"This is hard," he said.

"It's my fault. I should have gone to the toilet with him."

"No, Nick. It's not your fault. We should have left Sky Pond sooner, when there were still other people on the trail. We should have insisted that you stay with us when it started to rain. I should have run after you, not let you get out of my sight. We should have picked up our pace, not screwed around watching the falls. We can come up with a long list of should haves, but it won't help get Henry back."

That made me feel a little better, I guess, if him and Mom weren't mad at me. I sat on his lap and finally stopped crying.

"Here comes Detective Carpenter," he said. "I see his car down by the gate."

I sat up. I watched the police car coming up the driveway then I turned around to say something to Dad. And I saw something that made me scared all over again. Dad looked different. He looked old. Like how I remember Grandpa.

"I got snot on your shirt," I said.

He smiled a little and looked like Dad again.

"It's not the first time I've had snot on my shirt. Hop up, big boy. My legs are going to sleep."

C H A P T E R

10

Paul

IT WAS PRETTY rough watching Carpenter and the cop he'd brought with him go through Henry's room and the boys' bathroom, bagging up *Frog and Toad Are Friends*, pieces of a floor puzzle, his toothbrush with a picture of Batman on its thick handle and bits of dried toothpaste on the bristles. Carpenter was thorough but gentle in his questioning of Nick and told him he was a fine big brother when they were finished. Nick seemed to handle it pretty well. Elizabeth came home while the cops were still there, and I left them to return to the command post.

Monroe wasn't around when I got there, but he arrived late in the evening. He'd taken a shower and changed clothes and looked like he'd gotten a little sleep. Carpenter was with him.

"Any leads yet?" I said.

Monroe hesitated, looked at Carpenter then back at me.

"Not much to go on yet. But it's something." He stepped behind the desk, his chair squeaking as he eased into it.

"I talked to all the rangers on duty at the entrance stations yesterday. One of them remembers seeing a truck with Alaska plates—she just happened to glance at the plates and visitors from Alaska are not exactly a common occurrence."

"Did she get a look at the guy? A make on the truck?"

"She doesn't remember anything about the vehicle or the occupants."

"Goddamn it. How could she not remember?"

"We get thousands of vehicles a day in August, Paul. That she even noticed the plates is fortunate. But the most helpful bit of information is that she's pretty sure the truck came through early in the morning. Just before sunup."

He paused. It took me a moment, then it hit me.

"That's when we got to the park. He was following us."

"It's possible. So. Elizabeth gave me a list of everyone she could think of involved in the Alaska case. Carpenter will start calling them in the morning."

"And ask them what?"

"Their whereabouts in the past few days," Carpenter said. "Whether they know of any reason someone might want to hurt your wife or your family. Did they notice anything especially peculiar about someone they came in contact with in Anchorage. That kind of thing."

"Whether they own a dark-colored pickup," I said.

"I'll probably ask what kind of vehicle they drive."

"Did Elizabeth single out anyone in particular for you to talk to?" I asked Monroe.

He hesitated.

"She doesn't think anyone connected to the case would have kidnapped Henry."

Monroe was careful with that answer, I thought. I made a mental note to ask Elizabeth about it.

"Any other leads?" I said.

He shook his head. "Nothing on the truck. We have checkpoints set up on roads throughout the park. Carpenter's talked to the registered sex offenders in the area, but they're all accounted for at the time Henry went missing."

I felt sick. I thought about asking how many there were in Larimer County, but decided I didn't want to know.

"You're sure of that?" I said.

"It's a small town," Carpenter said. "We know who they are. Where they work, where they live. We keep pretty close track." He held out his hand. "Nick's a fine boy. I know Henry is, too."

I watched him leave, took a few minutes to swallow the lump in my throat before turning back to Monroe.

"I've worked with him before," Monroe said. "He's a good cop."

"Let's hope so."

"You planning to be here all night?"

"Yes. I came a little better prepared—sleeping bag and a pillow so I can stretch out in the back of the Jeep. Elizabeth and I agreed that I'll take the night shift, she'll be here during the day. One of us needs to be with Nick."

I poured myself a cup of coffee, looked at the park map on the wall behind Monroe.

"Do you have enough volunteers? My sister suggested maybe we should contact Texas EquuSearch."

"We have all we need, and more we can call."

"Elizabeth's law firm offered to post a reward for information leading to Henry's safe return. Fifty thousand dollars."

Monroe's eyes widened, and he leaned back in his chair. "That could be helpful."

We sat for a while without saying anything. I kept going back over in my mind the details of the hike, the thunderstorm, the realization that Henry was gone. I looked at my watch.

"Twenty-eight hours."

"Yes."

"It seems a lot longer." I was tired. "What's the date today?"

"August 16."

"August 16. The boys have to be back for school on August 23."

Monroe didn't say anything.

"I don't know what we'll do if we haven't found Henry by then," I said.

"You'll take Nick back to Houston. Get him to school, involved with his friends and activities."

He stood up, put his hand on my shoulder. "If Henry is in Rocky and we haven't found him a week from now, this won't be a search and rescue, Paul. It'll be a recovery."

* * *

I spent a couple of restless hours in the Jeep, not sure how much I slept. It made me appreciate even more the people who were camped out on rough terrain looking for my son. I rolled out of my sleeping bag as the sun came up, made a stop at the men's room, and went to the command post. Monroe was still there, looking at the updated map tacked to the wall. I sat with him a couple of hours, talking to rangers who came and went, listening to radioed reports from the teams, the areas they'd covered, where they were searching today. Nothing new. No trace found. Thirty-eight hours missing.

"I guess I'll go home for a while," I said. "Elizabeth will be here later."

"I'll let you know if we hear anything," Monroe said.

I stopped at the Donut Haus, bought bags of apple fritters, long johns, chocolate and cherry-iced donuts. It wouldn't be a trip to the Donut Haus without donut holes, Henry's favorite, so I bought a dozen of those. I got a cup of coffee and sat outside for a while, ate an apple fritter, and watched the kids on the giant slide, one of Nick and Henry's favorite spots in Estes. Trek up five flights of beat-up metal stairs, grab a ratty scrap of carpet to ride, enjoy a few seconds of bumpy glee screaming down the slide. Repeat. Repeat. Repeat. Repeat. Henry always anxious about whether

Nick really knew the secret to which lanes were the fastest on any given day.

I threw my coffee cup in the trash, collected the donut bags, and got in the Jeep. Traffic through town was heavy, tourist season drawing to a close in a few weeks, but the streets and sidewalks still jammed with visitors seeking T-shirts and souvenirs. I called Elizabeth, asked if we needed anything from Safeway. She didn't think so. I drove up Devil's Gulch Road and threw on the brakes when the gate to our property came into sight. I pulled off to the side of the road. *Shit.*

The press had found us. I called Elizabeth.

"Have you looked outside this morning?"

"I was out at sunrise, but now I'm lying on the couch. Nick's still asleep. What is it?"

"Half a dozen news vans parked outside the gate. Waiting for us to come out, apparently."

"Oh God."

"I can turn around and go back to the command post. Let them sit there all day."

"No. I'll walk down and meet you."

The reporters saw Elizabeth coming, jumped out of their vans, got cameras and microphones ready. Adjusted their clothes and smoothed their hair. When Elizabeth was almost to the gate, I drove the final few yards, stopped, and got out. Elizabeth unlocked the gate, came to me, and took my hand.

Questions hit us from all sides. I turned in the direction of one of them, saw the microphone inches away, and opened my mouth to answer. Nothing came out. I couldn't speak, couldn't form the words to respond. I looked at Elizabeth and shook my head. The strain and anguish were visible on her face, but she touched my cheek then held up her hand, silent for a few moments, until the reporters fell quiet.

"You all know that our beautiful boy, Henry English, is missing. He's six years old and, along with his brother, Nick, the light of our lives." Her voice cracked, tears ran, and I don't know how she went on. But she did.

"We don't know if Henry is lost in Rocky Mountain National Park. We don't know if he's been kidnapped. We are grateful for the many professionals and volunteers who are searching tirelessly for our son. A fifty-thousand-dollar reward has been established for information leading to his safe return. Please bring Henry back to us. And that's all we're going to say now."

She led me to the Jeep, and I got behind the wheel. She held the gate open while I drove through, then locked it behind me, some reporters still shouting questions, some turned to their cameraman, making a report. Elizabeth got in the Jeep beside me, the chatter fading but, no doubt, the cameras still rolling as we drove away.

* * *

"I'm sorry." I dropped the donut bags on the kitchen counter. "I don't know what happened. It was like I couldn't move my mouth. I couldn't say a word."

Elizabeth came up behind me, put her arms around my waist.

"It's okay." We stood like that for a while then I turned around and kissed her.

"I brought donuts."

"I saw that. Do you want some scrambled eggs?"

"Nah. I'd hate to ruin a good sugar high."

I poured a glass of orange juice and sat on a bar stool at the kitchen island. Elizabeth ate a cherry-iced with a glass of milk then started on the donut holes.

"I think we should send Nick back to Houston," she said. "He's bored and scared, and all the time on his hands just gives him more opportunity to worry. And now with the media, we're trapped."

"I agree. He can stay at Kathleen's. A few days with his rowdy cousins would do him good." I finished my long john, licked the chocolate off my fingers. "I'll call her."

I put my glass in the dishwasher and turned back to Elizabeth.

"Monroe says the truck with Alaska plates came through the entrance station a little before dawn."

Her jaw dropped. "How do they know?"

"The ranger manning the booth noticed the plates. But nothing else."

She picked up the bag of donut holes, looked inside, set it down again.

"It drove in around the same time we did," she said slowly. "It was at the trailhead when we came out. So someone from Alaska went on a hike yesterday."

She folded her napkin, swiped it across the counter, collecting sugar crumbs in her hand.

"Or someone was following us." She looked up at me. "I still don't believe that. But if it's true, he knows where we live. We have to get Nick out of here today."

"We do. Monroe said you gave him a list of names of people connected to the Alaska case."

She nodded. "Everyone I could think of—our team, our opponents, witnesses. Even court staff."

"Do you think anyone on that list could possibly be a suspect?"

She shook sugar crumbs into the sink.

"I don't think anyone connected to the case would have kidnapped Henry."

I waited for a moment, then took out my cell phone. "That's exactly what Monroe said when I asked him your take on it."

She rinsed her hands, reached for a towel, stared out the window while she dried them. "That's my opinion. Let's hope I'm right."

CHAPTER

11

Elizabeth

I WAS MORTIFIED TELLING Monroe about Brad Riegle. I didn't think he would tell Paul, and apparently, he hadn't. If it became necessary, I would do it. But not until then—I wouldn't voluntarily raise the possibility that our son was kidnapped because I got drunk and slept with a member of my trial team.

I hadn't had a drink since that last night in Alaska. I admit, though, a powerful urge to stop at the liquor stores I passed on the way home from the command center.

Paul went out to the porch to call Kathleen. I joined him just as he was ending the conversation. He said goodbye, then looked up at me.

"We got Nick on a Southwest flight leaving Denver at 7:05 tonight. Kathleen said don't worry about washing his clothes, just throw what he needs to bring home in a suitcase and she'll take care of it."

"Good. I'll go wake him."

Nick was not happy at first about being sent home, but as the day went on, the tension I'd seen in him since Henry's disappearance seemed to ease a bit. He needed distance from our nightmare, needed kids and television, swimming parties before school began, soccer practice and fantasy football. He ate donuts until I told him to stop or he'd be sick on the plane, then showered and sat on the bed watching me pack his clothes.

"You'll board first, with any other unaccompanied minors. Aunt Kathleen will be waiting for you when you land."

"Mom. This isn't the first time I've flown by myself."

True. He was a seasoned traveler, having been on trips with Paul and me from the time he was born, to London, Paris, Mexico, all over the U.S. and Canada. But as I packed, a scene kept playing in my mind. Nick walking down the runway in Denver, disappearing into the plane—never to be seen again.

"I know. You'll be fine."

I zipped the suitcase and set it on the floor. Nick took the handle and rolled it into the living room.

"Ready to go?" Paul said.

"Yup."

We'd agreed that Paul would take Nick to Denver, buy him dinner at the airport, and stay with him until the plane took off. The press was still camped out beyond the gate. We put Nick's suitcase in the Jeep in the garage, with the door closed. He lay down in the back seat, and I sat beside Paul in front. Paul opened the garage door and backed out, turned the Jeep around, and headed down the driveway. As we approached the gate, I said, "I love you, Nicky," and he said, "I love you" back. I hopped out and unlocked the gate, opened then closed it after Paul had driven through. Cameras clicked and whirred, still and video shots of Paul driving away, me walking back to the cabin as the reporters shouted, "Is there any news of Henry, Mrs. English?" "Have they found anything—any articles of clothing?" "It's been almost forty-eight hours since Henry went missing . . . Do you believe he's still alive?"

* * *

I heated a can of soup in the microwave, poured it into a thermos, and got a large bottle of water from the refrigerator. I pulled on a flannel shirt and jeans, grabbed my field jacket, locked up the house, and threw everything in the truck. I hated the thought of running the gauntlet of reporters again but hated the thought of being cooped up in the house alone for the rest of the afternoon and evening even more.

This time I spoke briefly to the reporters as I opened and closed the gate, telling them there was no news. Two of the vans followed me as I drove to the Ranger Operations Center, but they didn't try to question me again.

I stayed at the command post until dark, a woman ranger I hadn't met before filling in for Monroe for a few hours. She was kind and sympathetic and answered my questions in detail until there wasn't anything else to say and she sat there awkwardly watching me drink my soup. I finally said I thought I'd go home.

"Good night, Mrs. English. I hope you can sleep."

No, I thought, *I won't sleep. I don't know if I'll ever sleep again.*

My cell coverage comes and goes near the park, and my phone started buzzing with voicemails and texts as I drove to town—some of them from Nick and Paul. Thunderstorms in Houston, the flight was delayed. We'll keep you posted.

The press was gone when I got back to the cabin. I unlocked and locked the gate by the lights on the truck, parked the truck in the driveway, and went inside. I stopped by the front door, hung up my jacket, and listened. The house was deathly silent. Something rattled in the kitchen, and I jumped. It rattled again. Ice dropping from the ice maker into the bin.

I shook my head. *Get a grip, Elizabeth.* I turned on a few lamps, lowered the living room shades. I opened the front door and stepped out onto the porch. It was a beautiful night, hundreds of stars visible in the cloudless sky. Not another soul in sight. But for some reason, I was uneasy standing on the porch alone. I stepped back inside and closed the door behind me, my heart beating a little faster, my fingers trembling. I couldn't shake the feeling that someone was out there. Watching me.

CHAPTER

12

Monroe

I STOPPED AT CARPENTER'S office on my way back to the command post after lunch.

"Checking up on me?" he said.

"I thought you might want some help with that list."

"Not really. But go ahead, since you're here."

My first call was to Bradford Riegle's office. Mr. Riegle was out of the office on vacation, I was told, and wouldn't return until after Labor Day. *Must be nice.*

"I'll try his cell phone."

"Mr. Riegle answers his cell phone during vacation only if his office calls."

"Does he respond to voice mail?"

"Rarely. He often goes for days without checking it."

Swell. "Would you call him for me?"

"I don't call unless it's an emergency."

"Ma'am, this is an emergency." I explained that it had to do with Henry English's disappearance and gave her my contact information.

"I'll certainly try to reach him," she said.

While I waited to hear from Riegle, Carpenter and I started down the list Elizabeth had given me. Lawyers, legal assistants, videographers, court reporters. The manager at the Marriott, the guy who made copies for them at Kinko's. The judge's office manager. I called Elizabeth.

"What about the jury?" I said.

"I'll ask my assistant to email you the juror questionnaires. We talked to them after the trial, and they were very complimentary of our team."

"They liked you?"

"They liked me. It probably would be best for you and me to discuss them individually after you've looked at the questionnaires. Those will give you basic information about age, occupation, marital status. If you decide you want to contact any of them, I would need to get approval from the judge."

"Good. How are you holding up?"

There was a pause before she answered.

"Not well." Her voice cracked.

"I know. I'm sorry."

There was another pause.

"We're sending Nick back to Houston. He'll stay with Paul's sister for now."

"I think that's wise."

"The press found us. They're camped outside our gate. Paul and I talked to them. I hope it was okay."

"Yeah, I saw you on the news. You did fine. And from what I hear, the tip line has been busy since the minute the reward was announced."

"It has?"

I hated to hear the hope in her voice. There'd been a lot of calls, but nothing worth following up on. The usual cranks looking for any chance to cash in on the reward. Psychics offering their services for a fee. A few callers asking for more details on what happened to Henry, like they couldn't get enough of it from their televisions and the internet.

"Nothing solid yet," I said.

"Okay." This time, disappointment. Sadness I could feel through the telephone line. "I have to go," she said.

I gave her Carpenter's email address. A message from her secretary hit his inbox ten minutes later. Per instructions from Ms. English, juror questionnaires scanned and attached. Carpenter sent them to print and handed them to me. He read them on the computer.

"You see anything interesting here?" he said.

I shuffled through the papers and shook my head. "Five women and three men. Kindergarten teacher, nurse, bookkeeper for an auto parts store, assistant manager at T.G.I. Friday's. Salesclerk at Nordstrom's, civil engineer, computer programmer, and a barista. All friendly to Elizabeth, so she says. But I'll follow up with her later."

Carpenter sipped his Diet Coke and stared out the window. "How's the search going?"

"We're coming up empty so far."

"It's not good."

"No." Most search and rescues are resolved in under twelve hours. We were going on forty-eight hours for Henry. We'd keep looking, but the most likely areas where he would be found had been scrubbed thoroughly.

"Cute kid," Carpenter said.

I had printed pictures of Henry and given Carpenter one. It was propped up on his desk.

"Yeah. He is."

My phone rang.

"Monroe," I said.

"Mr. Monroe. This is Bradford Riegle."

I motioned to Carpenter that this might take a while. He nodded, and I stepped outside.

"Mr. Riegle. Thanks for returning my call."

"My secretary said it has something to do with a missing child. Elizabeth English's son?"

"Yes, you may have seen it on the news?"

"No, Mr. Monroe. I'm on my bike. My annual trip—no television, no newspapers, and to the extent possible, very little phone."

"Your bike?"

"Harley. Not Schwinn."

"Got it." I told him about Henry's disappearance, the pickup and the Alaska plates.

"What's this got to do with me?"

"The Alaska plates may just be a coincidence. But we're talking to everyone connected with the case Mrs. English tried in Anchorage."

"I drive a Mercedes, Mr. Monroe. Which is parked in my garage in Houston because I've been on the backroads on my Harley for the past two weeks."

Well, good for you.

"Where are you now, Mr. Riegle?"

"Not far from Taos. Camping tonight in the Sangre de Cristo Mountains."

Not far from Taos. Not far from the Colorado border, either. Tomorrow was my day off. Which I hadn't planned to take, until now.

"Would it be possible for you to meet me in Colorado Springs, Mr. Riegle? Tomorrow afternoon? If you don't have to be somewhere else, that is."

"I don't have to be anywhere for the next month. And I don't have any plans. But it sounds like a waste of your time and mine."

"Maybe. I understand that you and Mrs. English had a little altercation in Alaska. In her hotel room, when she asked you to leave."

There was silence on the other end of the line. I thought he'd hung up on me or we'd lost the connection. But he finally spoke.

"That bitch. Tell me when and where in Colorado Springs."

CHAPTER

13

Paul

NICK WAS QUIET on the ride to the airport. He flipped through his CD case and put on *Jock Rock* and *Jock Jams* and stared out the window, occasionally singing along. I'd thought I might say something about Henry while we drove, but realized I couldn't without breaking down—and that Nick didn't need to see my emotions on full display.

We checked his bag at the Southwest counter, and I got a pass to accompany him to the gate. His flight was delayed due to thunderstorms in Houston. The long lines at security were typical of Denver International in August, and Nick was randomly selected for additional screening. Watching the TSA agents wand my son, an elderly man in a wheelchair, and an eighteen-month-old baby made me feel safe as hell. Nick rolled his eyes when they patted him down, but complied patiently with arms outstretched and sock feet planted on the shoeprint templates as instructed. We found a McDonald's near the gate; Nick asked for a double quarter pounder with cheese and fries, and I ordered a milkshake. We took the food to a table by the windows and ate while we watched the planes take off and land.

"If Henry was here, he'd want a Happy Meal," Nick said. "Just so he could get some stupid toy."

"Yes, he would." It wasn't so long ago that Nick was equally excited about Happy Meals, but the about-to-be-a-fifth-grader was way too cool for that now. Not to mention that it would take at least three of the things to fill him up. He finished the last of his fries and crumpled up his burger bag.

"You want some dessert?" I said.

"I guess."

I handed him a five. He went to the counter and came back with a hot fudge sundae.

"Keep the change," I said.

"Okay."

That reminded me to give him a couple of twenties. "Aunt Kathleen will take care of anything you need until Mom and I get home, but here's a little money."

"Thanks, Dad." He stuffed the bills in his pocket and focused again on his sundae. He'd eaten about half of it when he pushed it across the table and asked if I wanted the rest. I shook my head. He folded his arms and rested his elbows on the table and looked out the window.

"If I was lost, would you look for me?"

"Of course we would, Nick."

"I mean like really look. Look hard."

"Yes, son. We would do everything we could to find you."

He was quiet for a moment, avoided my eyes.

"Then how come you're not looking for Henry?"

It was like he'd kicked me in the stomach.

"What are you talking about? We've been looking for Henry since the moment we realized he was missing."

He turned to look at me squarely, accusation written on his face.

"No, you haven't. The park rangers are looking for him. The search teams are looking for him. The cops are looking for him. But you and Mom are just sitting around."

There have been only a few times since my sons were born that I became so angry I had to walk away from one or both of them. Shut my mouth and turn around and remove myself before I lost control. Like the morning we were late for school for the third time in a week when Elizabeth was out of town, and Henry, in pre-K that year, fought me about getting dressed, complained that his breakfast was disgusting, refused to brush his teeth. Nick was in the car and I was by the back door yelling for Henry until finally I went to the boys' bathroom to get him, and what I found was not only Henry, but Henry's pee. Everywhere. Puddling on the floor, dripping down the wall behind the toilet, painting lines on the glass shower door. Pee sprayed on the hand towels, soaking the roll of toilet paper, soiling Henry's white socks and Velcro tennis shoes.

"What the hell happened?" I said.

Henry zipped his shorts and glared up at me. "I missed."

He must have been saving up all night. I took one more look, turned around, and walked out. I went to my bedroom and closed the door and sat with the lights off until I knew I could talk sternly, but calmly, to Henry as opposed to knocking his block off. When I came out, he was in the car with Nick. He had changed his socks and shoes.

And now here was Nick, accusing Elizabeth and me of not trying to find his brother. All the stress of the past two days was waiting to explode.

I picked up his sundae cup and the other trash on the table and threw it away. There was a flight monitor across the walkway from McDonald's. I went to it and found the flight to Houston. Still delayed, another two hours minimum. I scanned the list of departing flights, breathing in on Albuquerque and out on Atlanta, breathing in and out all the way down to Tulsa and Washington, DC. When I got to the end of the list, I started over again. I read the departing flights, breathing in and out, until I realized that someone was standing beside me and had been for a while. I looked at Nick, at the tears streaming down his face, and pulled him to my chest. *I don't know how we can survive this,* I thought. *This will kill us all.*

We went to the gate and found two seats, with an empty seat between us. Nick reached into his backpack for a deck of cards, and we played gin until the flight finally boarded. I held him close and told him I loved him. "We'll find Henry," I said. He nodded. I watched him down the jetway until he disappeared, then went to the window and found him again on the plane. I waited until the plane pushed back from the gate, turned and nosed toward the runway. I looked at my watch; he wouldn't arrive in Houston until after midnight. I called Kathleen and talked to her as I walked to the parking lot.

"Take care of him," I said as I unlocked the Jeep.

"You know I will. You and Elizabeth take care of yourselves."

"Yeah. Well. That's not really possible right now."

I said goodbye and got in the Jeep. The airport was deserted. Peña Boulevard was quiet as I drove toward I-25. The mountains to the west were dark and silent. I had never felt so miserable in my life.

* * *

Elizabeth was in bed when I got back to the cabin. I kicked off my shoes inside the front door, went to the kitchen, and filled a glass with water from the tap. I stopped at the hall bathroom, then turned off the lights and lay down on the sofa, cell phone in hand, waiting, in the dark. At 11:30, a text came from Kathleen. "Nick in H-town. Got him."

I pushed myself up from the couch, walked quietly down the hall to our bedroom, and stripped down to my shorts, then slipped into bed beside Elizabeth. I sighed and closed my eyes.

"Everything okay with Nick?"

"Yeah. I just got a text from Kathleen saying that he made it to Houston."

"How was he when he left?"

"Hurting."

My throat tightened. She let out what sounded like a cough that turned into a sob. I rolled over on my side to her and put my arms around her and we held each other and wept for our son, our little Henry. After a while I wiped my eyes and let go, sat up on the side of the bed, and gulped the rest of my water. I went to the bathroom, filled my glass, asked Elizabeth if I could get her anything. "No," came the response, low and muffled against the pillow. I sat down again, rested my elbows on my thighs and held my head in my hands.

"Nick accused us of not trying to find Henry."

"What?"

"He said the park rangers are looking, the search teams and the cops are looking, but you and I are just sitting around."

She was quiet for a moment.

"He's right," she said. "We have to do something."

"Like what?"

"Make flyers. Advertise the reward money, put Henry's picture on them, distribute them all over town."

"His picture's already on television and the internet."

"People here are on vacation. They're not necessarily glued to a TV set or on the internet every day. A lot of places don't even have internet."

"Okay. I'll check in with Monroe in the morning, let him know what we're doing."

I lay down, pulled the covers up to my ears. Elizabeth liked to sleep with the windows open; it must have been sixty degrees in our room. I closed my eyes but couldn't sleep, my mind racing with images of Henry. Curled up under a rock, shivering, terrified of the wind howling in the trees and calling for me and his mother. Bobbing and gasping in whitewater rapids, struggling to stay afloat, then disappearing without a sound. Unconscious, his skull cracked open, just out of sight from a well-traveled trail. Eyes wide open, bound and gagged. In the back of a dark-colored pickup.

CHAPTER

14

Monroe

I ARRANGED TO MEET Riegle at the Cracker Barrel off I-25 at two o'clock the following afternoon. I figured it would take him four hours or so to get there. I woke up early the next morning and took a long walk by the river. I wasn't getting much exercise, and eating my killer cowboy chili three days in a row had me feeling a little sluggish. My daughter told me I should get a dog, that I'd walk more if I had one. "I might do that," I told her, but then thought about me and a dog in a 580-square-foot cabin in the dead of winter and decided against it.

I heard my cell phone ringing while I was in the shower. I let the hot water run on my neck a while longer, then got out and wrapped a towel around my waist. Elizabeth English had left a message. I carried a cup of coffee to the porch and returned her call. We talked a few minutes, then she put Paul on the phone.

"I'm just wondering how the phone inquiries went yesterday," he said.

"No real leads yet. I'm following up with one of the members of Elizabeth's trial team, though. I'm leaving in a few minutes to meet him in Colorado Springs."

"Who?"

"A guy named Bradford Riegle."

"Oh, sure. The jury consultant. Elizabeth was really upset when Bob Simon made her hire Riegle. She thinks he's an asshole."

"That's what she told me."

"What's he doing in Colorado Springs?"

"He's camping near Taos. It's not that far."

"Any particular reason you want to meet with him in person?"

I thought about telling him to ask his wife. *No.* I didn't need to add any more stress to their lives right now.

"He's in the area." I stood up. "I have to go, Paul. I'll be in touch."

* * *

I got to the Cracker Barrel early and sat outside in one of the rocking chairs. I figured I wouldn't have any trouble spotting Riegle, and I was right. He was the only guy to pull up on a $30,000 Harley with Texas plates. I watched him walk from the parking lot. He had on the whole get-up. Leather jacket, chaps and gloves, black boots with metal buckles, bandanna and sunglasses. He hadn't shaved in a while. And sported an earring. Quite the look for a guy who most days of the year puts on a suit and tie to go to the office. Not that it was anything unique. We get a lot of bikers in Estes Park looking just like Riegle. You'd be surprised how many of them are lawyers and accountants.

I got up to meet Riegle as he stepped toward the front door of the restaurant.

"Mr. Riegle?"

He pulled off his gloves and held out his hand. "Monroe, I assume."

The place was half-empty, and we got a table by the windows. Riegle hung his jacket on the back of his chair and ordered chicken-fried chicken with extra gravy and a lemonade. I got the all-day breakfast. Pancakes, eggs over easy, bacon, grits, and biscuits. At least it wasn't chili.

"I went to a Starbucks in Taos this morning," he said. "Got on the internet and looked at reports on the kidnapping. Terrible thing."

He didn't seem too broken up about it. Or even very sympathetic, really.

"You think it's a kidnapping?" I said.

"What else could it be? Don't you think you'd have found him by now if he was just lost in the park?"

I shook my head.

"There are so many ravines and creeks, so much vegetation in Rocky, we could have passed within ten feet of him and not seen him."

"You mean if he's dead."

"Or unconscious."

Our food came. I doused my pancakes with maple syrup and slid the eggs on top. Riegle dumped the extra gravy on his chicken and sprinkled it liberally with pepper. We ate for a few minutes without speaking.

Riegle finally put down his knife and fork and wiped the gravy from his mouth and fingers with half a dozen paper napkins. He drained his lemonade, motioned for the waitress to bring him a refill. I started on the biscuits and grits.

"Back to the kidnapping angle," he said. "Alaska plates, so you're looking at everyone with any connection to the Alaska case."

"Correct."

"That's a stretch."

"It probably is."

"If anyone had a beef with Elizabeth, they wouldn't take her kid. They'd go after her. If it's a kidnapping, it's probably just a crime of opportunity. He's there, he sees the kid alone, he takes him."

I couldn't decide if he'd seen too many crime shows on TV or not enough.

"I don't have any theories at this point, Mr. Riegle."

"Right." He picked up his knife and fork and lit into the chicken again, swirled a bite in gravy and stuffed it in his mouth.

"You mentioned an altercation between Elizabeth and me."

"Yes. Why don't you tell me what happened."

He wiped his hands and mouth again. By this time he had a pile of paper napkins beside his plate. I was having issues with their absorbency myself.

"Elizabeth English is a cockteaser," he said.

I put down my fork and leaned back in my chair.

"Cockteaser?"

"Cockteaser."

"Is that even a word anymore? I mean, who says that?"

He shrugged. "It may be antiquated. But it gets the point across."

Sure. It was one of my favorite expressions in high school, back when I was desperately trying, with very little success, to interest every girl I knew in my nether regions. A cockteaser would have been a significant upgrade. But a grown man using the word to describe Elizabeth English? Especially given what transpired in her hotel room.

"Mr. Riegle, why don't you tell me your version of what happened between you and Mrs. English in Alaska. With as little disparagement as possible about a mother whose six-year-old boy has gone missing."

His face reddened slightly. He took a long draw on his lemonade.

"Elizabeth resented that I was hired on the case."

"She said it was Bob Simon's decision. And that you're a good friend of his."

"Bob and I have become friends. After many years of mutual professional respect. But it wasn't just Bob's decision. It ultimately was up to the client, and after meeting with Bob and me and seeing the value I could bring to the case, they hired me."

"I don't know much about how lawsuits work," I said. "Exactly what value did you bring?"

He smiled slightly. "Elizabeth was in over her head. It was a very complicated, high-dollar matter, with dozens of witnesses, expert opinions, construction and contractual issues. I had to bring it all together for her. Basically, tell her how to try the case, every step of the way. She would have fallen apart if I hadn't been there."

The waitress appeared and cleared the table, stacking the dishes up her left arm.

"Save room for dessert?" she said. "Double chocolate fudge Coca-Cola cake? Baked apple dumpling?"

"The cake," Riegle said. "With ice cream."

"None for me. Just a cup of coffee and another one to go." The all-day breakfast likely would challenge my ability to stay awake on the drive home.

"So, Elizabeth came to rely on me more and more as the trial went on. It became obvious that there was an attraction there, but of course she was married."

"You have some scruples about that?"

"It depends on the circumstances."

"And the circumstances in Alaska were what?"

The waitress slid Riegle's cake and ice cream in front of him, and for a moment I looked at my coffee glumly and reconsidered my decision on dessert. Fortunately, Riegle brought my focus back to the reason I was there. "She was drunk, but she knew what she was doing. I guess she had a moment of crisis when the family called. So, I left. End of story."

"A real gentleman."

"I can be. And frankly, in the light of day, she wasn't all that attractive."

Frankly, I thought, *that's a damn lie.*

He scraped the last bite of cake and ice cream from the plate then pushed it aside. "She's a very calculating woman. She'd been leading up to that evening for quite a while. I think she was worried about what I might report back to Bob Simon. On how she'd handled the case. Maybe she thought if she kept me interested, I'd keep my mouth shut."

None of this squared with my impression of Elizabeth English. Then again, I'd only known her for a couple of days, under circumstances that would make any decent human being feel sympathy for her.

"Maybe you were the one who was worried," I said. "Worried that she'd tell Simon, in detail, why hiring you was a waste of money. You don't like women thinking they're in charge, that they know more than you. You know she's tired, she's missing her kids. You get her drunk on the weekends, you come on to her, and then one night you follow her to her hotel room. You knew that if she slept with you, she'd never say a thing to Bob Simon."

Riegle got angrier by the minute.

"The next morning she realizes what a horrible thing she's done. But you, having no moral compass, don't like it when women don't do what you want. She has to fight to get you off her, and you think about going through with it anyway, but a rape charge wouldn't do much for your career, either."

I thought he might blow, come across the table at me. He didn't. It was quite a transformation to watch. He collected all that anger, bottled it up just beneath the surface, and stored it in a package of rage. I wondered what he would do with it later.

The waitress brought the check. I pulled out my wallet, counted enough cash for my share and a tip, and tossed it to Riegle.

"And your report to Bob Simon?" I said as we stood.

He paused, put on his jacket. "I don't know yet. I fucked his drunk partner?" He looked at me and smirked. "Anything I do say, of course, will be divulged with utmost sensitivity to Elizabeth's current circumstances."

I've thrown a few punches in my time, but never one in a Cracker Barrel in the middle of the afternoon. I turned and walked away from Riegle before I sullied my record of good behavior. I went to the can then waited outside while he paid the bill. He stepped out onto the restaurant's porch and stopped in front of me, shifting a toothpick from one corner of his mouth to the other. Also part of the bandido look, I supposed.

"This your first time in Colorado in the past week or so?" I said.

"It is."

"Mind telling me where your travels have taken you so far?"

"I do mind. But I'll tell you anyway. Texas, down the Gulf Coast. Up through Laredo, Big Bend, and El Paso to New Mexico where you found me. Many stops along the way."

"I suppose you can back that up with credit card receipts and such."

He shrugged, put on his sunglasses. "Some of it. I also like to pay cash."

I stared at myself in the mirror of his sunglasses for a moment, then followed him as he walked to his Harley. "Thanks for making the trip up here, Mr. Riegle."

He pulled on his gloves and cracked his knuckles. "Give Elizabeth my regards and tell her I'm sorry to hear about her son." He settled himself on the bike, started the engine and revved it a few times for my benefit. "I'll be off the grid for the next month. But leave a message if you need to reach me again."

"Right. Off the grid." I watched as he maneuvered slowly through the parking lot then laid tracks onto the highway in a loud burst of backfire and headed south.

I got behind the wheel of the Bronco, picked up the spiral notebook I'd left on the passenger seat. I thumbed through my notes of the phone calls I'd made, found the direct dial number for Matthew Feldman, one of the lawyers on Elizabeth's trial team.

"Matthew Feldman."

"Mr. Feldman, Hollis Monroe again."

"Have you found Henry?"

I liked this guy. Genuine concern.

"No. But I have another question for you. How would you describe Mrs. English as a trial lawyer—her performance in the Alaska case? Competent, in control, or over her head?"

Silence on the other end of the line. Then, "What does this have to do with Henry's disappearance?"

"I can't tell you that, Mr. Feldman. I know it's an odd question. All I can tell you is that it does have something to do with the investigation."

Another few moments of silence before he answered. "She was brilliant. From the moment she got the case three years ago until the jury came back with the verdict. I learned more from her than any other lawyer I've worked with. I just hope I can be that good someday."

I turned my gaze south to the highway. From what I'd learned in the past couple of days about egos and the legal profession, Feldman's words said as much about him as they said about Elizabeth.

"Thanks, Mr. Feldman. That's all I needed to know."

CHAPTER

15

Elizabeth

I finally fell asleep after Paul returned from the airport, waking every hour until I rose just as the sun came up. Sixty hours missing.

I brewed coffee and took a cup to a table in the corner of the living room that served as a desk. My laptop was connected by cable to an old printer, slow but still functional. I sat down, logged on, and opened Word.

I typed in bold, 26-point across the top: "$50,000.00 REWARD."

The next line: "For information leading to the safe return of"

I left a large white space for photos, then: "Henry Oliver English."

Underneath his name, "Disappeared on August 15 at Glacier Gorge parking lot, Rocky Mountain National Park." Then "Age 6, Height 47 inches, Weight 51 pounds, Hair brown crew cut (wavy when longer), Eyes blue with long eyelashes. Wearing a blue poncho, T-shirt, yellow shorts, and hiking boots." At the bottom of the page, telephone numbers for the hotline and the park's dispatch center. I saved and printed it and was proofreading as Paul came in from the bedroom.

"Coffee's ready," I said. He turned and went to the kitchen, and I followed him. I waited until he had poured a cup then handed him the flyer.

"Pictures here?" he said, pointing to the blank space. I nodded.

"Maybe we should add that he's missing his two front teeth." I nodded again, blinking as my eyes watered.

"Should we put our cell numbers on it, too?" I said.

Paul shook his head. "I don't think so. We can ask Monroe."

"I'll call him."

Paul glanced at the clock. "It's still early. But he's probably up."

Monroe didn't answer, but he returned my call a few minutes later. "Good morning, Elizabeth."

"Good morning." I told him about the flyers, asked about our cell phone numbers.

"No, no, no. The weirdos will be crawling out of the woodwork. Let us handle the calls."

"Is there any news?"

"No. Carpenter's making the rounds at motels and gas stations, asking for any surveillance tapes they might have. He got a lead on a truck that turned out to be an El Camino owned by a neighbor the caller's been feuding with for years. An old lady who lives up by Mary's Lake said she saw Henry in her backyard. Carpenter went out to check. She took him around to the back of the house and introduced him to Henry. No one was there."

Paul motioned for the phone, and I handed it to him.

"Monroe, this is Paul. I'm just wondering how the phone inquiries went yesterday."

I didn't want to hear their conversation. I went back to the computer and on the line under the description of Henry's eyes, typed "Two front teeth missing." I searched in the photo file and pasted onto the flyer three shots of Henry taken at different angles, one with a crew cut, one with short hair, one slightly longer. I printed the flyer again and went to the bedroom to dress. I was tying my shoes when Paul came in and handed me my phone.

"Is Monroe still on?"

"No. We're finished."

Paul dropped his sweatpants and shorts, tossed them in the closet hamper and stood naked at the door to the bathroom.

"He's meeting Brad Riegle in Colorado Springs this afternoon."

"Oh. Wow. Riegle's in Colorado Springs?"

"He was in Taos. Camping. He agreed to drive up and meet Monroe."

I tied the final knot on my shoelace. "Monroe's very thorough. He's checking out everyone connected to the Alaska case."

Paul stepped out of sight to turn on the shower then came back to the doorway.

"There's something you're not telling me, Elizabeth. About Riegle and about why Monroe would drive to Colorado Springs to talk to the guy."

The sheets and blankets on the bed were in a rumpled pile, the comforter had fallen to the floor. *I should make the bed*, I thought, then shook my head. *Who cares. Who cares whether the bed is made.*

"I can't talk about it right now."

He folded his arms and leaned against the doorframe. "When can you talk about it?"

I put my cell phone in my back pocket and grabbed a faded Longhorns sweatshirt from the closet shelf.

"I don't know. I'm leaving for town in ten minutes, if you're planning to go with me."

I heard the shower door slam as I left the room.

* * *

We took the flyer to a copy store in Estes Park and asked for a thousand copies, then went to Starbucks to wait. We sat at a table outside by the Big Thompson River and checked our emails.

My inbox flooded with messages when I opened it, the screen scrolling down as more were loaded. A number of them related to the Alaska case; Matthew Feldman, the young partner who had tried the case with me, had agreed to assume the lead while I was gone. Opposing counsel had asked for and gotten, with no objections from our side, an extension to file a motion for new trial. Matthew, anticipating some of their arguments, was handing out research assignments to the associates for our response.

I skimmed and deleted the general firm emails, saved the case-related ones for later. There were dozens, maybe hundreds, of personal messages from colleagues and friends, asking what they could do to help. I wanted to reply, "Nothing. There's not a damn thing you can do. A massive search, now covering the whole of Rocky Mountain National Park, grows more futile by the hour. Monroe and Carpenter are spinning their wheels looking for an Alaska connection because Nick thought he saw an Alaska license plate. Nick's a child, he was alone and wet and cold under the Jeep. It could have been Arkansas, Alabama, or for that matter, Nebraska. So, no. My baby is missing and there seems to be not a thing anyone can do about it."

I took out my cell and called Alex.

"Alexis LaDay's office."

"Missy, it's Elizabeth."

"Oh my God." Alex and I had been best friends since we started at the firm. Missy had been Alex's secretary for almost as long.

"How are you?" Missy said. "Have they found Henry?"

"I'm tired. And no, they haven't found him."

"Everyone's thinking about you. Waiting for word."

"Thank you. It means a lot." I didn't think I could say much more. "Is Alex around?"

"Hang on. She's in a meeting but she told me to interrupt if you called."

She put me on hold. I looked out over the river while I waited, watched two fishermen standing in the current, casting their flies on the surface of the clear water. Nick and Henry loved playing by the Big Thompson. We were there only a few days before, walked along the river after dinner and heard music, a flute and a violin. A concert on the square, two street musicians entertaining the crowd that gathered, violin case open for donations and copies of their CD for sale. Nick and Henry were captivated and insisted that we buy one. We put it on when we got back to the cabin, and Henry went to his room and returned with the ukulele he'd gotten for Christmas. The four of us lay by the fire in the dark, listening to the melancholy melody while Henry strummed quietly. He didn't know how to play the ukulele, didn't know any chords, but even Nick didn't object to his plucking on the plastic strings.

"Christ, Elizabeth. What the fuck is going on?" Alex was on the line. "Why haven't they found him?"

Alex was Henry's godmother, a role she'd assumed only after I extracted promises that she wouldn't curse or smoke in his presence and would make no attempt to turn him into a Georgia Bulldog. Alex had grown up in Atlanta and was runner-up for Miss Georgia before heading to Stanford for law school. She was every bit the southern beauty, with a honey drawl, peaches-and-cream complexion and sparkling teeth, perfectly coiffed hair that looked like her tiara was missing, and three-inch heels. All of which served her well in a mergers and acquisitions practice, where in late-night meetings of investment bankers and corporate lawyers she often was the only woman in the room.

"Am I interrupting something important?"

"Just the usual. The boys have their dicks on the table to see which is the biggest. I'm about to cut them off. What's the latest?"

"Nothing. They're searching the entire park, but other than Nick's flashlight that they found the first night, there's no trace of him."

"Anything on the truck?"

"No. And no contact from anyone claiming to have him."

"Jesus. How the hell can he just vanish?"

I rubbed my eyes, put my elbows on the picnic table, and hunched over my phone.

"Would you do something for me?"

"Anything. You want me to come out there? I can be on a plane tonight."

"No. Not yet." I didn't want to think about the circumstances under which I might need her in the future. "Would you draft something and send a firm-wide email? Something like, 'Elizabeth and Paul English and their family appreciate all the support. As soon as we have any word on Henry, we'll let everyone know.' You know—something like that."

"Sure."

We were quiet for a moment.

"You still there?" Alex said.

"Yes." It was all I could do to get the word out.

"I'm here for you, honey."

I gulped, struggled to speak. "I know." I thought I was going to make it through the conversation. Then I heard Alex's voice break, the high-pitched, nasal tone as she said to call her day or night.

"I love him," she said. "He's like my own."

Paul nudged me, showed me the text from the clerk at the copy store. The flyers were ready.

I took a deep breath. "I have to go."

"Call me," Alex said.

"I'll call you."

* * *

Paul and I divided up the flyers. I grabbed a handful and stuffed the rest in my backpack. I took the south side of Elkhorn Avenue; Paul took the north. My first stop was Beartooth Mountain Antiques. A small brass bell rang over my head as I pushed open the door. The shop was lined with shelves of old books, glass cases of antique jewelry and pistols. A wooden cigar store Indian stood next to an Edison home phonograph with a metal horn.

I'd met Aaron Laine, the owner, when he opened the shop seven or eight years ago. But I didn't recognize the woman behind the counter who greeted me.

"Is Aaron here?"

"He's not. He's on a buying trip and won't be back for a couple of weeks. May I help you?"

I gestured with the flyers in my hand. "I'm wondering if I can post something on the front window."

"No, I'm sorry. We don't allow ads on the windows."

"It's not an ad." I peeled off one of the flyers and handed it to her. My hands were shaking. "It's about a little boy. A little boy who's missing."

Her face softened as she looked at the flyer. "I saw him on the news. You're his mother."

I nodded.

"Of course. It's fine. Put it right by the door so people will see it when they come in."

I went to the front window, stood there for a moment then went back to the counter.

"Could I possibly borrow some tape?"

She looked pityingly at me for a moment, bent down and rummaged under the counter then held out a roll of masking tape. I took it and went back to the window, tucked the flyer under my arm and picked at the tape with my thumbnail until a jagged strip peeled free. I flattened the flyer on the window, Henry's face to the outside, taped one corner and picked again at the roll until another strip tore loose. I taped a second corner to the glass and glanced out the window. That's when I saw him. Standing on the sidewalk across the street, watching me. Mustard-yellow and orange plaid shirt, jeans and running shoes, knit cap pulled down to his brows. Our eyes met. For a second or two, there was a twinge of recognition, something about him that was familiar. He turned and walked away, disappearing in the crowd of tourists.

"Do you know that man?" The clerk had come up behind me.

I shook my head.

"I don't think so."

"I noticed him when you came in. He was looking this way for a while."

"At the window display, no doubt."

"No, I think he was watching you."

I scanned the passing crowd for a moment, but he was nowhere in sight. I finished taping the flyer to the window, offered the roll to the clerk.

"Keep it."

"Thank you."

I turned left from the antiques store and made my way down the street, stopping at every shop—T-shirts, ceramics, camping and fishing gear, Colorado decorative items that would look hopelessly out of place back home, a source of regret when the credit card bill with the vacation charges came. The proprietors were unfailingly kind; some hung the flyers themselves and said they were praying for Henry every day.

"That means a lot," I said. "Those prayers will bring him home." Then felt guilty for all the Sundays we'd slept in or I'd been at the office or we'd spent the day worshipping at the altar of the NFL. *Don't blame Henry for that, God. It's not like he could drive himself to church.*

I walked south on Moraine Avenue, posted flyers at more shops and the old movie theater. I hesitated for a moment at the liquor store, then opened the door and went in. A tall, thin man with a drooping mustache and gray ponytail nodded at me from the cash register and told me to go ahead when I explained what I was there for. The grimy front windows were covered with notices and ads; I put Henry next to a poster for an end-of-summer beer fest and turned to thank the store clerk again.

"Anything else I can get for you?" he said.

"I guess I'll look around."

I went up and down the aisles, glanced at the dusty bottles of wine, the cases of beer. I grabbed two pints of Jack Daniels from the shelf and took them to the counter.

"It's cheaper if you buy the bigger bottles."

"These are fine." I couldn't remember if I'd brought my wallet, rummaged through my backpack and found it in a side zipper pocket.

"Yeah, it's too bad about that kid," the clerk said as he rang up my purchase with nicotine-stained fingers. "Seems like every summer something happens. Some kid drowns or dies in a car accident. Couple of years ago this boy got attacked by a mountain lion. The mountain lion didn't kill him—the kid choked on his own vomit."

"I don't need a bag." I handed him cash and put the bottles in my backpack under the flyers as he counted out my change.

"Yeah," he said. "Scared shitless, you know?"

I slung the backpack over one shoulder and left before he could say anything more. Before I started to scream.

I walked back to the corner of Elkhorn Avenue. I pulled out a stack of flyers and handed them, one by one, to the people waiting to cross at the red light. Some waved me off, some took them. "Thank you," I said. "For any help you can give. Thank you." Over and over again. "Thank you. Any help you can give." One man offered me a ten-dollar bill. "No," I said. "Thank you. Just help us find him. Help us bring him home."

A group of middle-schoolers clattered up on skateboards. I handed them flyers and moved down the sidewalk a few steps out of their way.

"Holy cow," one of them said. "Fifty thousand dollars?"

"For his safe return," another one said.

"Yeah," said a third. "Like that's gonna happen. That kid is dead."

"Dead meat," said another, twirling his skateboard on one end. "Coyote snacks." He held the flyer up so his friends could see, laughed, and dropped it to the ground. Then looked at me, shocked, as I kicked the skateboard out of his hands.

"He's a human being, you little shit. Pick it up!" I pushed him. "Pick it up!"

I was vaguely aware that a crowd was gathering as I continued to scream, "Pick it up!"

He backed away from me and I lunged at him—stopped short by someone's arm around me from behind.

"Elizabeth." It was Paul. "Let's call it a day."

"Yeah," said the boy. "Call it a day, you crazy old witch."

Paul glared at him. "Don't push your luck, son." He dragged me, struggling and screaming, more than a block before I calmed down, people stopping to stare as we passed, then kept his arm tight around me as we walked the remaining blocks to where we'd parked the Jeep. He pushed me gently into the passenger seat and closed the door, then went to the driver's side and got in. He waited and watched as my breathing slowed. I pulled off my backpack and set it on the floor in front of me, rested my elbows on my knees and dropped my head into my hands. I was shaking.

"I'm sorry. I lost it. I just lost it."

"It's okay," he said quietly. He leaned over and rubbed my back. "It's okay." He started the Jeep. "Let's go home."

He backed out of the parking space and turned out of the lot onto Elkhorn Avenue. I sat up and fastened my seat belt. And caught a brief glimpse, as we turned onto the street, of mustard-yellow and orange plaid.

CHAPTER

16

Eddie

SHE'D CHANGED ALREADY.

When I first saw her in Estes Park, I was surprised at how little she seemed to have aged. She was a bit weathered, as expected, but still so like that fresh-faced lawyer sitting across from me for days, months, years as the case dragged on. Ever at the side of Bob Simon, his trusty girl, handing him exhibits, making notes, huddled in whispered consultation whenever there was a break in the questioning.

I could have used a trusty girl like that. But trusty girls are reserved for the Bob Simons of the world, with their custom suits and Italian shoes, their Ivy League law degrees and corner offices. Bob Simon has a black bean for a heart. But you—you could have shown me a little kindness, Elizabeth. Some small measure of compassion. Some respect.

So. Henry gone for only two and a half days and the suffering was wearing her down. It does that to you, Elizabeth. Live with it for ten years and then see what kind of shape you're in.

She saw me. There was a brief moment of hesitation as she looked right at me. Do you know me, Elizabeth? Do you know who I am?

No. It's no surprise. I don't even recognize myself sometimes. I turned and walked away.

* * *

I followed her at a distance as she wound her way through town, handing out flyers, taping them to storefront windows. Watched with amusement her scuffle with the little skateboard snot and hubby dragging her away.

I picked up a discarded flyer and studied the photos. Henry. Missing since August 15.

It's really very sweet, Elizabeth. Shaved head, missing front teeth, no matter. The boy looks just like you.

CHAPTER

17

Monroe

THE SEARCH FOR Henry was eight days in when the superintendent summoned me to her office.

"It's time to call it off, Monroe."

"I know."

"Has Carpenter made any progress on the kidnapping investigation?"

"No."

"Well, then. We'll keep eyes out for Henry in the park, but our role in this case is over."

I didn't say anything.

"Monroe."

"Yeah?"

"If Henry's not in Rocky, we have no jurisdiction. Remember what I told you when I hired you."

"Yeah. You're not looking for cowboys."

"It's still true."

I stood up to go. "Don't worry, ma'am. My cowboy days are over."

I got the task of telling Paul and Elizabeth. I tried Elizabeth's cell phone first, then Paul's, early in the morning, hoping to catch them before they left for town to hand out flyers. They'd been doing that for several days, standing on street corners, going door to door in neighborhoods. I'd seen them briefly the day before; they were sunburned and exhausted.

Paul answered and I told him I'd like to meet with them in person. No, I said in answer to his question. There wasn't any news about Henry.

"Come on over," he said.

It was the first time I'd been to their place, a comfortable mix of family history and money well spent to modernize it a bit. Too much house for me, but I'd sure like to have the land it sits on. Elizabeth, hair still wet from the shower, poured me a cup of coffee and the three of us went to sit on the front porch. Elizabeth pulled her knees to her chest and gazed at the mountains. Paul watched me while I studied my coffee and had a hard time figuring out how to begin.

"We know why you're here," Elizabeth said. "You're calling off the search."

I grimaced and rubbed my forehead. "We've had over a hundred people covering the entire east side, rangers on the lookout throughout the park. Dogs, helicopters. We're ending the formal search. But we won't stop looking for him. Our personnel are out there on the trails and at their stations every day. And there's always a chance that hikers may find him."

"But not alive," Paul said.

"No. If he's in Rocky, alone, he's not alive."

Elizabeth covered her mouth with her fist and made a muffled choking sound. She stared at the mountains still, tears streaming down her cheeks.

"What about the truck?" Paul said.

"Nothing on the truck."

He rose from his chair, paced the length of the porch and back again, slammed his fists on the rail.

"Goddamn it," he said. "Goddamn it."

Paul hunched over the porch railing. Elizabeth curled into a tighter ball on her chair. Finally, she spoke.

"We went to San Francisco for Thanksgiving last year, Monroe."

"Okay," I said, not knowing where this was going.

"I'd been in a two-week trial in Houston and hadn't made one preparation for the holidays. We all decided at dinner one night that we would pack our bags and fly out the next day. The boys were so excited. We spent Thanksgiving Day wandering around Chinatown. They'd never seen anything like it."

She wiped her nose on her sleeve and looked up at Paul. "Do you remember what Henry said?"

"Yeah. 'Dad, there's a lot of Chinese people in Chinatown.'"

"We gave the boys five dollars each to buy a souvenir. Nick spent his immediately, but Henry held onto that five-dollar bill and fingered every trinket in every store until I finally told him he had to make a decision because it was time to go back to the hotel. Then I noticed that he didn't have the money in his hand.

"'Did you lose your money?' I said. He shook his head. 'Well, where is it?' He pointed to a homeless man sitting on the sidewalk. He'd given the man his five dollars."

She buried her face in her hands and sobbed silently, and I just sat there, knowing there was nothing I could do or say to comfort her. After a while the sobs slowed, then subsided. She wiped her eyes and turned to me.

"He's so tender-hearted, Monroe. The world doesn't just take away a little boy like that, does it?"

I knew the answer to that question. Yes, it does. It happens every day. All the times I'd done this over all my years as a sheriff, it was still tough to know what to say. The car wrecks, the overdoses, the suicides. All the senseless ways that sons and daughters die, leaving their mothers to suffer for the rest of their lives. This one was hitting me hard. Six years old.

"There's always hope," I said.

Elizabeth stood. "I'd know if he was dead. Henry's alive."

I wasn't about to argue with what a mother knows or doesn't know. It was uncanny the way my Maggie could sense things about our daughter before I even had a clue. *If he's alive,* I thought, *he's probably a long way from here.* But I wasn't about to say that, either.

"There's not much more you can do in Estes Park," I said. "I promise I'll keep in touch—you can call me every day."

"We can't leave him," she said.

Paul turned to face us.

"I'll stay. I'll call U of H and ask if I can defer until next year."

"No," she said. "You've waited too long for this opportunity. The firm will give me time off. Bob Simon told me to take whatever I need."

I didn't like the idea of Elizabeth staying out there by herself, and I thought she'd be better off in Houston with Paul and Nick. I said as much, and the minute the words were out of my mouth, boy, did I regret it. She leaned over me and gave me a look that made me shrink a couple of sizes.

"You've called off the search for our son. You have no clue where he is. You have no idea how to find him. Yet you feel compelled to give me advice on how I should handle this situation."

She was just starting her windup, but before she could light into me further, Paul jumped in.

"Honey. Monroe's just concerned about the welfare of all our family."

"Yes," I said. "I don't mean to meddle." I stood up to go. "Will you call me if you need anything?"

She paused, took a deep breath then nodded. "Thank you. We're very appreciative of everything you've done." She pulled the screen door open and went inside.

"Sorry," Paul said.

"No, I'm the one who's sorry. Sorry at opening my big mouth, but mostly sorry that we haven't found your boy."

"I know. Elizabeth has stayed here alone many times since she was a teenager. Under normal circumstances, I wouldn't worry about her one bit. But now, the stress she's under . . . the creeps out there."

"Creeps? Has someone been bothering you?"

He shook his head. "Handing out the flyers, we've met all kinds. Most of them sympathetic and kind. But a few who ask for details about how Henry went missing, do we feel guilty about it, do we think he's dead. Morbid curiosity. And Elizabeth thinks a guy was following her a few days ago."

"Following her?"

"Well, more like watching. The first day we were posting flyers, there was a guy in an orange and yellow plaid shirt. She hasn't seen him since. But she gets this feeling sometimes that he's out there. Still watching."

I looked out over the expanse of their land, the quarter mile to the road, the thick stands of fir and pine, outcroppings of rock, brush lining the fences. Plenty of places for a man to hide.

"Please tell her to call me if she sees him again. A grieving mother in the public eye, especially a pretty one, you don't know what might crawl out of the woodwork."

He walked me down the steps to my Bronco, reached in through the open window to shake my hand after I got behind the wheel.

"Does Elizabeth have a gun?" I said.

"Yeah. A safe full of them in the garage—they were her dad's—and she won't tell even me the combination. She hasn't opened it since Nick was born."

I turned the key in the ignition. "Tell her to open it." I put the Bronco in reverse, swung it around, and headed for the road.

CHAPTER

18

Paul

I WATCHED MONROE'S TRUCK until he rounded the curve on Devil's Gulch Road and was out of sight. I wasn't crazy about Elizabeth staying at the cabin by herself, either. She's respectful of the mountains and their inhabitants, the terrain, the weather. She doesn't take anything for granted. And she's comfortable here in a way that I'll never be. I suppose, in the end, that's why I didn't fight her. I called Southwest, made a reservation for a flight that evening, and went inside to pack.

I looked for Elizabeth in the kitchen, then in the master bedroom, but she wasn't there. I crossed back through the living room, went down the hall to Nick's room, then Henry's. She was curled up on Henry's bed, holding Dolphie, a stuffed dolphin we'd bought at Sea World in San Antonio a couple of years ago. I sat on the edge of the bed beside her.

"I can smell him," she said. "His hair on the pillow. The little boy smell on the mattress."

I took her hand. We were quiet for a while. Then I said, "I can stay."

"No."

"I'm worried about you."

"I'll be fine. I can take care of myself."

I didn't say anything.

"What?"

"I found the Jack Daniels. Both bottles." She had a hiding place in the pantry, another one in the storage closet in the garage. I'd discovered those when we were first married, when she was drinking to the point that I wanted out. She'd suck one bottle almost dry, then partially refill it from the other, thinking she could disguise the amount of her consumption. The first day we handed out flyers, when I had to pull her off the kid with the skateboard, I'd heard the *thunk* of glass in her backpack and known immediately what it was.

She pushed herself up and sat beside me.

"I assume you noticed that they haven't been opened."

"I did."

"I wanted a drink. I've wanted one every night since Henry went missing. But I was afraid to take one. Afraid that I'd have one drink, and another. That I'd keep drinking and then Henry would call, he'd need me to come get him, but I wouldn't be able to, maybe not even able to answer the phone because I'd had too much to drink."

She rested her head on my shoulder. I stroked her hair and kissed the top of her head.

"That gives me some comfort," I said.

She stood. "Nothing comforts me. Not one thing."

She turned to go, but I pulled her to me, facing me while I sat on the bed. I raised her shirt and unzipped her jeans and kissed her belly.

"Here. For a little while."

She sighed and arched her back as I traced my tongue lower.

"I'm running out of room. There's a zipper in my way."

She unbuttoned her shirt slowly and slid her jeans to the floor. "Not anymore."

I put my hands on her hips and pulled her to me.

* * *

I dozed for a few minutes, woke when Elizabeth got out of bed and stepped into her jeans. I picked my clothes up from the floor, carried them to the master bath and got in the shower. I toweled off and dressed, threw the few things I would take to Houston in a duffle bag, put my computer and notebooks in my backpack. Then I went to the kitchen to find Elizabeth.

"What time is your flight?"

"It's the 7:05. The same flight Nick took." I plugged my phone in to charge and set it on the counter.

"Do you want me to take you to the airport?"

"No, there's no reason for you to make the drive. I reserved a spot on the shuttle. You can drop me off at the Stanley."

She ran water over a red bell pepper, set it on a cutting board next to green onions and a slice of ham. "Omelet?"

"Sounds great."

"We need to call Nick. To let him know you're coming home."

I drank orange juice, popped a couple of English muffins in the toaster, and watched her chop then sauté the vegetables and ham. She whisked eggs, added them to the pan with spinach and cheese, folded the omelet expertly and slid it onto a plate when it was done. She cut a third of it for herself and gave me the rest. I buttered the English muffins and handed her a jar of jelly. We sat on stools at the counter and ate. For a minute or two, life seemed almost normal.

"We also have to tell Nick that they've called off the search," she said.

"Shit." I got up and poured a cup of coffee. It was lukewarm and bitter from having sat on the burner too long. I dumped it down the drain, asked if she wanted me to brew another pot.

"No. My stomach's a little upset." She pushed her plate away, most of her portion of the omelet untouched.

"You don't want the rest of that?"

She shook her head. "Go ahead."

I finished it then set her plate in the sink. "You think we have to tell Nick today?"

"Yes. It'll be on the news. He should hear it from us."

She looked at the clock. "He'll be home from school in an hour or so. Soccer practice doesn't start until next week."

I shook my head, opened the dishwasher, and started to load it. "Shit."

Elizabeth got up and left the room. I was scraping dried egg crust from the omelet pan when she reappeared beside me. She set one Jack Daniels bottle on the counter, cracked the other one open and held it upside down over the sink, the contents gurgling and splashing on her hands. When it was empty, she rinsed it, and did the same with the second. She tossed both bottles in the trash and gave me what might have been intended as a smile but was more of a grimace.

"I'm going to take another shower," she said. "Then we'll call Nick."

I bent to kiss her. She smelled of whiskey and sex, her perfume of long ago. After she'd gone and I turned back to the sink, I remembered that she'd never told me what happened in Alaska.

* * *

The call with Nick did not go well. We went out to the porch, put him on speaker on my cell, and asked him to get his Aunt Kathleen to sit with him while we talked. He was thrilled at first that I was coming home, then shocked and angry that the search for Henry had come to an end. He insisted that it was all his fault that Henry was missing and that he would come to Estes Park to look for his brother if he had to walk the whole entire way. Elizabeth assured him that she would keep looking, and that the park rangers would keep looking, but he called her a liar. Then he hung up. The violence of his sobs and the depth of his misery left us both shaken. We tried his cell again, and when he didn't answer, I called Kathleen on her home phone.

"Poor little guy," Kathleen said. "He's having a hard time. He went up to the guest room and locked the door."

I rested my elbows on my knees, held my head in one hand, cell phone in the other. I was so fucking tired.

"I'll be home late tonight. I'll come over first thing in the morning to take him to school."

"He'll be glad to see you. He misses his mom and dad." Kathleen's voice broke. "And Henry."

"Okay, thanks. Thanks for everything." I hung up.

Elizabeth looked as if she'd been slapped.

"He needs us," I said.

"Yes. But he needs more than that. I'll call the school and ask for a recommendation for a therapist."

I leaned back in my chair and stared mutely at the snow-capped mountains in the distance, a view that most observers would call breathtaking. I had come to hate it in the past week, swore under my breath that I would never come to this place again.

"What do we do, Paul? I would give my life for Nick, would do anything for him. But the one thing he needs most from me right now—is me. And I can't give him that."

"You can. We can lock up the cabin and both of us go home."

"You mean give up. Give up and accept that Henry's dead."

"No. Not give up. Just accept that there's nothing more we can do here."

She shook her head. "I refuse to believe that. If I go home now, I'll never stop asking myself what else I could have done. I can't live with that."

"I understand. I just hope Nick can." I went inside to collect my bags.

* * *

The Stanley Hotel was a short drive from our place. Elizabeth drove, and I got out to open and close the gate. When I got back in the Jeep, I had to ask, couldn't let it go any longer.

"What happened in Alaska?"

She stared out the windshield, both hands on the wheel.

"Nothing. Nothing to do with Henry's disappearance."

"Goddamn it, Elizabeth. It had enough to do with Henry that Monroe drove to Colorado Springs to talk to Riegle. I'm not leaving until you tell me."

So she told me. All of it. The drinking, the come-ons, the fucking, the ugly scene the last morning they were there. Big-time lawyers having big-time fun. She finished just as we pulled in front of the Stanley. She put the Jeep in park and we sat there a few minutes without talking.

"I'm sorry."

"You goddamn well should be."

"I hate myself, Paul. I don't know that I'll ever be able to forgive myself."

"Yeah, well, I understand both of those sentiments."

I turned away from her, looked out at the old hotel. Beautiful, stately, and haunted. Before Nick was born, Elizabeth had insisted we stay there one night in hopes that one of the ghosts that roam the place would visit our room. No ghost showed up, but I didn't sleep the whole miserable night.

"You have some fun, don't you Elizabeth. You do your thing, whatever it is, whatever makes you happy, whenever you want. And your children pay the price."

I turned back to her.

"Are you blaming me for Henry? Are you saying it's my fault he's missing?"

I couldn't speak for a minute. Then I shook my head. "I don't know what I'm thinking right now."

The airport shuttle drove up. I got out of the Jeep, pulled my bags from the back seat, heard her say, "Paul," as I slammed the door.

CHAPTER

19

Elizabeth

I WATCHED PAUL HAND his duffle bag to the shuttle driver, his jaw clenched, so angry that the driver noticed and looked at me then back at Paul. Paul boarded the bus and I saw him take a seat toward the rear, but there was no acknowledgment that I was still there, not even a backward glance as the shuttle pulled away. I waited until it was out of sight then reached for my purse. The hotel bar was open. *One drink*, I thought as I reached for the handle of my door. Then caught myself. *No. No.* I dropped my purse on the seat beside me and willed myself to drive.

I stopped at Safeway on the way home to pick up something for dinner. Nothing appealed to me. I had no appetite. I finally bought some fruit, an assortment of frozen dinners, and several boxes of macaroni and cheese—*a shopping trip harkening back to my law school days*, I thought, watching with little enthusiasm as the cashier scanned and bagged the items.

I put the groceries in the back of the Jeep, closed the tailgate, and turned to push the cart to the front of the store. That's when I saw him—standing just inside and to the left of the automatic doors, by the lines of shopping carts. He had on a different plaid shirt—this one a faded green—but the same knit cap pulled down to his eyebrows. Our eyes met, and he quickly ducked into the store.

"Hey!" I shouted. I let go of the cart and broke into a run. I stopped just inside the store, then trotted through the produce section to the back and thought I caught a glimpse of faded green disappear a few aisles down.

"Hey!" I shouted again, then walked quickly by the meat counters and dairy section, checking each aisle as I went and vaguely aware of the startled looks of the other shoppers. I looked through the bread section and the deli, rounded the corner to the long row of checkout lanes. No sign of a plaid shirt.

"Damn it," I said. "Damn, damn, damn."

"Can I help you, ma'am?"

I glanced up at the concerned face of a young man whose name tag identified him as Ricky Alvarez, assistant manager.

"Is there a problem?"

"No. Just someone I thought I knew."

I gave him a little smile. "Thank you. This really is a very nice store. Very nice." I walked slowly past the lines of customers leaning on their overloaded carts or peering over the tops of *Star* and *People* and *Us Weekly*, pretending not to notice their curious stares. I gave the cashier who'd rung up my groceries a nod, considered for a moment seeking out Ricky Alvarez again to ask if tongue piercings and nose rings were a job requirement for grocery stores these days, and did he think his customers, trapped in line and unable to escape, appreciated the sight.

I walked out to the parking lot, stood behind the Jeep for a few moments watching the parked cars, the people loading their bags. Sunburned hikers, short-tempered parents, whiny kids, locals with their dogs. No green plaid shirt in sight.

* * *

"Are you crazy?"

Monroe was furious. I'd called him on the way home from the store, and he made it to the cabin in record time.

"No, I'm not crazy. I don't know if the guy is following me, or he just showed up by coincidence. But what if he knows something about Henry's disappearance?"

"What would you have done if you'd caught him?"

I had no idea. "Don't patronize me, Monroe."

He gaped at me for a moment, then shook his head.

"Elizabeth. A concerned citizen with information would go to the police. Anyone else who might know something about Henry is unlikely to be hanging around in plain sight. He's a creep. He saw you on TV, and he apparently knows where you live because he showed up at Safeway when you were there."

I reached into a grocery bag.

"Would you like some macaroni and cheese?"

"Jesus. No."

I dumped the macaroni in a pan, poured in water and set it on the stove.

"You're really going to eat that?"

I shook the packet of neon-orange powder that passed for cheese and my eyes started to burn, the tears finally brimming over and rolling down my cheeks and neck. I turned to the stove, kept my back to Monroe. "It doesn't matter. I can't taste anything."

He sighed and leaned his bulk onto a stool at the counter.

"In the interest of not getting my head bit off, I won't tell you that you shouldn't stay here alone. But you do need to take precautions. Paul said you have a gun safe in the garage."

I stirred the goop in the pan, put a lid on it, and slid it off the burner.

"Shotguns and hunting rifles. They were my dad's."

"Do you know how to use them?"

"Yes."

"Paul said you haven't opened the safe since Nick was born."

I wiped my eyes and nose on my sleeve, turned to face Monroe.

"I haven't opened the safe when Paul and the boys were here. But it's been opened in recent years. The guns are in good condition."

"May I see?"

I wanted to tell him no. My father and I, and my brother, Sam, hunted duck, quail, and deer in South Texas from the time I was a little girl. Sam and I were good shots, and we loved being outdoors with our dad, but as we grew older, we quietly parted ways with the hunting life. The guns, though, were memories, personal, part of a past that I had no interest in sharing with Monroe.

"Just to ease my mind, Elizabeth."

"All right." He followed me to the garage, waited while I flipped on the light. The safe was in the far corner, past the Jeep and the pickup. I spun the combination and opened it. Monroe let out a low whistle.

"That's quite a collection." He admired the safe's contents a while longer.

"Well?" he said.

"Well what?"

"Which one of these are you going to remove from the safe and put, fully loaded, by your bed tonight?"

I blew out a slow breath. "The Remington, I suppose. It's not pretty, but it's dependable. And accurate."

"Good choice."

I lifted the rifle from its barrel rest and took a box of cartridges from the shelf, then closed the safe. We went back to the living room. I set the rifle and ammunition next to the fireplace, and walked Monroe to the door.

"I'd like you to work with a sketch artist to come up with a picture of this guy," he said. "I'll set it up with Carpenter in the morning and call you about a time."

"Okay."

He looked as if he wanted to say more, but didn't. I stepped out onto the front porch with him, watched as he climbed into his Bronco.

"Be safe," he said.

"I will."

I locked the door behind me and went to the kitchen. I sat at the counter and ate lukewarm macaroni and cheese from the pan, washing it down with a cup of green tea. I ate what I could, dumped the rest in the trash, and set the pan in the sink. Shutting off the lights behind me, I retrieved the rifle and ammunition from the living room and carried them to the bedroom. I sat on the edge of the bed and loaded four rounds in the chamber, set the safety, and propped the rifle against the nightstand. I pulled off my clothes, got into bed naked then thought better of it. I rose, put on flannel pajama bottoms and a T-shirt, and crawled back under the covers.

I lay there in the dark for an hour or more, listening to the night. The wind picked up, a gentle roar in the trees. The cabin creaked in response. I thought for a moment that I caught the sound of a child's restless sleep, a low whimper, a whispered murmur. But then it was gone. *No*, I thought as I finally lost consciousness. *Nick and Henry aren't here.*

* * *

I woke the next morning to my phone buzzing on the nightstand. I grabbed it, disoriented for a moment, wondered why there was a rifle by my bed before remembering that I had put it there. I answered without looking at the caller's name.

"It's awfully early, Monroe."

"Who's Monroe?"

It was Alex. I sat up, pushed my hair back and rubbed my eyes.

"The cop. The park ranger in charge of the search for Henry. Sorry. He's supposed to call me this morning."

"Any news?"

"No. Nothing."

She blew out a long sigh. "Okay, so I talked to Paul. He says he's back in Houston and you're in Estes Park by yourself."

I slipped on a pair of flip-flops and went to the kitchen to make coffee while we talked.

"They called off the search, Alex." My throat tightened. I filled the coffee pot with water, dumped heaping spoons of grounds into the filter, and turned the machine on to brew.

"I know, honey. Paul told me."

I opened the refrigerator door, found a carton of skim milk. I unscrewed the cap with one hand, sniffed, then poured it down the drain.

I drew a shaky breath. "We decided Paul should go home. To be with Nick and to start his program at U of H."

"I understand. But you shouldn't be alone. I'm coming out there this weekend."

"You really don't have to do that, Alex."

"Of course I don't. But I am. I have all-day meetings on Friday and Saturday that I can't get out of. Missy will get me a flight Sunday morning."

I poured a cup of coffee. "What day is this?"

"It's Wednesday, honey."

My phone beeped, another call trying to get through. I looked at the screen. "Okay. I'll talk to you before Sunday. I have another call—it's Monroe."

I hung up with Alex and said hello to Monroe.

"Everything go okay last night?"

"Fine. I didn't have to shoot anyone."

"That's good."

I waited. What else did he want me to say? What else was there to say?

"The sketch artist has to come over from Loveland," he said. "She can't get here until late Friday afternoon."

"I'll check my calendar. Oh, wait—no need to check. The only thing on my calendar is the daily note that Henry's missing and no one, it seems, can find him."

He was silent. I opened the front door and stepped out. It was cool, in the midfifties. Deer grazed a few yards from the porch. Two does and a young buck who looked up at me cautiously, three fawns on the move constantly, heads down, nibbling, oblivious.

"Hello," I whispered. "Hello." I wanted Nick and Henry to see, to open the screen door slowly so it wouldn't creak, tiptoe in their socks across the porch, whispering excitedly and shushing each other until they inevitably scared the deer away.

"Sorry," Monroe said. "I didn't hear you."

"I didn't say anything."

"I'll see you Friday, then."

"Yes. Friday."

"Do you have any plans for the day?"

The buck leaped gracefully and bounded away. The others followed. I went to the west end of the porch, watched them disappear into the woods.

"Yes. I'm going to look for Henry."

* * *

I hiked to Emerald Lake that day, an easy hike, one of Henry's favorites. He could have come this way, I thought, gotten confused, set out to meet Paul and me and walked in the wrong direction. I scanned the terrain on both sides of the trail as I walked, searching for what, I didn't know. Anything. I stopped to rest when I got to Emerald Lake, ate an apple and a hunk of cheese and stared at the luminous green water, striking against the intense blue of the Colorado sky. Steller's jays and chipmunks lurked nearby, eyeing my snack. I finished the cheese, put the apple core in my backpack, and started down. Not ready for the hike to end, I headed southwest, crossed Tyndall Creek, and switchbacked up a shady ridge toward Lake Haiyaha.

The trail rounded a bend to reveal a sweeping view of the valley, Estes Park visible in the distance. I stopped for a swig of water, then cupped my hands around my mouth and called as loud as I could. "Henry!" No response. I called again. "Heeeennnnrrrryyyy!" Stood as still as I could, listening for Henry's answer. Nothing. Other hikers passed, asked if I'd lost someone, and I kicked myself for not having brought flyers to give them. I descended into a forest of fir and spruce and walked up again over rocky terrain until Lake Haiyaha came into view. I scanned the boulders surrounding the lake, the clear water, the twisted limbs of a timber pine that revealed its struggle. Nothing. I felt the dull ache of disappointment and grief slowly taking hold. I turned back to the trail before it overwhelmed me.

* * *

I woke early the next morning, reloaded my backpack with food, water, and flyers, and drove to the Glacier Gorge parking lot. I didn't want to go back to Sky Pond, didn't want to relive that day, but I had to. I had to find Henry.

The hike seemed harder and longer with no one to keep me company. When I reached the rocks at Sky Pond where we'd spread a picnic lunch that day, I collapsed, chest heaving, throat dry, every muscle in my body aching. I lay on my back, closed my eyes, and nearly drifted off to sleep, vaguely aware of the voices and laughter of a few other hikers scattered around the shores of the pond.

A gust of cold wind snapped me back to consciousness. I sat up and unzipped my backpack, pulled on a sweatshirt and jacket. I choked down handfuls of trail mix, stared at the barren cliffs and the desolate sky, and tried not to cry.

"Henry," I said in a loud voice. "I know you're out there somewhere. I know you're alive. Don't give up." I stood, slung my backpack over my shoulder. "Don't you ever give up. Because I will find you. Don't. Give. Up."

A young couple passed, glanced up at me, startled, then exchanged a look and picked up their pace. Was I shouting? I didn't know. I climbed down from the rock and started back. I had crossed Glacier Creek and started up the last incline to the trailhead when something caught my eye. A flash of royal blue under the brush a few yards off the trail to the right. I stopped, wondering at first if it was a bird, then climbed down for a closer look and saw that it was likely a piece of plastic discarded by some idiot who had no regard for the sanctity of the surroundings. I bent down to retrieve it, scratching my arms on the brush, but the thing was caught in a tangle of branches. I yanked harder and pulled it loose. It was larger than it first appeared, a sheet of nylon that fell open when I shook it at arms' length.

It took me a minute to realize what it was. I stared, almost disoriented, as the thing flapped, and I clutched it in both hands to spread it out into a familiar shape. And then, I started to tremble. It was a poncho. A child's rain poncho. The same size and the same color as the one Henry was wearing when he disappeared.

CHAPTER

20

Monroe

"YOU HAVE TO start the search again," Elizabeth said.

She'd called me, hysterical, like the day Henry went missing, and I met her at the Glacier Gorge trailhead. She showed me the poncho and where she'd found it.

She looked bad. Thinner every time I saw her, dark circles under her eyes, scratches on her arms and legs. I put the poncho in an evidence bag and set it in the truck.

"We went over this area with a fine-toothed comb," I said. "We didn't overlook the poncho. Some kid probably dropped it in the past day or so."

"Or Henry was here. Recently."

"If he was here, Elizabeth, he was close to the trail. He would have seen people, would have called for help."

She pulled at her ponytail in frustration, then pointed to the evidence bag.

"It's the same color. The same size, the same brand that Henry was wearing."

"And every camping store in Estes sells ponchos just like that one."

She curled her hands into fists, turned away and paced back and forth across the short distance between my truck and the trail.

"What if he was hiding from someone," she said. "He couldn't call out because he was afraid that person would hear him."

A six-year-old hiding from a bad guy, surviving in the park for ten days on his own? The idea was ridiculous.

"It'll be dark soon," I said. "I'll look around while there's still light. And I'll get a couple of people out here tomorrow to search this area again."

"I'm going with you."

I sighed, rolled up the windows on the truck and locked it. She followed me down the trail, and I pointed to a rock outcropping overlooking the creek.

"Just sit here, okay? Wait for me."

I guess she was too worn out to argue. I left her there and went down to the creek, walked along it then back again, crossed the trail and went in the other direction. Every few minutes, I heard Elizabeth calling, "Heeeennnnnrrrryyyy!" I didn't find anything, not that I expected to. I climbed back to the trail before it got too dark to see, and told her it was time to call it a day.

"Let me buy you dinner," I said. "A big plate of lasagna at Mama Rose's sounds pretty good to me."

She shook her head, then apparently changed her mind. "Okay. But we're going Dutch."

"That sounds even better. I have to stop at the office first and get my Bronco."

I followed her Jeep through the park. She waited while I swapped the park vehicle for my own, then I drove behind her into town and parked near her across the street from the restaurant. We went in together and got a table by the window overlooking the

Big Thompson. The waitress took our order and Elizabeth excused herself.

She was gone for a while. Our salads came and I was starting to get a little worried, then saw her making her way back to the table. I stood up and held her chair for her. She'd brushed her hair and washed her face, but I could tell she'd been crying.

"You should have started without me."

"I'm in no rush."

She ate a few bites of salad, then put her fork down and stared out the window at the river.

"I keep thinking I'll see him. Skipping down the sidewalk. Throwing sticks and rocks into the river."

She picked up her fork and poked at her salad. I was finished with mine.

"How's Nick doing?" I said.

"Not well. I called him last night, but it's hard for him to talk to me. He asks me why this is happening, why we can't find Henry. I don't have any answers for him."

The lasagna arrived. I was happy to see her dig in with a little more appetite.

"And Paul?"

"We haven't talked much since he went back to Houston. Just about Nick. And whether there's any news."

I looked up from my plate. She grimaced.

"I told him about Alaska. Brad Riegle. All of it. He's very angry with me."

I mopped up the last bits of meat sauce with a piece of garlic bread. She put down her fork and called it quits. We passed on dessert, ordered coffee, and paid the check.

"I understand him being angry," I said. "But you have more to deal with than that right now. You need each other."

She rested her chin on the heel of one hand, played with her spoon with the other. "I think he's been carrying a lot of resentment for a long time. With that . . . Alaska . . . Henry gone. I don't think there's much hope for the marriage."

"Resentment over what?"

She shrugged. "My career. My salary. The money my dad left me when he died. It wasn't a huge amount, but Paul comes from a working-class family. It seemed like a lot to him."

"He's a smart guy. He knew what he was getting into."

"He should have known. He took me bowling on our first date—it was a thing in his family to go bowling on Saturday nights. I crushed him. Every single game."

"Jesus. You couldn't let him win one?"

"No. Even if it meant that would be our only date."

"You obviously didn't scare him off."

She gave a little smile. "He wrote a poem for me the next day. 'Ode on a Ten-Pin Goddess.' I think I fell for him right then."

She took a sip of coffee, stared out the window again. "A lot has happened since then. All the times I wasn't there for him. For the boys." Her eyes filled. "I won't be able to forgive myself for that. I can hardly ask Paul to."

"I'm guessing your family didn't suffer much from you being gone. I—"

"Oh my God!"

Elizabeth jumped up and banged against the table, knocking her coffee cup to the floor.

"It's him!"

For a second I was confused, thinking she meant Henry. She ran for the door. I grabbed the jacket she'd left on her chair and hurried after her.

I found her by the river, turning to look in one direction, then the other. There was no one in sight.

"The guy in the plaid shirt?"

She nodded.

"Did you get a good look at him?"

"No. I only saw him for a second."

I held out her jacket. She put it on, and we started back to our cars.

"What time is the appointment tomorrow with the sketch artist?" she said.

"Three o'clock. I'd like to be there if you don't mind."

"I don't mind."

I walked her to her Jeep. "I'll follow you home. Just to the gate."

"That's really not necessary."

"Maybe not, but I'll feel better if I do."

Devil's Gulch Road was dark and quiet. I pulled in behind Elizabeth when she stopped at her gate. She got out of the Jeep, left it running with the door open, and I leaned out my open window.

"You have a taillight out," I said.

"Gee, Officer, I'm sorry. I've had other things on my mind."

"You might want to get it taken care of tomorrow."

She shook her head. "I'll be at Glacier Gorge in the morning. And at the police station in the afternoon."

"Be safe. I'll lock the gate behind you."

"Thanks." She unlocked the gate and pushed it open then came back to her car. "Don't worry, Monroe. If that guy comes around here, I'll blow his head off."

I had no doubt that she would. I opened my door and went to close the gate, kept an eye on the Jeep with its one taillight bouncing up the drive. The garage door rose and she pulled in, then it drew shut behind her. Lights went on in the house. I went back to my Bronco and turned off the engine. I sat there until after midnight, watching the house and the road. No one came by.

* * *

I spent the next morning and early afternoon on patrol, then went to meet Elizabeth and the sketch artist. They were in an interview room, chatting while the sketch artist fastened a blank piece of paper to a large clipboard and took out her pencils. They looked up as I came in. The artist stood and introduced herself as Officer Audrey McDowell with the Loveland police department. Elizabeth nodded hello, and I sat down out of the way.

Officer McDowell started by asking Elizabeth to recall what she was doing when she first saw the man watching her. Elizabeth described in detail standing at the window of the antiques store, taping a flyer about Henry's disappearance near the front door, looking up and seeing the man across the street.

"Did he look familiar to you?"

"I don't know. Maybe just for a second—I had a feeling he was someone I'd seen before."

"Okay. And the other times you've seen him?"

"I saw him again at the grocery store Tuesday evening. But I've had this feeling sometimes that someone was watching me."

"Every day?"

"No. Not every day."

"Tell me about Tuesday at the grocery store."

Elizabeth told her about that sighting, and then seeing him again last night outside Mama Rose's. McDowell picked up her pencil.

"What can you tell me about what he looks like?"

McDowell didn't start to draw. She took notes as Elizabeth described the man.

"He was maybe five ten, five eleven. Overweight."

"Race?"

"Oh. Caucasian. He looked about fifty-five or so, but he could be younger."

"What makes you say that?"

"He was out of shape. He didn't look like he's spent much time out of doors. Pasty skin, from what I could see."

"What about the color of his hair, his eyes?"

Elizabeth shook her head. "He wears a stocking cap pulled down to his eyebrows. And I was too far away to see eye color."

"Was there anything that stood out to you when you saw him?"

"The bags under his eyes. I could see those, even at a distance."

McDowell was ready to draw. "I'm going to make up a guy based on what you've told me so far. It's not going to look like him, but it's better than looking at a blank page. Then we'll start moving the features around. Okay?"

Elizabeth nodded, and McDowell went to work with short precise strokes, the soft scraping of pencil on paper the only sound in the room. Then she and Elizabeth discussed every detail—shape of the face, nose, mouth, cheekbones, jowls. Bridge of the nose, marks on the face, wrinkles, a day's worth of stubble. Placement of the stocking cap on his forehead, a roll of fat under his chin. They consulted pictures in a facial recognition catalog, and McDowell erased here and there and redrew. Finally, she held up the sketch and asked Elizabeth, on a scale of one to ten, how she would rate it on likeness to the man she'd seen.

"Maybe an eight."

"Do you have any suggestions for how I could change it to get it up to a nine?"

"I can't think of anything else."

McDowell smiled at Elizabeth, then at me. "Okay, then. Good work." She had Elizabeth sign and date the back of the sketch.

"Elizabeth," I said, the first time I'd spoken in over two hours. "Look again. Do you recognize the guy? Does he look even vaguely like someone you might know?"

McDowell slid the sketch across the table to her again. She rested her elbows on either side of it, head in her hands, and stared long and hard, her eyes darting back and forth across and up and down the page. Finally, she looked up.

"No. I have no idea who he is." She pushed the sketch in McDowell's direction. "Could I have a copy to take with me?"

"Of course." McDowell stood up and went to make the copies.

"Sorry, Monroe," Elizabeth said.

"Don't be sorry. We'll pass it around, see if anything turns up on him. And maybe it'll come to you who the guy is."

"Maybe." She shook her head. "Maybe."

CHAPTER

21

Eddie

BUYING THE BLUE poncho was a stroke of genius, I have to say. Just like the one Henry was wearing when he disappeared. I didn't have any idea what I might do with it, but then, then—she takes the one hike that makes the poncho scenario perfect. Poetic, even. I had tailed her through town, well behind in the traffic.

There was a moment when I thought I'd lost her. The ranger at the entrance station stepped out of the booth, circled my truck and took a look at my Oklahoma plates, then waved me through. I guessed at a left turn onto Bear Lake Road and spotted the Jeep after a mile or so. I followed her through the park, and couldn't believe my luck when she pulled into Glacier Gorge. I drove on past, pulled over at a lookout point, waited for a while then turned around. When I got back to Glacier Gorge, the Jeep was there. Elizabeth was nowhere in sight.

Why would she hike to Sky Pond? At least I assume that's where she went. She was gone for hours. But I'm a patient man. The past ten years have taught me that. I planted the poncho, parked the truck up the road, and sat in the trees across from the parking lot to wait.

The first few times Elizabeth and I met, I had a feeling that there was this connection between us, an understanding at least, that could turn into something more. I tried to get to know her, not as an adversary but as a colleague, hoping she would warm up to me as time went along. She soon disabused me of that notion, rebuffed my simplest questions and observations.

It was the little things that played over and over in my mind. Little movements, little expressions, things that would have gone unnoticed to most, but not to me.

The slightly raised eyebrow as she scanned the sport coat I wore to my deposition, a bit shiny and worn but still passable, I thought. The minutest curl of the lip when I answered Bob Simon's preliminary questions about my education and experience, my work as an auto insurance adjuster while I pursued my law degree at night. The barest, barest hint of a smile, the flick at a piece of lint on her skirt, crossed legs, a glance at her watch during my explanations of why the land deals, the stock trades, the development projects were all perfectly legitimate.

From what I'd seen in the past few days, I was pretty sure the days of the subtle gesture were gone. And she did not disappoint.

She emerged from the trailhead on the run, poncho in one hand, cell phone in the other, frantically looking in all directions. I almost laughed out loud. There's no cell service up here, Elizabeth. You'll have to drive down to call your park ranger friend.

Which is what she did. I watched as she jumped in the Jeep, squealed out of the parking lot, and hit Bear Lake Road driving much too fast. Slow down, Elizabeth. Slow down. We wouldn't want anything to happen to you.

I stepped out of the trees and walked to my truck. I had to take a minute to catch my breath. The altitude was killing me.

I hadn't driven far when Elizabeth passed me in the Jeep, on her way back up to Glacier Gorge. The park ranger wasn't long behind her.

It's a terrible thing when a child is lost. What if he's never found? I wouldn't wish that on the poor kid.

On the other hand, even tragic circumstances can have their amusing moments. Like watching Elizabeth run.

C H A P T E R

22

Paul

IT WAS GOOD in some ways to be home, hell in other ways. Nick was clingy and wouldn't let me out of his sight around the house. I couldn't even go to the bathroom without him hovering outside the door. But that was okay. Several of the moms in Henry's class had organized dinners to be brought to us every evening. We read kind little notes taped to casseroles and Tupperware, filled our plates and stuck them in the microwave. We ate watching TV then curled up together on the couch until bedtime.

Hell was the reminders of Henry everywhere. The night I got home from Colorado the house was hot, the air conditioner set at eighty degrees while we were gone and the Houston heat oppressive even at midnight. I adjusted the AC, got a beer from the refrigerator, then went upstairs. I dropped my bags, stripped down to boxers and a T-shirt, picked up my beer, and went to Henry's room. I hesitated before flipping the light switch, the thought running through my mind that I didn't want to wake him. Which made no sense, of course, because he wasn't there.

I sat on his bed and drank my beer and looked around. It was a kid's room, decorations by Henry. Baseball pennants tacked to the wall, a large map of the United States with pushpins on all the states he'd been to. Stuffed animals, Power Rangers, a bookcase filled mostly with Hot Wheels and snow globes and other junk. A corkboard over his desk with photos and ribbons and a large gold star proclaiming, "Henry English, Star of the Week!" And hanging on his closet door, a white shirt and navy shorts, his new school uniform. He'd hung it there before we left for Colorado and set his new sneakers on the floor beside it. Ready to go on the first day of school.

I lost it.

It didn't get any easier. I took Nick to school in the mornings, and in the few days before my classes started went back to the house and tried to write. Henry's bike and roller blades were in the garage. A pair of flip-flops and a bathing suit in the mudroom, a cup marked with the letter "H" in the kitchen. Framed photos everywhere, six years of a happy life.

It sounds corny, I know, but I write the old-fashioned way—pencil and paper. I have a little study off the kitchen that looks out over the backyard. I watch the hummingbirds in late summer and early fall, the cardinals in the spring. The neighbors' fat yellow cat in a crouch on the fence, eyes on a squirrel. Falcons high in the oak tree, an occasional opossum or raccoon. Crazy what you see in the middle of the city. Not long ago a coyote killed a dog just a few blocks from our house.

I sat with my pencil in hand, staring at the blank page. Usually, something would come. A line, a phrase. People ask me how that happens. I can't explain it. But then I sat for hours, and when Jimena poked her head in to tell me she was leaving to pick up Nick, the page was still empty. I knew we'd never see Henry alive again. I just wanted them to find his body, so we could bring him home.

Elizabeth called late one night after Nick had gone to bed. She'd hiked up to Sky Pond and on the way back found a kids' poncho, the same color and size as Henry's. She was convinced it was his. I tried to talk her through the logic of it, there's no way it could be, but she wouldn't hear it. She accused me of giving up, and I said, "I'm just being rational about the situation," and she said she can't even talk to me anymore, and I said, "So call Brad fucking Riegle, maybe he'll talk to you." She hung up.

Elizabeth and I met in a Shakespeare class our sophomore year at UT. She was passionate about Shakespeare, studied and read his plays over and over, and still keeps a volume of complete works in her office. She said it was like she'd found something she'd been looking for her whole life. I knew what she meant. I'd been looking for Elizabeth my whole life. I wanted to dive in and never come up for air.

I couldn't get it out of my head. Images of Riegle and Elizabeth in the bar, the looks, the signals. Did they make out in the elevator? Grope each other on the breathless, anticipatory walk down the hall, jam the key card in the door impatiently, fall on the bed tearing at their clothes?

Nick was torn. He wanted Elizabeth home, but he also wanted her to stay in Colorado, to keep looking for Henry. As for me, she could stay out there and hike as long as she wanted, for all I cared. I didn't think she had any real hope that she'd ever find him. She was just feeling guilty.

CHAPTER

23

Elizabeth

I TAPED A COPY of Officer McDowell's sketch to the refrigerator door. I sat at the bar in the kitchen before dawn on Saturday eating a bowl of cereal, looking alternately at a trail map of the park and the pale, doughy man in a stocking cap.

I'd gone to Sprague Lake after leaving the session at the police station. I walked around the half-mile loop, I'm not sure how many times, until the sun started to go down. I sat on a bench, watched mallards paddling with their ducklings in tow and heard the occasional splash of a brook trout, audible from across the lake in the profound silence. We took Nick and Henry there to fish at the beginning of our vacation, as we'd done for several years, the chances of catching anything slim, but they loved casting their lines in the water. Paul and I spent most of our time baiting the hooks, attaching new ones when they snapped off on a submerged log, untangling the lines. This year Nick managed somehow to hook the hood of Henry's sweatshirt. Henry yelled as Nick, confused about where his line had landed, started to reel it in. They fell over laughing, and that was it for fishing for the day. We stowed our gear in the Jeep, lit a fire, and made s'mores as the night fell.

I turned back to the trail map. I had marked on it the trails Henry might have taken, all of them accessible in some way from Glacier Gorge, the routes I'd covered so far, the location of the poncho. I thought I would save the easier hikes for when Alex arrived. Mills Lake, then on to Black Lake, was a good choice for me. About ten miles round trip. I put my cereal bowl in the sink and packed a lunch and water. I locked up the house, took the rifle with me to the garage and returned it to the gun safe, got in the Jeep, and headed for the park.

The hike took most of the day, and it was almost dark when I got back to the cabin. I parked the Jeep in the driveway, collected my backpack and boots. I dropped the boots on the porch to air out overnight, put my key in the deadbolt and turned it. Then I froze.

The front door was unlocked.

My heart started to pound. I went over in my mind the events of the morning, packing my lunch and water, putting the rifle in the gun safe. Locking the front door. I backed slowly down the steps and picked up a rock from the flower bed. Holding the rock ready, I went to the door, turned the knob carefully, and opened it. I stood at the threshold for a minute or two that seemed like forever, listening for anything out of the ordinary, then flipped on the living room lights. I almost jumped at the sudden appearance of something looking at me with glazed eyes. The deer head over the fireplace. I should take that damn thing down.

I turned left into the dining area, then to the kitchen, on to the master bedroom. Turning on lights as I went and opening closet doors, floorboards creaking as I crept across the living room. Nick's room, the guest room, then down the hall to Henry's. I stopped. The door to Henry's room was closed.

I stood for a moment, my heart pounding again and barely able to breathe, looking at the door. Was it closed when I left this morning? I wasn't sure. But why would I ever have closed it?

"Henry?"

Nothing.

"Henry?"

I reached for the knob and slowly opened the door. "Henry?" I flipped the switch, and almost jumped again. Seven feet of Hakeem Olajuwon looking at me from the poster across the room.

"Sheesh. You scared me, Hakeem." I checked the closet, then stepped to the middle of the room. I turned in a full circle. Nothing appeared out of the ordinary. But something didn't feel quite right. I bent down and looked under the bed. Nothing.

I took a deep breath, blew it out, and turned off the light as I went into the hall. I peeked in the garage, started back down the hall. Then had a thought.

I had bought a fake rock some years ago to hide a spare key to the house and put it in the flower bed. Paul and the boys and I were the only ones who knew it was there. I went back to the garage and found a flashlight on the work bench. I walked through the house, turning off most of the lights, then went outside to look for the fake rock.

It took me a while to find it, crouched under the bushes and moving the flashlight a few inches at a time. It wasn't in the precise place that I remembered, and it blended in well with the other rocks, especially in the dark. I carried it up onto the porch and opened it. The key was gone.

I stared at the empty halves of the rock, then closed it. I walked to the edge of the porch, pointed the flashlight out into the yard, and swept it slowly back and forth.

"Is someone out there?" I meant to say it in a loud, commanding voice, but realized it came out in a whisper. "Henry?" Louder this time. "Henry, are you there?" Nothing. I heard a car start in the distance but couldn't tell how far away it was. I turned off the flashlight and waited. No cars came by on Devil's Gulch Road. I stood there a few more minutes, then went inside.

I locked the front door behind me, carried the fake rock to the kitchen, and set it on the counter. I needed to eat something. I wasn't thinking clearly, and I was lightheaded after the adrenaline rush of the past hour. I opened a can of sardines and a sleeve of crackers, cut up an apple, squeezed a lemon over the sardines, and sat down at the bar. I was halfway through dinner when it hit me.

I wiped my mouth with a paper towel, slid down from the bar stool, and went to Henry's room. I turned on the light and said hello to Hakeem. I looked in the closet, the toy box, under the bed, and opened every drawer. I looked everywhere, just to be sure.

Dolphie the dolphin was gone.

* * *

"Is anything else missing?" I was on the phone with Monroe.

"I don't know." I went through Henry's closet carefully, but I couldn't be sure. I had lost track of what was in Colorado and what was in Houston.

"Back up," he said. "When was the last time you checked to see if the key was still in the rock?"

"I can't remember. Last summer, probably."

"So Paul or one of the kids could have taken it out and forgot to put it back."

"No. There was never a situation where they would have needed it."

"How about the boys playing with it? They think it's cool, they're playing robbers or secret agents or something, and they lose the key."

That was possible, I had to admit.

"The door was unlocked, Monroe. The dolphin is missing. The only way someone would know about that key is if Henry told him. Which means that Henry's alive."

"Or some really sick person wants you to think Henry's alive. And he's getting his jollies watching you."

He was quiet for a minute. Then said, "Check the windows."

"I'm sure they're locked." I crossed Henry's room and tugged at one window. It didn't budge. Moved to the other one. A gust of cool air as it slid up easily.

"Okay," Monroe said. "So someone could have gotten in without a key. I'll call Carpenter. He'll probably want to come have a look around. Be sure everything's locked up until he gets there. Then please, please get out. Go to a hotel. If you insist on staying in Estes, rent a condo or something in town."

"No. I'll get the locks changed tomorrow. But I want him to come back. He knows where Henry is, I'm sure of it now. Sorry to bother you."

He sighed. "You're not bothering me, Elizabeth. I just don't want anything to happen to you."

"Thanks." My voice cracked. "But nothing could be worse than not finding Henry."

CHAPTER

24

Eddie

IT WAS COMICAL watching her poke around in the dark. Standing on the porch, calling, "Henry, are you there?"

I waited until she went inside, then made my way back to the truck. I waved as I passed her place, then headed south of town.

* * *

The cabin I'd rented in the woods was pitch black. I unlocked the front door, flipped on a light. Dropped my bundle in the bedroom then went to the kitchen and poured a drink. Cereal and tequila for dinner. Beats prison food any day.

I finished a second bowl then took the tequila bottle with me to the living room. I pushed back in the old leather lounger and turned on the TV.

The cabin wasn't much, but it suited my purposes. Quiet, back from the road. Blessed solitude after not one moment of privacy for ten years. No fights over what to watch on TV.

I scrolled through the channels and settled on a rerun of *Home Alone*. I needed a laugh. That kid Kevin, what a brat. I really liked him.

C H A P T E R

25

Alexis

I TOOK AN EARLY flight to Denver on Sunday and rented a car, drove to Boulder and stopped at Whole Foods. Food choices are limited in Estes Park, in my opinion, and I suspected that Elizabeth was eating nothing but crap with all the stress. I bought produce, fresh-squeezed orange juice, ribeyes, salmon, and pork chops. Three cheeses, bread and crackers, paté and olives, and some decent coffee. Over four hundred dollars' worth by the time I was finished. Some wine would have been nice, but keeping Elizabeth sober was more important.

Despite the circumstances of the trip, I found myself enjoying the drive north out of Boulder. I'd been to Colorado a number of times with Elizabeth for girls' weekends, a few times by myself to get away. Elizabeth gave me a key to the cabin years ago and said to let her know whenever I wanted to use it. Each time I did, I thought a little harder about buying a place in the mountains, hanging out a shingle in Estes Park and leaving Houston and corporate law behind. Elizabeth laughed and said I'd get bored in a year if not before. I wasn't so sure.

Elizabeth saw me coming and walked out to greet me as I parked in the driveway. I got out of the car and we put our arms around each other, held each other tight, and wept. I finally pushed away.

She looked like shit. I don't think she'd showered in a couple of days, and it had been longer than that since she'd washed her hair. She was sunburned, lips chapped, nails jagged, scratches on her arms. She'd lost ten pounds that she didn't need to lose.

"You're limping," I said. "Are you hurt?"

"Just sore. And I have a couple of blisters on my feet from all the walking in town and hiking."

"Okay, honey. Let's get the groceries in, then we're going to do a little work on you."

"Are you sure we'll have enough?" she said as we carried the bags to the kitchen, then went back to the car for more.

"You know me and food. It's the Southern thing."

I went to the refrigerator, stopped when I saw the drawing of a man's face taped to the door.

"Who's this?"

"The creep who's been following me."

She told me about the times she'd seen him in town, at Safeway, outside the restaurant.

"And I'm pretty sure he was here yesterday."

I turned to look at her.

"Here? What do you mean by 'here'?"

She set the nectarines I'd bought on the counter, stacked apples and pears in a wrought-iron basket.

"In the house."

I heard the rest of the story—the front door and a window unlocked, the key gone from the fake rock, Dolphie missing. The police coming to check the house. Elizabeth propping kitchen chairs under doorknobs to barricade herself in after they'd gone. I watched her calmly put away groceries as she spoke, rinse a colander of grapes at the sink, unwrap cheese and paté, and open a box of crackers. All the while, every detail she described raised a few more goose bumps on my arms.

"I don't like this, Elizabeth. I don't like this at all."

"I had a locksmith out this morning. I'll give you a new key."

"Changing the locks won't keep the guy out if he wants in."

"No. But it'll slow him down." She poured tea over ice in two glasses and set them on the table. "And give me enough time to grab the rifle."

"Oh, that makes me feel a whole shitload better."

We sat down to lunch. Elizabeth unfolded a large map on the table and pointed.

"Here's where Henry disappeared." She drew her finger across the map. "This is the trail we hiked that day. I've gone back over it and hiked these other trails that connect to it." She pointed. "This is where I found the poncho."

She'd told me about the poncho. It seemed pretty farfetched that it could have any connection to Henry. But she was grasping at anything.

"Do they have the DNA results on the poncho?"

"Not yet." She pushed the map closer to me. "I thought we'd start with something easy tomorrow. Maybe Bierstadt Lake. Nothing too strenuous on your first day out." She traced the loop of the trail and, fingers trembling slightly, brushed her hand in a wider arc, then stopped. She sat motionless for a few minutes, staring at the map with vacant eyes. I leaned toward her, watching her.

"So much ground to cover," she whispered. "So many places he might be."

That was the moment it hit me. Elizabeth may not survive this. I sat back in my chair and for a few seconds, I couldn't breathe. Tears welled in my eyes, and I blinked to keep them from falling. Then I reached out and took her hand. "Let's go sit on the porch, honey. I need some fresh air."

I led her outside. We sank into rocking chairs, side by side, and rocked quietly, looking out over the mountains. After a while, I stood up, then knelt in front of her. She wore old, beat-up sneakers that used to be white. I unlaced one, then the other, and pulled them off. Then took off her socks, stuck to her skin in a few places with dried blood and pus. When I saw her feet, I shook my head. "Oh, Elizabeth."

Strips of moleskin and bandages covered her heels, the balls of her feet, and her toes. I pulled them off gently. Underneath were raw skin, several new blisters that hadn't popped, and a couple of places that looked almost infected.

"Sit here a minute," I said. "I'll be right back."

I threw the bandages in the kitchen trash, then went to the master bedroom and started a warm bath. I found gauze, antiseptic cream, and aloe vera in the medicine cabinet and a pair of ankle socks in a drawer. I went back outside and handed the socks to Elizabeth.

"I'm running you a bath. Put these on to protect your feet until you get in the tub. We'll doctor them when you get out."

She slipped on the socks and stood.

"I look pretty awful, don't I?"

"Yes. But it's okay."

I followed her inside and found my purse in the living room.

"There's an ashtray in the cabinet over the refrigerator," she called from the hall.

"You know me too well."

I waited until I heard her close the door to her bathroom, then found the ashtray and went back to the porch. I sat down, lit a cigarette, and leaned back in my chair. I'd only taken a couple of puffs when I heard a phone ring. It wasn't my ring tone, so I ignored it. Elizabeth could return the call when she got out of the bath. The ringing stopped. Then a few seconds later started again.

"Shit." Maybe it was Paul, or Nick. I stubbed out my cigarette, went inside, and followed the sound of the ringing to the kitchen. Elizabeth's phone was on the counter. I picked it up and said hello.

There was silence on the other end.

"Nick? Paul?"

A pause, then a man's voice. "Uh, no."

"Then who the hell is this?"

"This is Hollis Monroe. I'm trying to reach Elizabeth."

"She's not available right now. May I take a message?"

Another pause. "I'm just calling to check in. Make sure she's okay."

"Oh, right," I said as I walked back outside. "You're the park ranger. Excuse me a minute. You interrupted my cigarette."

I sat down, lit another, and blew smoke away from the phone.

"Okay," I said. "Now I can talk."

"May I ask who this is?"

"Sure. Alexis LaDay. Elizabeth's best friend."

"Pleased to meet you, Mrs. LaDay."

Mrs.? I let it slide. "Call me Alex."

"Thank you. Elizabeth is okay?"

"She's fine." I inhaled, blew out again. "Actually not fine, but you know what I mean."

"Yeah. Well, I won't trouble you anymore."

"Hold on a second, Mr. Monroe."

"Monroe. Just Monroe."

"Okay, just Monroe. What the fuck is going on here? Why haven't you found Henry? I assume you have other law enforcement agencies helping with this."

"Yes, ma'am, we do."

Mrs. Ma'am. I tapped ash into the ashtray, inhaled furiously.

"Do you have even one clue what happened? Or where he might be?"

I thought he might get defensive, perhaps raise his voice and argue. He didn't. His voice was softer. Maybe even a little sad.

"There are two likely scenarios. The first is that he wandered off in Rocky. Got lost, fell off a cliff or into a lake, and our search teams haven't been able to find him. The second, which I now think is more likely, is that he was taken."

He was quiet for a moment. "I'm sure you watch the news. You know what happens to little boys when they're kidnapped."

I looked up at clouds gathering over the mountains and saw the first drops of the afternoon rain, images of what might have happened to Henry racing through my mind. I wanted to stand up, kick the porch rail, and scream. And scream and scream and scream. But I didn't. I was there for Elizabeth.

"You think he's dead," I said in a low, flat voice.

"Yes, ma'am. Alexis. I think Henry's dead."

* * *

I'd finished my third cigarette when the door opened and Elizabeth stepped out onto the porch. Her hair was wet and she'd put on a clean T-shirt and sweatpants and a pair of fur-lined moccasins. She sat down beside me and sighed.

"You look better."

She nodded and pointed at her phone. "Who were you talking to?"

"The park ranger. Monroe."

"Any news?"

"No, he was just calling to check on you."

She pulled a rattan stool over to her and propped up her feet.

"He's a good man," she said. "I have been unkind to him on more than one occasion."

"Yeah, well, I wasn't so nice to him myself."

"What did you say?"

"I asked him why the fuck he hasn't found Henry."

"And what did he say?"

I reached for the antiseptic cream and the aloe vera, got up and lifted Elizabeth's feet, then sat on the stool and put them on my lap.

"That he's doing the best he can."

I pulled off her moccasins and rubbed her feet with the cream and aloe vera. Every now and then she twitched and drew her foot away.

"Sting?"

"Yes."

I stood and carefully rested her feet on the stool.

"Let them air out for a while. When you're ready to go inside, I'll wrap a layer or two of gauze around them."

"Thank you, Alex."

I sat down in my rocking chair and lit another cigarette. "You have to stop, Elizabeth."

"Stop what?"

"Hiking all over the park. Losing weight, wearing yourself down."

She leaned over, picked up my pack of cigarettes, took one and lit it. She smoked maybe once or twice a year, and only with me.

"It's the only thing keeping me sane, Alex. And I can't just give up."

"I'm not telling you to give up. I understand what you're doing. You have to keep moving, keep looking, because it's all you can do. Rest for a couple of days. Let me take care of you. Then you can decide what your next steps should be."

She took a deep drag and frowned, crossed her legs and accidentally scraped her left heel against the rattan. She clenched the sides of the rocker, and I thought she might jump out of her chair. I didn't say anything. She looked at me with a grimace.

"Okay. Maybe for a couple of days."

* * *

She went to bed early that night and slept late the next morning. I cooked breakfast, and after she'd eaten she lay down on the couch and slept most of the afternoon. I read, grilled the salmon for dinner, and not long after I'd done the dishes, she turned in for the night. I was drinking coffee on the front porch the next morning when she came out with a stricken look, cell phone in her hand.

My heart sank, fearing the worst. "What is it?"

"Monroe called. The test results came back. Henry's DNA isn't on the poncho."

C H A P T E R

26

Monroe

I CALLED ELIZABETH TUESDAY morning to give her the news about the poncho. I hated to hear the disappointment in her voice, the desperation when she asked what was next, the frustration when I told her there wasn't much more we could do. I said I was sorry, hung up the phone, and looked at the picture of Henry on my desk. If we ever found him, it most likely would come from an anonymous tip or a random traffic stop or some unexpected link to another crime. I opened my spiral notebook and for about the hundredth time, went back through all my notes. There was precious little to go on. I turned a page.

Bradford Riegle. I still didn't think he had anything to do with Henry's disappearance, but something else occurred to me. Elizabeth said Riegle was actually good at analyzing jurors and reading people's reactions. Maybe he'd seen something during the course of the Alaska trial—a gesture, an expression, anything—that might reveal a grudge against Elizabeth. It was a long shot, but worth a try. I called Riegle's office and got the same spiel from his secretary that I'd gotten the first time I called. Mr. Riegle was away, doesn't answer his cell phone, responds only to his office in an emergency. But she would try to reach him. I told her thanks—and please have him call me as soon as possible.

I didn't hear from Elizabeth for a couple of days. I felt better about her staying at the cabin now that her friend was there, and I doubted either one of them wanted to hear from me unless I had something to report. But late Thursday afternoon I was in my office, filling out paperwork after coming in from patrol, and heard women's voices in the hall. There was a knock, and Elizabeth was at the door.

"Alex wanted to meet you," she said as I got to my feet. She turned slightly and moved aside, and I got my first look at Alexis LaDay. She was in faded jeans and a plaid shirt with the sleeves rolled above her elbows. Dark brown hair past her shoulders, gold hoop earrings, a leather watch band and scuffed suede loafers. And oh, damn, she was the prettiest woman I'd ever seen.

She stuck out her hand. "Alex LaDay."

I stood there like an idiot for what seemed like a long time, then took her hand and said, "Monroe."

"Just Monroe. Elizabeth told me. Nobody calls you Hollis."

I couldn't think of a thing to say. She shook my hand with a firm grip, then pulled hers away. I motioned for them to sit down and retreated behind my desk.

"You're looking at my tattoo," Alex said.

She held out her left arm, turned it up so I could see the inside of her wrist. I hadn't even noticed the tattoo. I was looking for a wedding ring.

"Elizabeth has one, too. We got them yesterday."

Elizabeth rested her left arm next to Alex's. They had matching tattoos that said, simply: Henry.

I'm generally of the opinion that no respectable woman would ever get a tattoo. But on the two of them, it looked natural. Even kind of elegant.

"Very nice," I said. "Was it painful?"

"It hurt like a motherfucker," Alex said. She looked at Elizabeth. "But it was worth it."

Elizabeth nodded. She sat back in her chair, but Alex leaned a little farther across my desk. She picked up the picture of Henry.

"I'm his godmother. We appreciate everything you're doing to find him." She put the picture back.

"We do appreciate it," Elizabeth said. "And we want to know what you're planning to do next."

Of course. I should have known that they weren't here because Alex LaDay was dying to make my acquaintance.

"Every law enforcement agency in the country knows about Henry," I said. "We've got eyes and ears out."

"I mean specifically," Elizabeth said. "Specifically, what is the next step in your investigation."

They stared at me politely but intently, two very nice ladies with "Henry" tattooed on their arms who were never going to give up. Not that I thought they should.

"It's Detective Carpenter's investigation. But specifically, I'm trying to get in touch with Brad Riegle again."

Elizabeth's face reddened. "Why would you do that?"

I explained my thinking about Riegle, told them it probably wouldn't lead to anything, but it was worth a try.

"It sounds like a waste of time," Elizabeth said. "I don't think there's any connection to Alaska."

Alex looked at her. "At this point, honey, nothing is a waste of time. You just have to get over your little indiscretion."

Elizabeth turned redder.

"Riegle may be an asshole, but he's fucking gorgeous," Alex said, arching an eyebrow and looking back at me.

"I've met him," I said. "I only noticed the asshole part."

"You haven't heard from him?" Elizabeth said.

"No. I'll let you know when I do."

We sat for a little while longer, them looking at me and me looking mostly at Elizabeth because I was afraid to look too much at Alex. Finally, they stood up to go. They said thank you and shook my hand and I walked them from my office, down the hall, and out to the parking lot.

"Elizabeth," Alex said. "We should invite Monroe to dinner tonight."

Elizabeth gave her a blank stare.

"Oh, no, ma'am. I wouldn't want to intrude."

There was what I would call an awkward silence before Elizabeth spoke.

"Not at all. Come around seven. Alex is cooking."

* * *

I went home after my shift, showered, and changed clothes. I wondered if I should bring something. Beer, maybe? No, Elizabeth didn't drink. I could stop at Safeway and pick up a pie. Something told me, though, that Alexis LaDay didn't eat many Safeway pies. Flowers? *Christ, Monroe, you'd look like a damn fool.* So, in the end, I sat on my porch, looking at my watch every few minutes until it was time to leave. I did not want to be late. I did not want to be early.

My palms were sweating a little as I steered the Bronco up the driveway. Elizabeth answered the door. I took off my hat, a leftover from my sheriff days, hung it on a peg alongside jackets and baseball caps, and followed her to the kitchen. Alex said hello and poured me a glass of ice water, and I sat at the counter and watched them cook. They moved effortlessly around the kitchen, like a dance, like they knew what the other one was about to do and staying out of the way, concentrating on their own tasks. Elizabeth tossed a salad, Alex heated a cast-iron skillet until it was smoking, then seared ribeye steaks and finished them off with herb butter. There was something almost intimate about it. I could feel their closeness as I watched. And their sadness. Images of church women serving lunch after my Maggie's funeral came to mind.

I couldn't remember the last time I'd eaten a meal like the one I had that night. There were pears and green beans and spinach in the salad. Smoked gruyère scalloped potatoes and steaks cooked to a perfect medium rare. And the company of two smart, pretty women, which likely gave my taste buds an even sharper edge.

I mostly listened as they told stories about their law firm—lavish, drunken summer recruiting functions for law students, partners who tried to engage a young Alex in grinding slow dances at firm parties, the backbiting, the affairs, and sexual episodes that occasionally made national news.

"Monroe," Alex said. "You remember the TV episode where two lawyers were screwing in the attic at a firm Christmas party and fell through the ceiling? That actually happened at our firm. We were the inspiration for that story."

"It seems like a lot of hanky panky going on," I said.

Alex threw back her head and laughed.

"'Hanky panky.' I love that, Monroe. You sound like my grandma."

It was a comparison I was not exactly happy to hear.

"We have cheesecake," Elizabeth said. "And strawberries."

"That sounds wonderful," I said. "But I'm going to pass."

We cleared the table, and Elizabeth insisted on doing the dishes, sending Alex and me out to the front porch. We sat under the stars, not saying anything while Alex smoked. Elizabeth finally came out and said she was going to bed. I stood, said I should go. Alex looked up at me.

"Stay a while, Monroe. Keep me company."

So I did. She asked, and I told her, about my life as a sheriff in Montana and Maggie's slow, painful death from ovarian cancer.

"That must have been so hard," she said. "Watching her suffer, knowing the best thing would be for her to go, but not wanting her to leave you."

"Yeah. I learned that the price you pay for loving that much is that one day you'll stare into the face of hell. And I did."

I went on to tell her about my daughter and her kids, my son-in-law who worked the night shift for a gas pipeline company. How I needed a change of scenery after Maggie died, loved my job in Rocky and my cabin on the river.

"It's a good life. Not without its heartbreaks, though. Like Henry."

She leaned back in her chair and slowly shook her head. "I can't even wrap my mind around the fact that he's gone. I keep thinking he'll walk out of his bedroom in his pajamas and snuggle up with me on the couch, and I'll realize that this was just some terrible nightmare."

She lit a cigarette, waved the smoke away from me. "He's the sweetest boy, Monroe. So sweet. And hilarious."

She laughed softly. "I have to tell you this one. Henry and Nick stayed with me one weekend this summer when Elizabeth was in trial. Just to give Paul a break. Henry set up a lemonade stand in front of my house and sat there for an hour in the ungodly heat."

"Very industrious for a six-year-old," I said.

"Yes, but there's almost no traffic on my street. He didn't make one sale. So he decided to go door to door. I got my wagon from the garden shed, and he put the lemonade and cups in it. I watched him go next door, then come back, pulling the wagon up the walk, all sweaty and red-faced. He rang the doorbell and I answered.

"'Would you like to buy some lemonade?'

"'How much is it?' I said.

"'Fifty cents a cup.'

"'Okay. Let me get my purse. I think I have fifty cents.'

"'Make it a dollar,' he said, 'and I'll have one with you.'"

We both laughed then.

"You must be very close," I said.

"We are."

"Any children of your own?"

She looked over and flashed a smile. "Oh God, no. The problem with children is that they usually come with a man attached."

I wasn't sure what that meant. And I didn't exactly know how to ask. Fortunately, she cleared it up for me.

"I got married right after law school. It didn't last long. I made the mistake of marrying a lawyer. Too many long hours, too much stress. And both of us knowing how to move in for the kill in an argument."

"No one since then?"

"Jesus, Monroe. You think I'm living like a fucking nun?" She paused. "That didn't sound quite right—nuns aren't supposed to be fucking."

That was pretty much all the information I wanted on the subject.

"Elizabeth was smart," she said. "I should have married a poet."

"Somehow I can't see you with Paul English."

"Oh, hell no. And I'm not saying their marriage is perfect."

"I hope they survive this," I said.

"They won't. Not if Henry's dead. Maybe not even if by some miracle he's found alive."

She stubbed out her cigarette. "She doesn't think he'll get over the Alaska thing. Not that Paul should be throwing rocks in that department."

"Oh?"

She shook her head. "I shouldn't have said that. But Elizabeth's already talking about moving here permanently. Bringing Nick with her."

"I'm sorry to hear it."

"Yeah. I told her that would be a terrible thing to do to Nick. That seemed to get through to her a little. I'm trying to get her to go home to Houston with me, at least for a few days, but I don't think she will."

"What's she going to do here?"

She frowned. "She'll walk, Monroe. She'll hike every trail in that park looking for Henry. And after she's hiked them all, she'll start over again."

"Why?"

"Because it's the only thing she can do right now. And she will never, ever give up on finding him."

Then I tried to ask the question casually.

"When are you going back to Houston?"

"Sunday."

We sat there a few more minutes without saying anything. Then Alex looked at her watch.

"Jesus. It's almost midnight."

I got up and went inside to get my hat. Alex was leaning on the porch rail when I came out.

"Thank you," I said. "I really enjoyed this."

She cocked her head and I swear to God, looked me up and down from head to toe.

"I enjoyed it, too."

I walked down the steps to my Bronco and opened the door.

"Monroe."

She leaned against the porch rail again and gave me a slow, lazy smile.

"Nice hat."

I nodded. "Thank you." Then I sat down in the driver's seat and closed the door. Before I dropped to my knees.

CHAPTER

27

Paul

ALEX CALLED MY cell phone Friday morning. I was on my way to U of H for a nine o'clock seminar. She was in Colorado with Elizabeth.

"Is Nick with you?"

"No, I just dropped him at school."

"Good. I didn't want to say anything that he shouldn't hear."

That was a concern born from experience. When Nick was about six, about Henry's age, Elizabeth was driving him to soccer practice when Alex called and immediately went into a tirade about something at the office. It was fuck this and fuck that and cocksucker this and asshole that, reverberating through the car on the speaker phone until Elizabeth, unable to get a word in, hung up on her. She looked over at Nick. He had tears streaming down his face. He was laughing that hard. He'd never heard anything like it, particularly from an adult, and Elizabeth had to speak sternly with him several times in the weeks that followed to stop him from repeating it to every kid in first grade. She also had a stern talk with Alex about the use of profanity in the presence of our children.

"What's going on?" I said.

"I'm worried about Elizabeth."

I turned left onto Kirby Drive, where traffic immediately slowed then, miraculously, picked up speed after a couple of blocks.

"Paul?"

"Yeah?"

"Aren't you going to ask me why I'm worried about your wife?"

"Aren't you going to tell me whether I ask or not?"

"Jesus, Paul, don't be a dick."

Said in that honey-dripping Georgia accent. Classic Alex.

"Is that what I am? A dick? For worrying first about my six-year-old son who's missing and probably dead? For worrying about my ten-year-old son who cries at least once a day, sometimes more, over his brother, and can't be convinced that it wasn't his fault?"

I was pretty wound up now. "You know what Nick does every night, Alex? He sits at the computer, looking at pictures of trucks. Makes, models, and colors over the past twenty years. Then he looks at images of Alaska license plates. Last night I found him searching for news stories about little boys who were missing or killed. Of course, Henry was among those he found. I had to cut him off from the computer, which is not an easy thing to do in this day and age."

I was shouting, driving too fast heading into Allen Parkway, and swerved back into my lane when the driver next to me honked angrily.

"Paul."

I lowered my voice. "What."

"It's not Elizabeth's fault, either."

"Did I say it was?"

I turned onto the entrance ramp for I-45 south. I didn't want to talk to Alex. I wanted to listen to NPR and relax for those minutes alone in my car before class.

"Then why are you so angry at her?"

I didn't say anything.

"She told me about Riegle," Alex said. "She's ashamed, beating herself up, and would take back every second of that night if she could."

Christ, do these women tell each other everything?

"Paul."

"What."

"Shit happens. People aren't perfect. She shouldn't have done it. But think about someone you know who shouldn't have done it, either."

I took the Cullen Street exit, came this close to being sideswiped by a jacked-up pickup going sixty on the feeder.

"I have no idea what you're talking about, Alex."

"I think you do. She found the poems, Paul. In their own little notebook at the bottom of the pile. 'For Claire.' You'd never shown her those."

My stomach turned. I'd stacked up every poem I'd written, planning to go back over them before classes began, and left them on my desk. I didn't think Elizabeth would have any interest in reading them. "When?"

"A few weeks before she left for Alaska."

"She didn't say anything about it to me."

"No. She was leaving town. Maybe it was just your poetic imagination. Not someone you actually knew. And when she got back, she couldn't exactly muster up moral outrage."

I blew out a long breath. "Maybe it was my imagination. It was a long time ago. Things were complicated."

"Oh, I get it," she said. "But I bet not as fucking complicated as things are now."

I was tired. I wasn't sleeping well, of course, and Henry and Nick were weighing heavy on me. The work at U of H was stressful, the level of talent around me and the expectations of the program exhilarating and intimidating at the same time. And the one thing Elizabeth has made very clear to me since the day I met her is that she can take care of herself.

"Just tell me, Alex. I have to get off the phone."

She laid it all out. The incessant hiking, hiking, hiking. Obsessing over the poncho, the missing Dolphie, the key. Blisters and not bathing and vacant stares. The creep that might be watching her.

"She's better this week," Alex said. "But I'm worried what will happen after I leave."

"Have you seen any sign of the guy in the stocking cap?"

"No. She was sure she spotted him in town yesterday, several blocks away in the crowd. She grabbed my arm and pointed, but I couldn't see him. She said maybe she was mistaken."

"Has Monroe seen him?"

"I don't think so."

"Does Monroe have any leads on who the guy might be?"

"No."

I pulled into my designated parking lot at U of H.

"Alex."

"Yes?"

"I never saw the guy, either."

There was a loud burst of static on the line, and then it went dead silent. I thought I might have lost the connection. Then heard her voice through the background noise.

"Jesus, Paul. You think she made it up? Elizabeth would never do that."

"Not intentionally."

Alex went quiet again. "Well, shit," she finally said.

Exactly. I didn't know which was worse. Some creep stalking Elizabeth. Or Elizabeth's encounters with a guy who was never there at all.

CHAPTER

28

Elizabeth

"PAUL THINKS I'M imagining the man?"

One of the things I usually appreciate about Alex is that she puts it all out there when it needs to be said. This time, though, she was really pissing me off. Worried about me, she called Paul. Now they were questioning whether I really saw the creep.

"He raised that possibility."

"And what about you? What do you think?"

Alex sighed. We'd been to the bookstore, browsed for an hour, and each of us bought a novel. We'd walked around town for a while, and now we were having tea and little sandwiches at Hey Diddle Diddle Café. Alex was determined to take me on these outings. She'd suggested manicures and a movie, and I told her absolutely not. Hoping every minute for news about Henry, and waiting for my nails to dry? I couldn't even begin to explain how ridiculous that sounded.

"You're under a lot of stress, honey." She held a teacup at her lips, blew gently and sipped, then set it down and took a bite of sandwich. "This is really good. I can't remember the last time I had pimento cheese."

I looked across the table at her. "Explain the sketch, Alex. I saw enough detail about him for a police sketch artist to come up with a pretty good likeness."

She dabbed at her mouth with a napkin, took another sip of tea. "When I was little, I had an imaginary friend. Her name was Dana. She had red hair and freckles and wore cute little pinafore dresses. We talked every day. I still remember what she looked like."

She picked up the tray of sandwiches and offered it to me. I shook my head and motioned to the waitress for our check. "I can introduce you to the salesclerk at the antique shop who saw him, too."

"That's not necessary."

"Then what's the point of this conversation?"

"I believe you saw him. At least once. Maybe more. But maybe he's also become like this stand-in for finding Henry. You can't find Henry, so you keep seeing this guy, and chasing him, and hoping he holds some clue."

I fumbled in my purse for my wallet. "Okay, maybe I'm losing touch with reality. Maybe looking for the creep is a waste of time. Maybe hiking all over the park looking for Henry is a waste of time. What's your point?"

She reached across the table and took my hand. "Another maybe. As in maybe it's time to go home."

"I'm ready when you are. As soon as we pay."

"No, honey. I mean home to Houston."

I pulled my hand away, gave my credit card to the waitress.

"Would you like those sandwiches to go?" said the waitress.

"Sure," I said.

She picked up the tray and headed toward the kitchen. I looked back at Alex.

"No way, Alex. No way. I am not going back to Houston without Henry."

* * *

Alex started to say something as we got into the Jeep, but I told her I didn't want to talk. We drove to the cabin in silence. I pulled off Devil's Gulch Road, stopped to unlock and open the gate. Alex unbuckled her seat belt.

"I'll get it," I said. I got out of the Jeep and went to the mailbox set on a post to the left of the gate, retrieved grocery ads and junk mail. As I turned to the gate, something to the right caught my eye. Ten yards or so down the fence, under the shade of a stand of aspens. I walked toward it. Then fell to my knees and screamed.

It was a small wooden cross. At the end of what looked like a small, freshly dug grave.

I heard Alex's door open, her feet pounding as she ran toward me, yelling, "No, Elizabeth, no!" Then her arms around me, pulling me back as I clawed at the dirt and started to dig.

* * *

Alex and Monroe and I huddled by the Jeep while Detective Carpenter and three Estes Park police officers taped off the area and did a slow, methodical search, measuring the grave, photographing all around it. It had been almost an hour since the police arrived, and they hadn't even begun to investigate what was in it.

"What's taking them so long?" I said.

"They're preserving the scene," Monroe said. "Collecting anything that might be evidence."

Detective Carpenter bent under the police tape and walked over to us.

"Elizabeth," he said.

"Yes."

He had spoken with us briefly when the police first arrived but was back with pen and notepad in hand.

"What time was it when you and your friend . . . "

"Alexis LaDay."

"What time was it when you and Ms. LaDay went to town?"

"Around one thirty."

"Did you exit your vehicle to open or close the gate as you left?"

"Alex did."

He turned to Alex.

"You didn't see the cross or anything unusual at that time, Ms. LaDay?"

Alex shook her head. "But that doesn't mean it wasn't there. Elizabeth and I were talking, and I wasn't really paying attention to anything but the Jeep and the gate."

He turned back to me. "And you didn't see anything then?"

"No."

"What time was it when you returned from town?"

"A little after four."

"Tell me again how you discovered the scene."

"You mean the grave?" I said. "That's what it is, isn't it? A grave?"

"We don't know that yet."

"Then why the hell don't you dig it up and find out?"

"We're working as quickly and carefully as we can."

"I've been hearing that for the past two and a half weeks, Detective. But my son is still missing."

"I understand, Elizabeth. Please help me out here."

"Carpenter." He looked up. One of the investigators waved him over. "We're ready."

Alex and Monroe and I went with him. We stayed outside the taped area while he tied a white mask over his nose and mouth and pulled on latex gloves. He squatted down and watched as two officers, similarly clad, used a small shovel and trowels to excavate the site.

"Here's something," one of the officers finally said. They brushed at the soil with their hands, and the fourth officer stood over the hole and took photographs from several angles.

"Anything else in there?" Detective Carpenter said.

“No. This is where the digging stops.”

“Sick bastard,” Carpenter said. He reached into the hole and pulled what was buried there out for us to see. It was covered in dirt but instantly recognizable.

Dolphie the dolphin.

CHAPTER

29

Alexis

I ALMOST LOST IT when Detective Carpenter held up the dolphin. I turned and walked back to the Jeep, went around it so no one could see, bent over, and tasted pimento cheese. I gagged and spit a couple of times, but the sandwich stayed down.

"You okay?"

It was Monroe. I straightened, rubbed my mouth with the back of my hand. He offered me his handkerchief, and I took it.

"Thank you. Not a pretty sight, I'm sure."

He shrugged.

I wiped my face with the handkerchief. "I don't know what that was about."

"Stress," he said. "Whoever did this dug the hole large enough to make it look like a child might be buried there. Carpenter didn't pull out any body parts. But it's not good."

He looked behind me and nodded. "Elizabeth."

She was quiet, almost calm, but very pale. I put my arm around her waist, and she let me, so I drew her close.

"It'll be a while before they're finished here," Monroe said. "You should go on up to the house. If there's anything else to report, I'll let you know."

"He knows where Henry is," Elizabeth said.

"Maybe," Monroe said.

"And he wants me to believe that Henry's dead."

"Maybe."

"What other explanation could there be?"

"We don't know who this guy is, Elizabeth. Obviously, what he's doing is directed at you. Did he have anything to do with Henry's disappearance? That's a good possibility, but there's a lot we don't know yet."

Elizabeth shivered. The temperature was dropping as twilight fell, forecast to be in the low forties overnight.

"I'm so tired," she said. "So tired of people telling me they don't know."

A pained look crossed Monroe's face, but he recovered quickly. I led Elizabeth around to the passenger's side, then got behind the wheel. I rolled down the window.

"Lock the house up tight," Monroe said.

"We will."

"Elizabeth has a rifle," he said.

"I know all about those rifles. I even know the combination to the safe."

"Good. You know how to use them?"

"Sure do. It's one of the things Elizabeth and I have in common. Our daddies taught us to shoot."

I started the Jeep. Monroe opened the gate and waved for me to stop as I drove through.

"Put my cell number in your phone," he said. "And don't hesitate to call me if you need anything."

"Will do."

* * *

Elizabeth was shaking by the time we got to the cabin.

"Do you believe me now?" she said.

"Yes. I believe you."

I told her to take a hot shower and I would find something for dinner.

"I don't think I can eat anything," she said.

I lit a fire in the living room, set the leftover sandwiches and some fruit on the coffee table, and turned off most of the lights. Elizabeth emerged from her shower in sweatpants and a flannel shirt. She sat on the couch and wrapped herself in a blanket. I made a cup of hot chocolate and brought it to her, found her cell phone in her purse so she could give me Monroe's number, then sank into a chair opposite her and put my feet up on an ottoman. We watched the fire.

"I thought I would know," she said.

"Know what, honey?"

"If Henry had died. I keep telling myself he's alive because I've been so sure that I would know if he died."

She drained her cup and set it on the coffee table, then wrapped herself tighter in the blanket.

"Maybe I just refuse to let that knowledge into my consciousness. Because I can't face it."

The tears streaming down her face glistened in the firelight.

"I can't bear this, Alex. I can't bear it."

There was nothing, really, that I could say. I got up and went to her, sat next to her on the couch and wrapped my arms around her. She put her head on my shoulder, and I held her until she fell asleep.

* * *

After a while, my arm started to go numb. I eased Elizabeth's head off my shoulder, whispered her name. She roused a bit and I helped her up, then walked her to her bedroom. I don't think she ever woke up. She slipped into bed and was sound asleep.

I carried the food back to the kitchen and put it in the refrigerator. Neither of us had touched it. I put on one of Elizabeth's jackets and went out on the porch to smoke.

The police were still there. I watched flashlights bounce along the ground, silhouettes in the headlights of vehicles. Voices drifted on the night air, but I couldn't make out what they were saying. It wasn't long before they packed it in, car doors slamming and engines revving as one by one they turned onto Devil's Gulch Road and headed toward Estes Park. Finally, the night was quiet. I sat and smoked and watched a falling star, then another.

I'd noticed that afternoon that the aspen leaves were starting to turn—gold, orange, red. The beginnings of a typical glorious fall in Estes Park. Followed shortly by a winter I didn't want to think about. Not with Henry out there somewhere.

The wind picked up, and I lit another cigarette and listened to it whistling across the mountains. Then heard another sound. A car approaching from the direction of town. It slowed as it passed Elizabeth's property, then stopped and made a U-turn. The headlights went off as it parked near the end of the driveway.

I stubbed out my cigarette, walked slowly to the front door. I went inside and locked the door behind me. I found my cell phone on the coffee table and, hands trembling, scrolled to Monroe's number. He answered on the second ring.

"Monroe, it's Alex."

"Hey, Alex."

"I think there's someone parked out by our gate. By the side of the road."

"Yeah, sorry. It's me. I thought I'd keep a lookout for a little while."

I blew out a long breath. "Well, what the hell, Monroe? You scared the shit out of me."

"Sorry."

"Give me a little warning next time, okay?"

"Okay."

I hung up. I went to the fire, warmed my hands, turned my back to it, and stood close until I could feel the heat through the jacket. Then I went to the kitchen and cut a piece of the as-yet-untouched cheesecake. I locked the front door behind me and walked down the drive.

Monroe saw me coming. He leaned across the seat and opened the passenger door just as I got to his truck. I handed him the plate, then climbed in and closed the door.

"That's a big piece of cheesecake," he said.

I dug into my pocket and pulled out two forks. "It's not just for you."

He took a bite. "This is a treat."

I took a bite and nodded. "Now if we only had something to drink."

Monroe passed the plate to me, leaned over, and reached far under the seat. He pulled out a flask and held it up.

"Does whiskey go with cheesecake?"

"Sweet Jesus, yes." I set the plate on the seat between us, opened the flask, and took a long drink. Then another. Sighed and handed it back to him.

"Do you always keep that in your truck?"

He took a swig and smiled. "For use only in case of emergency." He handed the flask back to me. I took another long drink and rested my head on the back of the seat.

"Hard day," he said.

"Yes. They're all hard days. But this was particularly hard."

I offered him the flask, but he shook his head. "What did you do with poor Dolphie?" I said.

"He'll have a nice home for a while with the Estes Park police. They'll send him and the cross to the lab, run for fingerprints, any other trace of evidence. They won't find anything. Whoever this guy is, he's careful."

"Do you think he took Henry?"

"If he did, he's taking a lot of risks hanging around here and tormenting Elizabeth. All of it combined would mean there's a guy out there who very badly wants to see her suffer."

We were quiet for a while. Monroe finished off the cheesecake, and I told him to put the flask away before I finished off the whiskey. It was getting colder in the truck.

"I'm going in before I freeze to death," I said.

"I can turn the heater on."

"No, that's not necessary. I don't want Elizabeth to be up there alone much longer." I picked up the plate and forks. "Thanks for the whiskey. And for everything you're doing. I'm sure you think we're real assholes sometimes."

"That's not a word that comes to mind when I think of you and Elizabeth."

I opened the door and jumped down.

"I can drive you up to the house," he said. "Or walk with you."

"Not necessary. I need the exercise. Watch me up the driveway, then go home. Don't stay here all night."

He looked at me and I looked at him.

"Well," I said. "I think I'll go now."

He nodded. "What time is your flight on Sunday?"

"I canceled it. I'm not leaving Elizabeth."

He looked away, then back at me again. "Then I'll see you again soon."

"Yes, you will, Monroe. Good night." I closed the door, locked the gate behind me, and walked up the drive. I turned and waved as I went into the house. He flashed his headlights twice. I took the plate and forks to the kitchen, got a glass of water, and turned off the lights. I closed all the shades on the front of the house and took a last look before going to bed. The dim shadow of Monroe's Bronco was still there.

CHAPTER

30

Monroe

I STOPPED AT POLICE headquarters Saturday morning on my way to work. Carpenter poured me a cup of coffee, and I sat in his office and drank it.

"You look tired, Monroe."

"Yeah. Henry English is weighing on me."

"On us all." Carpenter leaned back and put his feet on the desk. "Nineteen days missing, and we're nowhere on finding the kid."

I rubbed my eyes. "I know."

"So the question is, does the dolphin killer have anything to do with that? Or is he just some sick bastard who's fixated on the grieving mother?"

"That's the question. At least we know he's in the area." I took a final drink of police-issue brew. "Keep looking for him."

"We're looking for him, Monroe. Don't you worry about that."

I checked in at the office and headed out for patrol. It was almost lunchtime when a call came on my cell.

"Monroe."

"Bradford Riegle."

I pulled over to the side of the road.

"Mr. Riegle. Thanks for returning my call."

"How can I help you?"

He asked, but truth be told, Bradford Riegle didn't sound all that anxious to be helpful in the search for a missing six-year-old. My approach to our last conversation may not have been the most productive, however, so I decided to take a different tack.

"Well, you may know that Henry English is still missing."

"I'm aware of that. I've checked periodically for any news that he's been found."

Big-hearted of you.

"Mrs. English has described to me on a couple of occasions during our investigation your unique skills as a jury consultant in reading people."

I paused. Riegle didn't say anything.

"What I'm hoping, Mr. Riegle, is that you'll agree to give us a few hours of your time. That you'll think back over every person you came across during the Alaska trial, really picture them in your mind, and see if you can remember anything—anything—that might suggest a desire to harm Elizabeth English."

Nothing but silence on the other end of the line.

"Mr. Riegle?"

He finally spoke.

"I'm willing to do that. But it probably would be best if Elizabeth and I did it together. She may remember things about the trial that I've forgotten, and vice versa."

"I agree, Mr. Riegle. That's a great idea. The only problem is, Mrs. English is still here in Estes Park. I don't know when she'll be back in Houston."

"Not a problem at all. I just happen to be in Estes Park."

Now it was my turn to go quiet.

"Monroe?"

"Yes. Sorry. When did you arrive?"

"A couple of days ago."

And you waited until now to return my call, you son of a bitch?

"What brings you here, Mr. Riegle?"

"It's one of my stops on the way back to Houston. I don't always come through Estes Park, but I have several times."

"Good, well, I hope you've been enjoying yourself."

"I have. Photography is one of my hobbies. I've gotten a lot of great shots on this trip."

Isn't that just dandy.

"When are you thinking we'll do this exercise?" he said.

"I'll have to talk to Mrs. English. How long will you be in Estes Park?"

"I don't know. We should get it done in the next couple of days, though. I don't plan how many days I'll be in one place. When I wake up in the morning, if I feel like moving on, I move on."

"Gotcha, cowboy." I couldn't resist. "I'll call Mrs. English right now."

* * *

"No," Elizabeth said. "No way."

"Elizabeth—"

"No. I don't want to even see Brad Riegle, much less sit down and talk to him for hours on end."

I know I shouldn't have, but I got a little fed up with Elizabeth English right then. "Grow up, Elizabeth. The only thing we have to go on is that Henry may have been taken by someone in a dark-colored pickup with Alaska plates. A conversation between you and Riegle probably won't come up with anything, but it's worth a try. So don't tell me your pride is more important."

She hung up on me. I sat there for a minute, resisting the urge to smash my cell phone on the pavement. Then I pounded my palms on the steering wheel and cursed Paul and Elizabeth English and Brad Riegle and the sick bastard who digs graves for stuffed animals and the son of a bitch who took Henry. I was feeling a little better when my phone rang.

"My pride is not more important than finding my son. Nothing is more important than finding Henry."

"Okay. Can you meet Riegle tomorrow? Before he rides off into the sunset?"

"Yes. But I would like you and Alex to be there."

"Done. Go to Carpenter's office at eight. I'll ask him to get a conference room."

C H A P T E R

31

Elizabeth

I HATED THE THOUGHT of seeing Riegle again. And, frankly, I didn't know what I would do if he made even the slightest reference to what happened between us in Alaska. *Just ignore it*, I told myself as Alex and I drove to Carpenter's office. *Don't be defensive, or cutting, or apologetic. Just ignore it.*

Fortunately, I didn't have to ignore anything. Riegle was gracious when we met and expressed his regret and concern about Henry. Monroe had told me about Riegle's road warrior get-up, but for our meeting he was dressed in dark slacks and a button-down shirt. Very professional.

We sat across from each other at a conference table, Detective Carpenter at my side, Monroe and Alex at opposite ends. I'd brought my laptop; it had everything on it we might need as a reference about the trial. Witness lists, juror information, depositions and trial transcripts. Correspondence, pleadings, disclosures.

Riegle and I went back over the people on the jury. There was nothing we could add to what Monroe and Carpenter already knew.

"What about the panel?" Alex said. "The people in the jury pool that didn't get picked?"

Riegle thought for a moment, then shook his head. "One guy looked like he'd had a hard night. Probably still high. But nothing else stands out."

"We had limited interaction with the panel during voir dire," I said. "Judge Albertson doesn't let the lawyers say much. He takes questions from each side in advance, but he does the asking. I don't think anyone on the panel would have formed an opinion about me at that point."

We went through every witness who took the stand. Court personnel. Nothing.

"Opposing counsel," I said. I read the list of names.

"You didn't have many friends on the opposite side," Riegle said. "That one guy, though, really despised you." I detected a note of satisfaction in his voice.

"Which guy?"

"The in-house lawyer. I can't remember his name."

"Bernard Wiest?"

"Yeah. That's him."

"He sat through the entire trial like a statue. I never once saw his expression change."

"That's true. But trust me. Wiest hates your guts."

That stung. Bernard Wiest had attended every hearing, every deposition, and then, finally, the trial as the company's representative. He always shook my hand when we met and, although we obviously never would be friends, I thought our relationship was cordial. Thinking back on it, there were a couple of times in depositions that I'd looked at him after the witness had given me an answer and seen pure venom on his face. But I still couldn't wrap my head around the idea that there might be someone who hated me enough to harm my son.

"Bernard Wiest is a seasoned lawyer," I said. "He's been paid very well for many years to supervise the company's litigation. This wasn't the first time they've taken a pounding."

"Yeah, but you have a way of getting under people's skin, Elizabeth. I saw it the first time we worked together, and you haven't changed much over the years."

"Wiest is German?" Monroe said.

"Yes," I said. "But he spends a substantial amount of time in Houston. They have a large office there."

Monroe wrote Wiest's name in his notebook. "It'll be easy enough to check where he was when Henry disappeared."

"That's it for anyone connected to the case," I said.

"How about at the hotel?" Carpenter said. "Desk attendants, housekeepers. Bartenders."

I felt my face get hot. I didn't dare look at Alex. I stared at my computer screen, stole a quick glance at Riegle. His expression was serious, brow knitted, lips pursed. And looked completely phony.

"No," he said. "I can't recall anything unusual about anyone at the hotel. Very friendly people."

We'd been at it almost four hours, and I'd had enough. I logged off and closed my laptop.

"Last try," Monroe said. "Spectators in the courtroom?"

Riegle snorted.

"This wasn't O.J. Simpson," I said. "There are not a lot of people sitting on the edges of their seats in a breach of contract case."

"There were not a lot of people sitting in the seats, period," Riegle said. "On most days, there was no one in the courtroom who didn't have to be there."

I shoved my laptop into my bag and gave Alex a *let's go* look.

"One more thing," Monroe said. He slid a piece of paper across the table to Riegle. "Do you recognize this man?"

Riegle bent over the sketch and studied it closely. "Doesn't ring a bell. Who is he?"

"Just someone Elizabeth has seen around town a few times."

Riegle picked it up, held it with both hands and looked at me. He shook his head. "Sorry." He looked back at Monroe. "May I keep it?"

"Sure," Monroe said. "That's your copy."

We all stood. Monroe and Carpenter shook Riegle's hand and thanked him for coming. Riegle paused, then came around the table to me. He held out his hand, and I took it.

"Thank you," I said.

"I hope you find him. And I wish you the best." He gave my hand a squeeze, nodded to Alex. "And I'll think some more about this guy." He held up the sketch as he turned to the door. Maybe it was the angle at which he held it. Maybe it was his reference to the first time we'd worked together. Maybe it finally just clicked.

"Wait," I said. "I know who he is."

* * *

"Eddie Marsh?" Riegle looked at it again. "I watch faces for a living. It could be him. But it's hard for me to imagine that it is."

"Why?" Monroe said.

"Because Eddie Marsh was a skinny little weasel. And I think he's still in prison."

Monroe and Carpenter looked at each other. I looked at Riegle.

"When you mentioned the first case we worked on together, my mind started running through all the crazy characters we met on that case," I said. "I may be wrong, but I think it's him."

"Okay, Elizabeth," Monroe said. "Tell us, who is this Eddie Marsh?"

"Eddie Marsh was convicted of swindling Allen Haas. Haas is a billionaire, a longtime client of Bob Simon, the managing partner of my firm."

"Billionaire?" Carpenter said. "With a 'b'?"

"With a 'b.' As you can imagine, Haas is bombarded regularly with investment opportunities. Hollywood movie projects—the 'have your people call my people' kind. Shopping centers, office towers, that sort of thing. Haas eventually crosses paths with one Clinton Scruggs. . . . Could I get some water?"

"Sure," Carpenter said. He left the room and reappeared shortly with bottled water for everyone. I cracked mine open, took a long drink, then continued.

"Scruggs owned most of the stock in a company called Transamerica Investment Corporation, TIC for short. Scruggs was looking for investors, and he latched onto Haas. He told Haas that TIC had land and mineral rights holdings, all slated for major development, but their value in fact was minimal. And the price of TIC's stock was highly inflated due to Scruggs trading it back and forth between shell companies he owned. It was all an elaborate scam, but Haas fell for it and bought $18 million of TIC stock."

"How does Eddie Marsh fit into all this?" Carpenter said.

"Eddie Marsh was Scruggs's lawyer. He set up the phony companies, forged signatures, helped with the stock manipulation. He filed fraudulent lawsuits, which were nothing more than attempts at extortion. It was all so complicated."

"But you unraveled it," Alex said.

"Oh, gosh, I was just a young associate. Thrilled to be working on a high-profile case with Bob Simon."

"I take it Haas eventually figured out he'd been cheated," Monroe said.

"Yes. Haas hired an investigator and in pretty short order demanded a meeting with Scruggs and Marsh. During that meeting, Eddie Marsh made a threat on Haas's life."

"Jesus," Carpenter said. "Some lawyer."

"Yeah. Scruggs and Marsh weren't your average white-collar criminals. They were scary guys."

"You think Marsh was serious?"

"I think Eddie Marsh was capable of anything."

"But Haas didn't back down?"

I shook my head. "Haas went after them hard. We got a jury verdict of $110 million against Scruggs and $38 million against Eddie Marsh."

"How did Marsh end up in prison?" Monroe said.

"Scruggs was already on the Feds' radar. I think an unsolved murder was suspected of being connected to one of his companies. Criminal charges were filed based on the evidence we uncovered in our case. They plea bargained—I think Scruggs got twenty years and Eddie got fifteen. And Eddie was disbarred, of course."

"Fifteen years," Monroe said. "How long ago was this?"

I thought back to the time frame. I remembered hearing shortly before Nick was born that Scruggs and Marsh were going to prison. "Maybe ten years or so."

There was a light tap at the door, then it opened. A uniformed officer handed Carpenter a file. Carpenter looked at it, then up at us.

"Eddie Marsh is out," he said. "I asked them to check when I went for water. His sentence was ten years, not fifteen. Served in full."

"When was he released?" Monroe said.

"Five months ago. April 17, from the federal facility in Texarkana." Carpenter took something from the file. "Here's a photo the warden's office sent over."

He held it up so we all could see.

"Holy fuck," Alex said.

It was him. The guy in the sketch. The man who'd been following me was Eddie Marsh.

* * *

I sat stunned, silent, after the confirmation of his identity.

"He doesn't look anything like I remember him," Riegle said. "He must have gained at least fifty pounds."

"It happens," Carpenter said. "Prison food, not much exercise."

"But why?" I said. "Why would he be following me?"

"One possibility," Monroe said, "is that he read about Henry's disappearance. You were involved in the case that ultimately sent him to prison. He follows you around, watching you suffer, out of morbid curiosity or maybe because he enjoys it."

I shuddered. "Or he's the one who took Henry. To get back at me."

Monroe nodded. "That's another possibility."

"That makes no sense," I said. "I was the lowest lawyer on the totem pole. Bob Simon made all the decisions. I did the grunt work—plowing through boxes of documents, legal research, memos, and briefs."

"But Bob took you everywhere," Alex said. "You helped prepare him for depositions and hearings. You sat through the entire trial. You uncovered some of the most critical links in Scruggs's criminal enterprise."

"And let me guess," Monroe said. "You were the only woman lawyer on the case."

Alex and I looked at each other. "Yes," I said.

"So, Eddie Marsh fixates on you," Carpenter said. "Ten years is a long time to think."

I bent over, head in my hands. Then pushed myself up from the chair.

"Ladies room?" I said to Carpenter.

He pointed. "Make a right out the door, then the next left."

I lurched out of his office and down the hall. Pushed open the restroom door and dropped to my knees in the nearest stall. I barely made it over the toilet before I started to vomit.

CHAPTER

32

Alexis

We sat quietly, waiting for Elizabeth to return. The minutes ticked by, and still no Elizabeth.

"Well," Riegle said. "I think I'll be on my way. Let me know if there's anything else I can do."

"I think I'll go check on her," I said.

Monroe and Carpenter nodded.

I cracked the ladies' room door. "Elizabeth?"

Legs and feet sticking out from under a stall, she was sitting on the floor, arms wrapped around the toilet, head resting on the seat, vomit floating in the bowl. She didn't look up.

"No, no, no," I said. "This is fucking disgusting."

"Sorry," she whispered.

"Not the puke." I put my hands under her arms and helped her to her feet.

"Growing up, my mother wouldn't even let me sit on a bare public toilet seat. Here you are, making out with the nasty thing."

I unwound a wad of toilet paper, pressed it on the handle to flush, and dropped it in the swirling water. Elizabeth went to the sink, scrubbed her hands and face, rinsed her mouth, and spat. I went to the adjoining sink to wash, then handed her some paper towels. She dried her face and looked at me in the mirror. I'd never seen her that pale.

"What if it's my fault, Alex? What if Eddie Marsh took Henry to get back at me?"

"Don't go there, Elizabeth. We don't know if that happened. But if it did, it's not your fault. It's Eddie Marsh's fault—no one else's."

She bent over the sink and gagged once, then a second time, but nothing came up. She rinsed and spat again, then straightened and wiped her watering eyes.

"Okay," she said. "Let's get to it."

* * *

Monroe stood when we entered the conference room. Riegle was gone. Carpenter was on the phone. He hung up as Elizabeth and I sat down.

"The warden's in a meeting," Carpenter said. "He'll call us back."

"We thought we'd have a chat with the warden of the Texarkana unit," Monroe said. "Find out anything we can about Eddie."

"I'd like to be part of that conversation," Elizabeth said.

"No," Monroe said. "It's been a productive day. But you need to let Carpenter and me take it from here."

He went to the door and held it open for us. "We appreciate you coming in. I'll walk you to your car."

* * *

"Can you believe that asshole?" Elizabeth was fuming in the passenger seat beside me.

"You're talking about Monroe?"

"Of course I'm talking about Monroe. Arrogant son of a bitch." She mimicked his Western drawl. "We appreciate you coming in, ma'am. There's nothing for you to do, little lady. I'll walk you to your car."

I had to smile. She had him down pretty good. "I don't think he actually said 'ma'am' and 'little lady.'"

"No, but he was thinking it."

"He's just doing his job. It won't help to have us in the way."

"Fat lot of good he's done so far."

"Well, he was the one who insisted on following the Brad Riegle inquiry. You didn't recognize the guy in the sketch until the meeting with Riegle jogged your memory."

She didn't respond. I glanced at her as I turned onto MacGregor. Her cheeks were red, her lips pursed tight. That one stung, I guess.

"You just want to fuck him," she said.

"What?"

"You just want to fuck Monroe. And why not? A little sport fucking would make the time go by. I'm sure you're tired of all this."

I looked at her in disbelief, not only because she was cursing, something I almost never heard her do, but also because of the attack on me. I pulled over to the side of the road and put the Jeep in park. We sat in silence for a few minutes. Which was not easy for me, because I really wanted to rip her a new one and that was my intention when I stopped.

"I'm sorry," she finally said. "I'm such a jerk."

I took a deep breath and stared out the window.

"I'm an expert on jerks. I see them every day. You are not one. You're under a lot of stress, honey."

I turned to face her. Tears dropped from her jaw onto the front of her shirt.

"We're going to find him," I said. For some reason, I was starting to believe it.

She nodded.

"You should go home, Alex. You've done so much. I can't ask you to stay."

"No way." I looked in the side mirror. A car was coming, then another. I let them pass.

"You know," I said as I eased back onto the road. "I don't think Monroe is the sport-fucking type."

She shot me a little smile, the first I'd seen in a while.

"I think you're right. And I can probably guess what's going through your mind."

"Yes," I said as I pulled into the driveway. "It's a shame. It's a damn shame."

CHAPTER

33

Monroe

THE WARDEN AT the Texarkana unit called us back in a few minutes.

"Yes, indeed," he said. "I know Eddie Marsh well. He served his term and was just released in April."

"He didn't come up for parole?" Carpenter said.

"His plea agreement with the prosecutor's office was ten years with no possibility of parole."

Carpenter laid out the background for our inquiry—Henry's disappearance, Marsh's ties to Elizabeth.

"What was Eddie like?" I said. "How did his time there go?"

"A model prisoner on the surface," the warden said. "He worked in the law library, as you would expect, and was helpful to inmates working on appeals or other legal proceedings. He'd show them how to do research, help them write letters to the court, and so forth. He's a smart guy. And, he supposedly found Jesus during his time here."

"You said on the surface."

"Eddie Marsh is a cockroach. A well-educated, slick-talking cockroach."

"How so?"

"Scuttling around behind the scenes, in the dark. Whispering, insinuating, stirring up one inmate against another. Making men doubt their wives, their friends. Any kind of altercation, you could bet Eddie had some hand in it, although it was never anything you could pin on him."

"For what purpose?" Carpenter said.

"Who knows? That's the damnedest thing—it's not like it got him anywhere. I think he just liked to see people suffer."

"What about finding Jesus?"

The warden snorted. "He carried a Bible around, went to church services, and curried favor with the local prison ministries. He might benefit from that scam now that he's out—congregations helping ex-cons get back on their feet. Lonely women fixing him dinner. You know."

"Yeah," I said. "I know."

"Did Eddie have a genuine religious conversion?" the warden said. "No way."

"Do you know what his plans were after he got out? Where he might have gone?"

"He was going to see his mother for a few days. After that, he wasn't sure—other than he thought he'd look up an old friend or two. At least that's what he told me."

"Do you have an address for his mother?"

"I can get it for you. I should remember it—she wrote me a stack of letters over the years. Complaining that the food was terrible, the prison staff were rude, there was trash in the visitors waiting room. That Eddie wasn't being treated fairly, he should be in a facility closer to home. And, of course, that he was innocent."

"Of course," Carpenter said. "Plea bargain notwithstanding."

"We won't take up any more of your time," I said. I gave him Carpenter's phone number and he said his secretary would call us shortly with the address.

"I can tell you this much," he said before he hung up. "The old lady lives in Tulsa."

* * *

"Tulsa," Carpenter said. "That's interesting."

He flipped through one of the files on his desk, ran his finger down a page. "Alaska plates reported stolen outside a motel in Tulsa. July 15." He looked up at me.

"Just after Elizabeth's trial ended," I said.

"I'll make some calls once we have the mother's address," Carpenter said. "Ask Tulsa police to go out to her place and take a look, stop by the motel. I'll put out an APB on the truck now that we have the license number."

I rubbed my eyes. "Eddie has to know we'd look for him at his mother's place. If he's left Estes Park, that's gotta be the last place he'd go."

"Probably. But it can't hurt. Maybe the old lady's heard from him, has some idea where he might be."

"She may have heard from him. But I doubt that he told her where he is."

The phone rang. It was the warden's secretary. Carpenter wrote down the address, repeated it to her to confirm he had it right, then thanked her and hung up. I picked up my hat.

"I think I'll go home and salvage what's left of my weekend."

"Uh huh. The usual big plans?"

"Yeah. A crossword puzzle and a nap."

"You live an exciting life, Monroe."

"I know."

"You should call Miss America. Ask her out for a beer."

"Miss Georgia. Runner-up."

Carpenter arched an eyebrow.

"I don't think she'd have much interest in spending time with me."

"One never knows," he said. "Unless one asks."

I made a point of looking at the picture of his wife and three kids.

"One doesn't know," I said. "But one is pretty damn sure."

CHAPTER

34

Nick

Mom and Dad weren't telling me everything going on with the search for Henry. One day Aunt Alex called Dad on his cell phone and I heard him say something about Dolphie the dolphin and then he went into his bedroom and closed the door. He looked kind of sick when he came out and I asked him about Dolphie and he said, "It's nothing, Mom just couldn't find Dolphie for a while and now she found him." Which is good, because Henry loves Dolphie and he'd be really sad when he came back if Dolphie was gone.

They weren't telling me everything, but I knew they thought they'd find Henry because Mom was still in Colorado and Aunt Alex was out there with her. Which was also good. Aunt Alex is cool. She cusses, and when she slips up and does it around me, it's so funny. I know I should be cool about it and not laugh, but I can't help myself because I'm not used to hearing grownups talk like that, especially a lady. And not only that, I caught her smoking one time when me and Henry were staying at her house a weekend Mom and Dad were out of town. She thought I was asleep but I wasn't, and I went looking for her and found her out on the patio and she made me swear I wouldn't tell Mom. So I don't think Mom knows she smokes, but I do. Which is cool.

I told Dad maybe we should go back to Colorado and help, but he said, "No, there's nothing we can do, and we both have school." So I started looking on the internet to see what I could find about missing children and what families should do when their children are missing. Dad found out and told me that I was not allowed to get on the internet anymore, but he usually stayed at U of H until almost dinnertime. Jimena picks me up at school, and she lets me do whatever I want. She pretty much let me do what I wanted before, but after Henry was gone, she really let me do what I wanted. She kisses me and cries almost every day. She loves me, I know, but she's just crazy about Henry. He calls her MeMe and she calls him Henny Penny, and she goes to Mass every morning and prays for him. So I tell her I'm going to do my homework, and I get on the computer and do my research.

There's all kinds of stuff on the internet. Like survival guides for families with missing children, checklists for what to do in the first twenty-four hours, the second twenty-four hours, the long-term search. Working with law enforcement, psychics, the media. Psychics! I thought maybe we should get a psychic. In English class we were learning how to write a research paper. It was just like a page and a half, but it had to have references. We were working on it all year and it wasn't due until sometime the next semester, but I thought I'd write mine about missing children, maybe psychics finding missing children. I wasn't telling Dad about it until after I turned it in because he'd probably be mad.

But here's something else I found. There are like hundreds of cases of people missing in NATIONAL PARKS. Under MYSTERIOUS CIRCUMSTANCES that CANNOT BE EXPLAINED. And they are mostly CHILDREN and OLD PEOPLE.

There are lots of people talking about this on the internet. Some of them say that the government does not want us to know about this because they don't want people to stop going to national parks. There's also talk about Bigfoot and End Times and I read some of the stuff about that and it's all crap. But this stuff about mysterious circumstances was information Ranger Monroe needed to know, which he probably did, but I decided to call him to be sure. When I got home from school that afternoon, I got a plate of Oreos and a glass of milk and told Jimena I was going to do my homework. I went to my room and closed the door. I pulled my English notebook out of my backpack and sat down at my desk. Ranger Monroe's card was stuck on my bulletin board with a push pin. I dialed his number.

"Monroe."

Crap, he answered fast. I thought maybe I'd get his voice mail. I had like a whole Oreo in my mouth. I spit it out on the plate.

"Hi, Mr. Monroe."

"Hi. Who's this?"

"It's Nick English."

"Hey, Nick. How are you man?" He sounded kind of surprised.

"I'm okay. How are things going out there?"

"Things are going fine. We haven't found Henry yet, but we're still looking for him. I guess your mom keeps you up-to-date on the search."

"Oh, yeah. She definitely does. But I just thought I'd call and get a report from you."

He didn't say anything for a minute. I dunked an Oreo in the milk and it turned to mush in my mouth while I waited.

"You know, Nick, I think it's better for you to get your reports from your mom and dad."

I knew he'd say that. Like he was going to tell me anything, but it was worth a try. I swallowed the Oreo mush and took a drink of milk.

"Actually, Mr. Monroe, the real reason for my call is that I'd like to discuss some information I have found on the internet." I thought that sentence sounded pretty good. I wrote it in study hall that morning, and I read it to Ranger Monroe from my English notebook.

He was kind of quiet again, and I thought, *Maybe he doesn't talk to kids much?*

"Okay, Nick. Tell me what you have."

I looked at my notes.

"So I read that there are a lot of mysterious disappearances in national parks, going back like a hundred years. There are these clusters of where the disappearances happened around the country, and Rocky Mountain National Park is one of the clusters."

"Okay."

"Most of them are kids, like under twelve years old, and old people. The kids who disappear, they're usually with their parents, but the parents turn around and they're gone. It usually happens in the afternoon, and then there's rain that washes out the footprints and any other clues. Sometimes the kids are found miles away from where they disappeared, without their shoes but no scratches on their feet, and there's no way they could have gone that far by themselves. Sometimes they're found right around where they went missing, even though the searchers looked in that area like a hundred times. The kids who are still alive say they don't remember what happened to them, and a lot of times they're running a fever. And a lot of times they're found near water, like a river or a stream."

I stopped for a minute here in case he had any questions and also because I wanted another Oreo. I ate a cookie and I guess he didn't have any questions at this point, so I told him the scariest part.

"In many of the cases, the area where they disappeared has the word *devil* in its name. Like Devil's Lookout or Devil's Punch Bowl."

I stopped again. I thought I heard him blow out some air.

"Mr. Monroe? Have you heard of this before?"

"Yes, Nick. I know all about it. There are people who believe that the devil or something supernatural is kidnapping and sometimes killing children in national parks. And that the park service is engaged in some kind of conspiracy to cover it up."

"Is it true?"

"No. You're a smart guy. Let's think about it. Kids can wander off in a minute without their parents noticing. Especially in the afternoons, when the family has been out all day and everyone's tired. And afternoons are when we often get rain in the mountains."

"What about the streams and rivers?"

"It would be natural for a person who's lost a trail to follow a stream or river, thinking that it will lead them to a place where people might be. The same as it's no surprise that people can suddenly be found in locations that have been searched many times. These are huge areas with lots of tree growth and underbrush. Searchers could pass within a few feet of an unconscious person and never see him."

"How can they not remember what happened to them?"

"Also pretty easy to understand, if they've been wandering around confused, frightened, cold, maybe sick and running a fever. Especially children."

"Okay. What about the devil thing?"

"Nick. Henry wasn't lost anywhere near an area with *devil* in the name."

"I know. But our cabin is on Devil's Gulch Road."

If that didn't convince him, I didn't know what would. He was quiet again. I wanted another Oreo, but I'd eaten all the ones on my plate, even the one I spit out. It was not the time to go to the kitchen for more.

"Nick, is your dad there?"

"He's at school."

"Are you at home alone?"

"No, Jimena's here. Our housekeeper."

"Okay, well, I think you should talk to your dad about this when he gets home."

No way was I doing that.

"But just for the record," he said. "I don't believe a devil has Henry. Do you?"

All of a sudden, I didn't want to talk about it anymore. I didn't want to get into a discussion about devils. And I didn't want any more Oreos. I just wanted Henry to come home. And Mom. I hung up the phone. I didn't want Ranger Monroe to think I was crying.

CHAPTER

35

Alexis

I LEFT ELIZABETH A note, took my laptop, and slipped out of the house early Tuesday morning. I drove to Starbucks, bought a latte, and sat down to check emails. I'd been in Estes Park for a week and a half and wouldn't be able to put off my return to Houston much longer. Another week would be pushing it, but maybe I could pull it off. I answered emails, reviewed documents and drafts, ordered another latte. I made phone calls to mollify the most insistent clients then checked the time. Almost ten. Time to get back to Elizabeth.

She was sitting on the porch, waiting for me. Dressed in nylon pants, a long-sleeve T-shirt, and hiking boots. Looking at a map.

I sat down next to her, nodded at the map.

"Is that a trail map?"

"No. It's a detailed map of the area."

"Good." I reached into my purse for cigarettes and lit one. She pushed the ashtray, now a permanent porch fixture, closer to me. "I was afraid you were thinking about a hike."

"I considered it. My feet are in good shape, thanks to you."

"The altitude really bothers me when we get up into the park."

"You've been hiking in the park for years."

"True. It just seems to be affecting me more this time."

She folded the map. "No need to worry. We're not going on a hike. We're going to find Eddie Marsh."

* * *

An hour or so later, we started our road trip. It wasn't actually a road trip, because we were coming home at night, but it turned into a five-day adventure, although I wouldn't call it exactly an adventure, either. We packed water and snacks and extra jackets in the Jeep. I told Elizabeth I'd drive. I waited in the Jeep while she went back into the house to get something. She came out a couple of minutes later with the Remington. She locked the house, stowed the rifle under the back seat, and got in beside me.

"What's the Remington for?"

She looked at me with a grim smile. "That, my friend, is for when we find him."

* * *

We drove every street in Estes Park that afternoon, looking for dark-colored pickups and pudgy guys with or without stocking caps and plaid flannel shirts. The first truck we saw that fit the bill was parked in a driveway in front of a one-story house with vinyl siding, an American flag and wagon wheels planted in the front yard.

"Pull over," Elizabeth said.

"It's got Colorado plates."

"Easily replaced."

Then, to my horror, she got out of the car, went to the front door, and rang the bell.

"Fuck, fuck, fuck," I said. The door opened a few inches, then wider to reveal an elderly woman who talked to Elizabeth for a few minutes. Elizabeth pulled something from her back pocket and handed it to her, then the door closed and Elizabeth came back to the car.

"What the hell, Elizabeth."

"What?"

"You can't walk up to a house and ring the doorbell just because there's a truck in the driveway."

She gave me a quizzical look and a quick shake of her head. "I just did."

"Yes, and I didn't know if I would have to pull out the Remington and come after you."

"Oh, for God's sake, Alex. You're so dramatic."

She buckled her seat belt, and we took off again. "I spoke with a very nice elderly woman. The truck belongs to her seventeen-year-old grandson. I gave her a Henry flyer."

"Great."

She did that three more times Tuesday afternoon, the trucks black and gray and dark blue. I told myself to relax because truth be told, this was a futile effort. As was the search for Eddie Marsh. I confirmed that there were a good number of beer bellies, plaid shirts, and stocking caps in Estes Park, just like everywhere else in America. None belonged to Eddie Marsh.

Wednesday, we wound our way through the park, then up Trail Ridge Road and down the western side to Granby and Grand Lake. Thursday, we headed north, to Glen Haven and all the country roads leading off Devil's Gulch. Friday, we set out to the east. It didn't really matter where we went. It was keeping Elizabeth occupied.

On Saturday, we traveled south on Highway 7, thinking we would end up in Boulder for dinner and a stop at Whole Foods. It was rainy, dark, and cold. I turned on the wipers and the headlights and we drove in silence, both of us tired and neither of us interested in small talk even in the best of times. We were a few miles past Allenspark when Elizabeth spotted a pickup parked at a general store next to the highway, a dark shadow in the gloom.

"Can we pass on this one?" I said. "Let's not stop every time we see a truck today."

"Okay."

Perhaps this exercise was getting tedious for her as well. She looked back over her shoulder as we passed, then suddenly twisted in her seat, fighting to unbuckle her seat belt.

"Stop, Alex!" she screamed. "Stop! Go back!"

I pumped the brakes. The Jeep skidded, and I stepped on the gas pedal again.

"What are you doing? Stop, damn it! Stop!"

"For God's sake, Elizabeth. The highway's slick, and there's traffic behind me. I have to find a place to pull over."

A little farther down the highway I signaled, slowed, and turned onto a gravel road. I stopped, reversed, and turned the Jeep until we faced the highway, then waited for the traffic to clear. Elizabeth was beside herself.

"Hurry, Alex! This is taking too long!"

"I'm hurrying, I'm hurrying. Jesus. You scared the shit out of me." There was a break in the line of cars in both directions. I gunned the Jeep and we bounced up onto the highway, heading north.

"I saw him, Alex. I think it was Eddie. At least it could have been him."

"Where?"

"Coming out of the store. Getting into that truck."

Traffic slowed, and we saw the cause at the next curve, a line of cars behind a dump truck slowly grinding its way. Elizabeth pounded her fists on the dash, then slumped back in her seat.

"Hang on, honey. We're almost there."

Another curve, and the store came into sight. Lester's General Store, the sign said. Groceries, Beer, Live Bait. The pickup was gone. I pulled into the gravel parking lot and stopped as close as I could to the entrance. The rain came down harder.

"What now?" I said.

Elizabeth drew the hood of her parka over her head and opened her door.

"We go ask." She jumped out into the rain.

"And me without an umbrella." I went after her.

It was only a few yards from the Jeep to the front door, but I was soaked when I stepped inside the store. Elizabeth, hair plastered to her head and rain dripping from her parka, was at the counter, talking to a girl behind the register who looked to be about sixteen.

"A man was in here a little while ago," Elizabeth said. "Overweight, wearing a parka."

The girl nodded.

"Do you know him?"

The girl shook her head. "I don't know him."

"Have you ever seen him before?"

She shrugged. "Maybe once. But I'm not sure. We get a lot of dudes looking like him. You know. Hunters. Off-roaders."

"Did he buy anything?"

"Yeah, I don't know. Cereal, milk, maybe some candy bars? I wasn't really paying attention."

"Did he use a credit card?"

The girl frowned. "I think he paid cash. Who are you, anyway? Are you the cops?"

"We're not cops. But if he used a credit card, we'd like to verify his name."

She frowned harder. Then, motioning to the only other customer in line, said to Elizabeth, "Could you step aside, please, ma'am?" Elizabeth stepped back until the girl had rung up toilet paper, charcoal lighter fluid, dog food.

"Do you know his name?" Elizabeth said.

"I think you should talk to my manager."

"I'm happy to talk to your manager."

"He's not here right now."

"When will he be back?"

The girl shrugged again. "Maybe in a couple of days?" She crossed her arms and leaned against the counter.

Elizabeth glared at her, but before she could say anything else, I took her arm and pulled her toward the door, then out into the rain. We ran to the Jeep, getting soaked again, and I started it and turned the heater to high. I pulled off my wet jacket and tossed it on the back seat, and Elizabeth did the same. We sat for a while, the heater and our breath fogging the windows, until we stopped shivering.

"If he's been here more than once, he may be staying somewhere in this area," she said.

"Or he passes by here. He could be anywhere for miles in every direction. And he's probably not even Eddie."

"But I saw him."

"You said it could be him. While passing by going fifty miles an hour in pouring rain."

"I don't think you were going that fast."

I closed my eyes and leaned back against the headrest. I'd prayed more in the past month than I had in the twenty years since walking out of the Southern Baptist church I was raised in, making good on my promise never to go back. Now I was praying for patience.

"We're talking hundreds of square miles, Elizabeth. We can't do it."

I opened my eyes. She was staring at me.

"We didn't pass him after we turned around," she said. "So he went north. Let's just drive around Allenspark. It won't take that long."

I sighed. "Okay."

We were in Allenspark in a few minutes. Population five hundred or so, unpaved roads leading off the town proper to small wooden houses with propane tanks and satellite dishes and turkeys in the yard. Roads west led farther into the mountains, where a number of large homes perched and construction was underway on more. We wound around west and north and then back to Second Avenue. The rain eased a bit, but fog was settling in. My damp clothes stuck to me everywhere, and I was ready for a hot shower. I turned up Ski Road again, then right, worried that the Jeep might get stuck but willing to take one more look. I caught a glimpse of something moving and hit the brakes.

A long-legged creature, taller than the Jeep, emerged from the mist and stepped into the road. It stopped in front of us and turned its head in our direction. I blinked, then blinked again, not sure if what I was seeing was real.

"What the hell is that?"

"A moose," Elizabeth whispered. "A cow moose. I can't remember the last time I saw one."

The cow looked over her shoulder in the direction she had come, then back at us. Elizabeth gave a soft cry and pointed.

"Look, Alex."

Two calves, half the size of their mother, trotted onto the road, spindly legged and comically clumsy. Bumping into each other, and with a nudge from the cow, they crossed to the other side. The cow stood her ground, holding us at bay and watching her offspring until they were safely across. She took a last glance at us, then broke into a slow run. The calves followed her, and we lost them in the fog.

"Wow," I said. "That was incredible. That was like—something magical."

Elizabeth didn't say anything. She was weeping silently, tears rolling unheeded down her neck. I patted her thigh.

"It was a sign, Alex."

"A sign?"

"Yes. That wasn't some random wildlife sighting, Alex. That cow came to see me."

I put the Jeep in reverse and backed carefully down the sloping road, then turned in the direction of the highway.

"With two calves. Not just one baby, Alex. Two."

We rolled back onto the highway and headed for Estes Park. "She came to see me. To tell me that Henry's alive."

* * *

We hadn't gone far when Elizabeth spoke in a low voice. "Wait." Then louder, "Stop!"

Heart pounding, I pulled over to the shoulder. "What now?"

"Back up a little."

I backed the Jeep slowly along the shoulder.

"There." She pointed across the highway to a rusty cattle gate with signs on it. Private Drive. No Trespassing.

"What about it?"

"A private drive leading up into the woods. Probably no neighbors around. Just the kind of place he could keep Henry without anyone noticing."

She opened her door.

"No, Elizabeth. No. You are not going up there."

She waited for cars to pass in both directions, then sprinted across the highway. She gave the gate a push, and when it moved a few feet, pushed it again until it swung open. She turned and motioned to me. I shook my head. She nodded hers furiously.

"Shit." I looked in the rearview mirror and let another car pass, then gave the Jeep some gas, steered into the opposite lane and down onto the drive. Elizabeth opened the back door, then came around to the front with the Remington cradled in her arms.

"We'll just take a look," she said as she got in.

I drove at a crawl, wincing every time a tire crunched rocks, wondering who or what might be listening and waiting for us. In three hundred yards or so, the road ended in a dark clearing where a log frame cabin with a sagging front porch sat. There was a satellite dish on the roof, a propane tank to one side. Window shades drawn, no sign of life.

"Well," I said. "I don't think there's anyone home."

Elizabeth stared at the cabin for a moment.

"You stay here. Be ready, in case we have to get out in a hurry."

"Oh God."

She got out of the Jeep and stepped up onto the porch.

She knocked. No response. She knocked again, then turned the knob and pushed. It was locked. She leaned the Remington against the frame, then pressed her face to the window to the right of the door, hands cupped at her temples. She slid to the next window and did the same, then turned to me and shook her head. She picked up the rifle, stepped down from the porch and walked around the side of the house, disappearing from sight.

I gripped the steering wheel and waited. I was just about to go looking for her when she came around the corner, turning to look in all directions as she walked slowly to the Jeep.

"You're giving me a fucking heart attack," I said as she got in. "Did you see anything?"

"No. There's a large shed around back with doors wide enough to drive a truck through, but they were padlocked. I couldn't see inside. The back door and all the windows to the house are covered over and locked."

"You tried the windows?" I was practically shrieking at her.

"Of course I tried the windows. It's Henry's life we're talking about. I'm thinking about breaking one to get inside."

"If you break a window, I will drive off and leave you. I swear I will."

She closed her door. "I'm not going to. But there's something about this place."

"Yeah, there's something about it," I said as I steered the Jeep back to the dirt road. "It's creepy and abandoned, and we need to get the hell out of here."

"Creepy, yes. Abandoned, no. I have a feeling, Alex. That Henry is somewhere near."

CHAPTER

36

Monroe

ELIZABETH CALLED ME Saturday afternoon just as my shift was ending. She told me about the sighting of what might have been Eddie Marsh and her conversation with the clerk at a store south of Allenspark.

"Okay. Thank you for the information."

"Well?"

"Well what?"

"What are you going to do about it?"

"I'll check it out."

"When?"

"As soon as I can get down there."

"Will that be today?"

"Yes, Elizabeth. I'll go down there today."

I hung up the phone. I leaned my swivel chair back as far as it would go, put my feet up on the desk, and closed my eyes. *Henry English, Henry English. Where'd you go, where'd you go? Everybody's worried about you, little fella. Your mom, your dad, your brother. I feel sorry for your brother. I don't think he's getting much help with this.*

And then I go and lie to the poor kid. I said, "I don't believe a devil has Henry." That wasn't just a lie. That was a whopper. I'm pretty sure a devil has Henry. Just not the kind Nick was thinking about.

I rubbed my face and pushed myself up. I found my hat and headed for Allenspark.

* * *

A bell tinkled over the door at Lester's General Store when I went in. A girl matching the description Elizabeth gave me was working the cash register. I waited until she had rung up the two customers in line, then stepped up to the counter.

"You a park ranger?" she said, eyeing my hat.

"I am." I took off my hat and introduced myself to her, then showed her my badge. Which would cost me my job if the superintendent ever found out. She'd fire me just for being there.

"Awesome," she said.

"What's your name?"

"Katie."

"Katie, I understand that two women came in earlier today asking about a man they'd seen at your store."

"Yeah. The one asking the questions was all wild-eyed and crazy looking."

"Do you remember the man they were asking about?"

"Sort of. He was kind of fat."

"Was he white, Hispanic, African American?"

"White. And I mean white like he doesn't get out in the sun much."

My heart started to beat a little faster.

"Can you tell me what he was wearing?"

"No. Just some old jacket."

"Did you see anything else he was wearing? Like what kind of shirt he had on?"

She shook her head. "No. I just remember an old jacket. With a hood pulled over a stocking cap."

"Great. Do you remember what he bought?"

She gave me a smug little smile. "I can tell you exactly what he bought."

She pushed a button on the cash register. It opened with a ding. She lifted the coin tray and fished out a strip of yellow carbon-copy register tape that had been folded several times and paper-clipped together.

"These are sales up until an hour ago. We tear off the top white receipt for the customer. We keep the yellow copy, and my manager checks it against the cash and credit card sales every night."

She unclipped the strip and scrolled through it until she found the entry she wanted. She pressed it against the counter for me to see and pointed.

"He bought milk, Froot Loops, and Lucky Charms. Four candy bars and two big bags of chips. Not exactly your healthy foods."

I examined the list. "Did he pay cash or use a credit card?"

She pointed again. "Cash. It says right there."

Katie, Katie, Katie. You've shown remarkable initiative compared to most of the teenagers I've run across in my line of work.

"This is kind of mean," she said. "But sometimes when I'm ringing up a customer, I'll have a conversation in my head about what they're buying or what they should be buying. You know, like 'Dude, how about a bar of soap and some toothpaste instead of that carton of Camels?' Or like, 'Seriously, girl? Diet Coke to go with the pork rinds and jumbo bag of M&Ms? Just go ahead and get yourself a regular Coke.'"

I chuckled. Katie was growing on me.

"How about this guy? Did you have a conversation in your head about him?"

"Yeah, I was like—'Dude, you need to lay off the sugary cereals and all this other shit. Because you look half-dead already.'"

"Half-dead?"

"Yeah. Like I told you—like he doesn't get out in the sun."

"Anything else you can tell me about him? Like what kind of vehicle he was driving?"

She shook her head. "It was raining up a shit storm yesterday. I didn't see what he was driving. Not that I was looking, though."

I had a copy of Eddie's photo folded up in my pocket. I pulled it out and showed it to her.

"Does this look like the man you saw?"

"Yeah. That could be him. I'm not a hundred percent sure—I didn't get a real good look at him under the hood. I couldn't really see his eyes."

I put on my hat.

"Katie, you have been most helpful. Does your manager keep those cash register tapes?"

"Oh, yeah. For the accountant. I'll tell him to hang on to this one, extra careful."

"Great." I fished a card out of my back pocket and handed it to her. "My office number and my cell phone are on there. If you think of anything else, give me a call."

She looked at the card and then up at me and smiled. "Awesome."

"And I'd appreciate a call right away if that fellow comes back in."

"Sure. Is he wanted for something?"

"No, I just need to talk to him. But stay away from him. If you see him again, let him buy whatever he's here to buy then go on his way. And call me as quick as you can."

"Okay. I'll at least find out what he's driving. Maybe get a license number."

"Thank you, Katie. You're the one who's awesome."

I smiled back at her and stepped outside. In spite of the rain, I felt better than I'd felt all week. Katie at Lester's General Store had kind of made my day.

* * *

I called the Boulder County Sheriff's office, the Nederland and Estes Park police departments, and told them Eddie Marsh might have been spotted just south of Allenspark, headed north. Then I took Highway 7 to Lyons and stopped for dinner on my way home. Nate Gibbs, owner of The Fork & Spoon, knows that I'm there for the rack of lamb and, as usual, did not disappoint. Nate sat across from me while I ate, and we talked baseball and college football and local politics until I was afraid he might charge me rent on the table, I'd been there so long. I took a piece of pecan pie to go, told Nate I'd see him next time, and headed for home a relatively happy man.

I'd left my cell phone in the truck, and when I checked it saw that Elizabeth had called me. Six times. I changed out of my uniform when I got home, put on a jacket, took a beer and the pecan pie out to the porch, and called Elizabeth back.

"Where have you been, Monroe? I've been trying to reach you all evening."

"I was at dinner, Elizabeth."

"Ignoring my calls?"

"No. I didn't have my phone with me. I generally do that so I can enjoy my meal in peace."

"Well? Did you talk to the girl at the store?"

"I sure did. Katie. Katie was very helpful."

"And?"

"I think it may have been Eddie Marsh."

Elizabeth was quiet for a second, then let out a loud whoop. "I knew it! I knew it was him!"

"I let local law enforcement know he was seen down there."

"Good. I feel like this is progress, Monroe. Don't you think? We're starting to make some progress."

I took a bite of pecan pie.

"I hope so, Elizabeth. I hope so."

I thought I heard a muttered profanity on the other end of the line, but perhaps I was mistaken.

"So," I said. "How are you? How's Alex?"

"We're fine."

I heard Alex's voice in the background but couldn't understand what she said.

"Alex wants to know if you need to talk to her."

I took another bite of pie. Tried to swallow, but it wasn't going down easy. I took a swig of beer and washed it down.

"Monroe?"

"Yeah."

"Alex wants to know if you need to talk to her."

I blew out a long breath. "No. I don't need to talk to her. Good night, Elizabeth. I'll be in touch."

I zipped up my jacket and finished the pie and the beer. Listened to the river and watched the stars. For what seemed like a long, lonely time.

CHAPTER

37

Elizabeth

I WOKE EARLY SUNDAY morning and dressed quickly, anxious to get on the road and scout the area south of Estes Park again. I put on a pot of coffee and made enough noise to wake Alex, who was not particularly cheerful when she appeared in the kitchen. She poured herself a cup and went to the porch for a smoke. I gave her a few minutes, then joined her, taking the coffee pot with me.

"You okay?" I said, refilling her cup.

"I'm fine."

She seemed to have perked up a bit. I took the coffee pot inside, then went back out and sat beside her.

"Listen," I said. "You don't have to go with me today. I know this must be getting tedious for you. Whenever you're ready to go back to Houston, feel free to go."

She closed her eyes and rocked slowly.

"It's not tedious at all. It's just so fucking frustrating. Not knowing where Henry is, nobody able to find him."

She opened her eyes and looked at me. "I woke up with the urge to call a meeting of everyone involved, pound the table, and say, 'Damn it, people, we will get this job done and we will get it done now. We will find Henry English today.'" She gave me a rueful smile.

"I know. Speaking from one type A to another."

"Well," she said, lighting another cigarette. "We type A women have to stick together. Because no one else can stand us."

I stood. "Do you want breakfast before we go? I can scramble some eggs if you'll eat them."

She shook her head. "There's only one thing you absolutely must do before we head out for the day."

"What's that?"

"Call your husband. You haven't talked to him in God knows how long."

"I talked to Paul a couple of days ago."

"No. You said two sentences to each other while waiting for Nick to get on the phone. I mean call him and really talk. About what's going on. How you're feeling, how he's feeling."

I shuddered. The last thing I wanted was to have that kind of conversation with Paul.

"You haven't even told him about Eddie Marsh."

"I don't want to tell him, Alex. If Eddie Marsh took Henry, Paul will blame me. He'll never let me forget it."

"He'll be even more furious the longer you go without telling him."

"Yes. Well. Maybe I don't really care."

Alex stood. "I'm going to take a shower. After which, you can give me a report."

I followed her inside. I retrieved my cell phone from the kitchen and, chilled from sitting on the porch, wrapped myself in a blanket and lay on the sofa. I dialed the home phone. Paul answered after the first ring.

"That was quick."

"Yeah, Nick's still sleeping. I didn't want the phone to wake him. He had kind of a rough night." His tone was stiff, detached.

"What happened?"

"We went to the Astros game last night. One too many hot dogs, I think."

"Poor baby. How's he doing otherwise?"

"He's suffering. He tries not to show it. His grades are off a little, not too bad. But—you know. I can see it."

Tears came to my eyes, and I swallowed, struggling to stay in control.

"Is he seeing the counselor?"

"Yeah. The school's been great. They let her come in twice a week now, to meet with him at lunchtime."

"Twice a week?"

"She thinks he needs more than weekly."

"Have you gotten any feedback from her?"

"He feels guilty—that it's his fault Henry's gone. And he's afraid. Afraid of what's happened to Henry. Afraid of losing you."

The tears were flowing freely now. I kicked off the blanket, went to my bathroom, and grabbed a wad of tissues. I closed and locked the door, lowered the toilet lid and sat down. The reluctance I'd felt earlier this morning was gone and suddenly, desperately, I wanted to talk to Paul.

"Paul. . . ." I didn't really know how to begin. "I don't know if you'll ever forgive me for what happened in Alaska. I want us to work this out, but I just don't have the energy for it. I can't deal with it right now."

"I get it."

"So how are you doing?" I wiped my eyes.

"It's killing me." His voice cracked.

"I know. It's killing me, too."

I bent over, elbows resting on my thighs, and sobbed. I could hear Paul on the other end doing the same. We cried together, until finally, for a while, the tears were exhausted. I blew my nose, stood, and paced around the bathroom, my leather moccasins shushing against the tiles. I told Paul about seeing the man who'd been following me at Lester's General Store. About our plans to keep looking, driving the roads off Highway 7 down to Allenspark and beyond.

"Be careful," he said.

"I will. And hey, I've got my badass friend Alex by my side."

"I don't know if that makes me feel better or worse."

Then I told him about the moose. The cow and her two calves, appearing like an apparition out of the mist.

"Wow. Very cool."

"That's when I knew, Paul."

"Knew what?"

"That Henry's alive."

He didn't say anything.

"The two calves, Paul. Two babies. The cow came to tell me that Henry's alive."

I heard him blow out a long breath.

"Okay," he said.

"Paul. Think about it. Remember a couple of years ago when we were driving west across the plains from Colorado Springs on the way to Crested Butte? We saw a white buffalo, in the middle of a herd on the side of the highway. A symbol of hope."

"I remember."

"Then last year, when we were rafting with the boys. Two eagles flew over us, turned around, and circled our raft. Twice. The guide said it was a blessing."

"Yeah."

"They all tie together, Paul. They're messages. That we will receive a blessing. That Henry will be found."

He took another deep breath and let it out slowly.

"You know I've never been very religious."

"This is something spiritual, Paul. It has nothing to do with religion."

"Okay, spiritual. Spiritual, religious, I have a hard time with it. You go up in the mountains, out in the countryside, you're bound to see some animals. I wouldn't read anything into the fact that you've seen them. The bottom line is, Henry is gone."

I sat down on the toilet again. The harshness of his words took my breath away.

"Elizabeth?"

"Yes."

"I'm trying to be realistic here. It's day twenty-seven. At some point—probably sooner rather than later—we have to accept that Henry's probably not coming back. And that you have to come home. For Nick's sake, if nothing else."

The sudden, desperate desire I'd felt earlier to talk to Paul was just as suddenly gone. I had nothing more to say.

"Tell Nick I love him. I'll be in touch."

I hung up the phone. I leaned over the sink, brushed my teeth and washed my face, then went to find Alex. She was waiting for me in the living room, thumbing through a stack of old magazines.

"We're stopping at the bookstore on the way home," she said, "and buying some new reading material." She looked up at me. "So how did it go?"

"Fine." I collected my purse, a cap, and a jacket. Alex tossed her magazine aside and joined me.

"There are times," I said as I locked the front door, "that I can't believe Paul's a poet."

"Why?"

"Because he has so little imagination."

* * *

We turned on every road off Highway 7 south of Mary's Lake, wound on gravel and dirt roads across creeks, through heavy forest and marshes. Some houses were visible, others completely hidden from the road. Private Property, No Trespassing signs were abundant. One that said "Trespassers will be shot. Survivors will be shot again." We saw pickup trucks, of course, but Alex told me if I got out of the Jeep like I'd done the day before, she would drive off and leave me.

"You see those signs? These people mean it. You march up to their front door, you'll get yourself killed."

So I made a list instead, of where the trucks were located, for Carpenter and Monroe.

"They'll be thrilled," Alex said.

"I'll let you deliver it. You can hand it to them and pound their desk and say, 'Damn it, Monroe, damn it, Carpenter, we will get this job done and we will get it done now. We will find Henry English today.'"

"It won't be the first time I've been thrown out of someone's office."

By late morning we'd made our way down to Lester's General Store. We stopped, picked up soft drinks and peanuts, and I went to pay while Alex went to the ladies' room. The cash register this time was manned by a boy who looked even younger than the girl we'd talked to. Katie. Monroe said her name was Katie.

"Is Katie here?" I asked as he rang up our purchases.

"She's off today."

I pulled a copy of Eddie's photo from my purse.

"We were here yesterday. We were hoping to talk to Katie again about this man."

"Well, she's not here."

"Have you ever seen him?"

He took one quick glance at the photo. "Nope." He pulled his cell phone out of his pocket, sat on a stool behind the counter, and started texting. I watched him for a minute, completely engrossed in his shiny little object, thumbs working furiously, oblivious to anything around him.

"Put down the damn phone and look at this picture."

He didn't look up. I said it louder. He ignored me, head bent, thumbs still working. I slapped my hands on the counter.

"I said, put down the damn phone and look at this picture."

He looked up, put his cell phone back in his pocket, crossed his arms, and glared at me. He didn't move from the stool.

"I looked at it already. I don't know the guy. I've never seen him before."

"Is there a problem here?" It was Alex. I hadn't heard her come up behind me.

"Yeah, there's a problem," he said. "You and your friend need to leave."

"Okay," she said. She tucked the soft drinks and peanuts under her left arm and grabbed me with her right.

"Little shit," I said.

"I have a baseball bat under the counter," he said.

Alex tugged at me. "Let's go, Elizabeth."

I picked up the photo and let Alex lead me to the door, looking back over my shoulder at the kid as we went outside.

"What the fuck, Elizabeth?" Alex said when we were in the Jeep.

I cracked open my soda and took a long drink. "I just asked him to look at the photo."

"You didn't just ask him. You were yelling at the kid. I heard you from the bathroom."

I took another drink, wolfed down a handful of peanuts.

"He wasn't being helpful."

"Jesus." Alex turned the key in the ignition. "Where to now?"

"Maybe another look at the cabin we checked out yesterday?"

"No way. Absolutely not."

"Then onward. South to Nederland."

CHAPTER

38

Alexis

I called Monroe Monday to tell him I had something for him. I dropped Elizabeth at the grocery store then drove on to Monroe's office. He stood when I entered the room, very polite. I halfway expected him to hold my chair, so I sat down quickly before he could get around the desk. I pushed the sheets of paper across to him. He took his seat and looked at Elizabeth's notes.

"What's this?"

"That is a list of every pickup truck we saw between here and Nederland this weekend, and either the address or the truck's approximate location. Which probably amounts to half the houses in that area. The trucks we didn't see are presumably parked at the remaining homes."

"And what I am supposed to do with this information?"

"You are to investigate, Monroe. To find out if one of these trucks, or one of the trucks that we didn't see, belongs to Eddie Marsh."

Monroe leaned back in his chair at a dangerous angle from my perspective and rubbed his face wearily.

"In other words, I'm to ask local law enforcement to go to every house in the vicinity of Highway 7 between here and Nederland and see if they can find him."

"That is correct. Which is better than Elizabeth marching up to houses unannounced to have a look."

"She's doing that?"

"Oh, yes."

"Tell her to stop. She'll get herself shot."

He looked at the papers again. "Single-spaced, two-sided. I take it this is her handwriting?"

"It is."

He folded the papers and slipped them inside his spiral notebook.

"I also assume she'll be calling for status reports?"

"You and Carpenter. She made a copy for me to drop at the police station. I'd check caller ID, if I were you. For the next several days."

He gave me a little smile. "I shouldn't say it. But there is a bit of humor in that."

"Yeah. I'd be laughing my ass off if it weren't so fucking sad."

He was serious again. "How is she?"

"Wound pretty tight. She is an altercation looking to happen."

"I'm glad she sent you, then."

"Me, too."

I looked at him and he looked at me. Uncharacteristically, I couldn't think of anything else to say. Neither, it seemed, could he. I sat there for another minute or so, then got up to leave. He jumped up, knocking the chair out from under him and sending it into the file cabinets behind his desk.

"I'll walk you out."

It was a cool, sunny day. Neither of us spoke until we reached the Jeep.

"How much longer are you staying in Estes Park?"

I squinted up at him. "You sure are interested in my departure date, Monroe. You ask about it every time you see me."

"I'm just glad you're here. For Elizabeth."

I unlocked the Jeep, and he opened the door for me. I rolled down the window, then got behind the wheel and closed the door.

"I keep pushing the return date. It was to be Wednesday or Thursday of this week, now it's maybe Sunday night. Spotting Eddie Marsh—if it was him—I can't leave now."

"It may take a long time to find him. If we ever do. And even if we find him, he may not know anything about Henry."

"I can wait. And who knows—maybe I'll get lucky and the firm will boot my ass out the door."

"Would they do that?"

"They very well might."

"What would you do then?"

I started the Jeep and gave him a smile. "Why, then, Monroe, I would move to Colorado."

* * *

I left Carpenter's copy of the list at the police station, then went to pick up Elizabeth. She was leaning on a cart full of groceries, waiting for me in the Safeway parking lot. I helped her load them in the Jeep.

"Any other errands we need to run?"

"No," she said. "Let's get the groceries put away then hit the road again."

I'd thought that once we gave Monroe and Carpenter the list, she might take a break from the hunt. It was a moment of insanity on my part. This was Elizabeth.

Back at the cabin, she got out to collect the mail and told me to drive on, that she'd like the walk up the drive. I took the groceries in, then sat on the porch to smoke, watching her as she slowly approached, thumbing through the mail. She stopped, opened an envelope, and pulled out its contents. She read what appeared to be a letter, looked up at me, and continued up the drive. She stepped up onto the porch, a sick expression on her face, and handed it to me.

"What?"

"It's from Eddie Marsh." She lowered herself into the chair beside me and buried her face in her hands as I began to read.

Dear Elizabeth,

I assume you remember me, although it has been some number of years since we last met. You probably heard that I was sentenced to 10 years in prison. I was released in April of this year, after having served the full amount of time.

I held a lot of anger and bitterness inside me the first few years. I lost everything—my career, my money, the good life I had made for myself. I thought a lot about the people who had a hand in that, you included.

I forgive you for all the times you looked at me with disgust. For all the times you turned away when I tried to speak to you. For your complete failure to show me one ounce of compassion in all the years that the cases against me dragged on.

I, however, am capable of compassion. I am truly sorry for the tragedy that has befallen your family. For your sweet little boy Henry. For you, for the sadness that overcame you when you pleaded, begged for Henry to be brought home.

I don't know what I can do to help, but if I think of anything I'll be in touch.

Sincerely,

Edward Marsh

The letter was undated and handwritten. The envelope was handwritten as well, with no return address. It was postmarked from Tulsa, Oklahoma, three days before.

"Jesus," I said. "That's about as creepy as it gets."

"He's evil to the core." She pushed herself up from the chair like an old woman whose every joint ached. "Let's go see Monroe and Carpenter. There's no doubt in my mind that Eddie Marsh has Henry."

CHAPTER

39

Monroe

I HAD TO GO back to my office and sit down for a while at the thought of Alexis LaDay moving to Colorado. I had pulled myself together and was reaching for my hat when the phone rang.

"Monroe," I said.

"How you doing, Monroe?" Roxanne Babcock was one of the chattiest operators in our dispatch center.

"Fine. Heading out for a late lunch." Hoping to cut the conversation short.

"There's a caller on line two. Says he has information that may be relevant to Henry English."

I'd talked to dozens, probably hundreds of people in the past month who claimed to have information about Henry. I wasn't in the mood right then to talk to one more nutcase.

"Can you take down his name and number, and ask him what information he has? Tell him someone will return his call? Or maybe even tell him to get in touch with Estes Park police?"

"Nope. He says he won't talk to anyone but you."

"Swell."

I hung up, looked at the light blinking on line two, picked up the phone again, and punched the button.

"This is Ranger Monroe."

"Mr. Monroe," the man said. "Thanks for taking my call."

"Sure. To whom am I speaking?"

"My name is George Erwin."

"How can I help you, Mr. Erwin?"

"I live over here in Fort Collins. Owned a heating and air conditioning business for forty years. I sold it last year, I'm retired now. Maybe you heard of it. Erwin Heating and Air?"

I put my elbows on the desk, one hand cupped around the handset, forehead resting on the other. I wondered how much more of the autobiography of George Erwin I might be subjected to.

"Sorry to say I haven't. But I'm fairly new to the area."

"Well, that's neither here nor there, anyway. I'm calling about that little boy that's missing. Henry English."

"Yes?"

"This might have something to do with him. Or it might not. I just thought I should call."

"Okay, shoot. Tell me what you've got." *Please. Or shoot me if this goes on much longer.*

"I've got a little old house back in the woods near Rocky Mountain National Park. I don't get up there much anymore, and I've thought about selling it. But my sons use it sometimes, so I've hung onto it. I rent it out most of the year. To hunters and off-roaders and the like."

He paused, to see if I had any comments on the wisdom of real property ownership, I suppose. I didn't, so he went on.

"Mid-July, I rented it to this fellow who said he was an attorney from Oklahoma. He wanted it for four months. Said he was taking some kind of sabbatical and trying to write a book."

An attorney from Oklahoma? George Erwin suddenly had my attention. I sat up straight, reached for a pen, and opened my spiral notebook.

"What's the man's name?"

"Russell Posey. P-O-S-E-Y. He sent me a money order for the full four months' rental. I told him where to find the key and told him the place was all his."

"You didn't meet him in person?"

"Nah. I've never had any trouble up there. And sure didn't figure I'd have any with a lawyer."

"But something's happened. Something made you call."

"Well, there may be nothing to it. I haven't talked to the man since the first day he arrived. He had some questions about trash collection and the like when he got there. After that, I never heard from him, so a few days ago I thought I'd call to see if everything was going okay. I called the number I had for him—his cell—and it's no longer a working number."

"I'll get that number from you in a minute. Finish your story first."

"I have a lady that cleans the house for me, at the end of every rental. I make my renters pay a cleaning fee, nonrefundable. She has a key, so I asked her to go over and check on the place. See if Posey was still there."

"The four months isn't up yet. He has a while to go on the rental."

Erwin chuckled. "Four months of solitude may sound like a good idea. But you're up there by yourself for a while, and you see your first bear or hear your first coyote—a lawyer might decide he'd had enough of playing Henry Thoreau."

Henry Thoreau. I was impressed.

"My cleaning lady went up there yesterday. She's actually a teacher. Had to wait until the weekend. It's a shame, isn't it? That a teacher has to clean houses to supplement her income?"

I didn't respond. I didn't want to derail this slow-moving train with a discussion about teacher salaries. Fortunately, he went on.

"She drove up to the property yesterday afternoon. She knocked several times, no answer. So she uses her key, and she's got the door about halfway open when she hears a shout from the kitchen at the back of the house."

"What kind of shout?"

"A man yelling, 'Hey.' Saying, 'I have a gun. I'll shoot.' She slams the door shut and runs to her car and gets the hell out of there as fast as she can."

"She didn't see the man?"

"No."

"Did she see any vehicles?"

"No. But he could have parked behind the house."

I leaned back in my chair.

"What makes you think this has anything to do with Henry English, Mr. Erwin?"

"It might not have anything to do with him at all, Mr. Monroe."

"What about this incident made you call me?"

He hesitated. "It's what my cleaning lady saw just inside the door."

I sat up straight again. "What did she see?"

"It was a pair of little hiking boots, Mr. Monroe."

"What do you mean, 'little'? You mean like kids' boots?"

"Yeah. It was kids' boots. And trust me, the schoolteacher would know."

My heart started to race.

"Maybe he has a kid," I said. "Or a grandchild."

"I asked him about that when I rented the place to him. Whether any other family or friends would be joining him. He said no, he didn't have any family."

I drew in a deep breath, blew it out again, afraid my voice would shake.

"Where's your place located, Mr. Erwin?"

"Not too far from you. It's off Highway 7, a few miles south of Estes Park."

"North of Allenspark?"

"Yes. Between there and Estes Park."

* * *

I got more details from Erwin, wrote down the address of his place, contact information for him, and the telephone number Posey had given. I thanked Erwin for calling and said I'd be in touch. I walked out to my Bronco and called Carpenter on the way. I gave him a brief rundown of my conversation with Erwin and said I'd swing by and pick him up.

"That's out of your jurisdiction, Monroe."

"I'm just here for support. You don't want me along?"

Carpenter grunted. "Yeah. Actually, I do."

He was waiting outside police headquarters. He jumped in and we headed toward Highway 7.

"I checked with the Oklahoma Bar Association," he said. "There's no Russell Posey licensed as an attorney in the state of Oklahoma."

"Then the cell phone's probably a burner."

"Count on it. We're checking that, too."

I filled Carpenter in on the details of my conversation with Erwin as we drove up the mountain, past Lily Lake and Longs Peak Road. I slowed and pulled onto the shoulder until I finally came to a stop by the private dirt road that Erwin had described. There were No Trespassing signs and a gate, but Erwin said it wasn't locked. Thick stands of Ponderosa pine and aspen hid the house from view.

"You think this could be the guy?" Carpenter said.

"He's some kind of guy. Let's find out."

Carpenter got out and pushed the gate open, then climbed in again. I drove at a crawl up the dirt road, and in three hundred yards or so, the road ended and the house was in sight. It wasn't much to look at. Dark log frame, a porch that sagged. Satellite dish on the roof. No vehicles we could see, no signs of life. I parked the Bronco in the front yard and waited while Carpenter went around the back. He returned, shaking his head.

"There's a barn with an old four-wheeler in it. No truck."

We stepped up onto the porch and I knocked on the door. No response. I knocked again. There were two windows off the porch, but the blinds were drawn. I knocked a third time. No response. I turned the knob. The door was unlocked. I pushed it open.

"Hello? Anybody home?"

Nothing.

I nodded at Carpenter, and we stepped inside.

"Hello. Hello. Anyone home?"

Nothing. I looked at Carpenter. He shrugged. "Let's take a look around."

Based on the appearance of the house's exterior, I wasn't expecting much inside. But it wasn't bad. The walls were the same dark log and the furniture looked like it had been purchased thirty years ago, but it was sturdy and in decent shape. The television was more recent. The front room was a combination living and dining room, with a fireplace at one end. At the other end, a short hall led to a kitchen on the left, two bedrooms and a bathroom on the right. The floors were wood plank, tile in the bathroom and kitchen.

One bedroom had a queen-sized bed, the other two sets of bunk beds. The mattresses were bare; Erwin had told me he didn't provide any sheets, blankets, or towels.

"I did at first," he'd said. "But some of those hunters make a real mess."

The closets were empty. Nothing in the bathroom medicine cabinet. We went to the kitchen, checked the cabinets. Dishes and pans all washed, all put away. No trash anywhere. Cast-iron sink, a small gas stove, and refrigerator that looked to be original to the house, all sparkling clean. And empty. A keyring was on the counter, a plastic house-shaped key tag printed with "Erwin Heating and Air" and a telephone number attached.

"Does something strike you as odd here?" I said. "For a guy who's paid a nonrefundable cleaning fee in advance?"

"Yeah," Carpenter said. "The place isn't just clean. It's spotless."

* * *

I dropped Carpenter at the police station to start the process of getting a forensic team over to Erwin's place.

"It's a long shot," Carpenter said. "There's fifty years of DNA in that place. The surfaces where we might find a fingerprint were wiped."

"Maybe we'll get lucky," I said.

I went across the street to Ed's Cantina, ordered bison enchiladas, and called Erwin while I waited for my food. I told him the renter was gone, but the police would need access to the place for a few days for a forensic team to go over it.

"Did you see any evidence that Henry English was there?" he said.

"No." I asked him for the name and number of his cleaning lady. I also asked him not to talk about this with anyone.

"I won't," he said. "It could be nothing at all."

CHAPTER

40

Elizabeth

I COULDN'T GET MONROE on the phone—I'd left several messages, but didn't hear back from him. I tried Carpenter's office. No luck there, either. I understood that finding Henry wasn't their only job, but I was frustrated that they weren't more responsive.

"We should be out looking for Eddie Marsh," I said, pacing back and forth across the living room. "Not waiting around for them."

"They'll get in touch when they can," Alex said. "Just rest for a while."

It was almost sunset when Monroe finally called.

"I need to bring you something," I said. "A letter from Eddie Marsh. Let me read it to you first."

"Okay," he said when I'd finished. "Bring it to Carpenter's office."

"He must have an accomplice. He wasn't in Tulsa three days ago."

"No. His mother lives there. He probably sent it to her and asked her to mail it. Elizabeth. . . . "

"Yes?"

"Bring Alex with you."

For a moment I couldn't breathe.

"Have you found something?"

He didn't respond.

"Monroe?"

"We haven't found anything. But we may have a development in the case. I think you should know about it. By the way, what kind of cereal does Henry like?"

"Cereal? Well, Henry likes Multi-Grain Cheerios. Shredded Wheat. And this homemade granola I make."

"Seriously? That's what he likes best?"

"No, Monroe, that's not what he likes best, that's what I let him eat. I'm not buying all that sugary crap. If I let him, he'd eat nothing but Froot Loops and Lucky Charms."

"Yeah," Monroe said. "Froot Loops and Lucky Charms."

* * *

"We got a tip earlier today," Monroe said.

Alex and I were across the conference table from Carpenter and Monroe. She grabbed my hand.

"A fellow in Fort Collins has a cabin in this area that he rents out."

Monroe paused.

"Earlier in the summer he rented it out for four months to a lawyer from Oklahoma."

Alex gasped. "Eddie Marsh?"

"The man said his name was Russell Posey," Carpenter said. "But we've checked, and there's no one by that name registered with the Oklahoma State Bar."

"Have you followed up? Gone to the cabin?" Alex said.

"Yes," Monroe said. "Carpenter and I had a look around. It's empty. Cleaned out. Whoever he was, he's gone."

"Did the owner give you a description?" I said.

"No. Posey, or whoever he is, paid by money order and gave a number for a disposable phone. Erwin—that's the owner—never even saw the guy."

"So, we're no further in the investigation," I said.

I looked at Carpenter, then Monroe, then back at Carpenter. He avoided my eyes.

"What? What?"

"Erwin sent his cleaning lady up there yesterday," Monroe said. "She used her key to get in, but Posey yelled at her as soon as she cracked the door, threatened to shoot. She got back in her car as quick as she could and got out of there."

"Did she see him?" Alex said.

"No. But she saw something else. A pair of boots just inside the door." He paused. "They were hiking boots, Elizabeth. A child's hiking boots."

I opened my mouth, but I couldn't speak. Alex turned to me and squeezed my hand tighter.

"The boots weren't there when you went in today?" she said.

"No. The place is clean as a whistle, nothing left behind."

"Where is the cabin?" she said.

"Off Highway 7 between here and Allenspark."

A horrible realization began to take shape.

"South of Longs Peak Road?" I whispered.

"Yes."

"Up a private drive with No Trespassing signs? A dark log house, sagging porch, satellite dish on the roof?"

Monroe nodded. "Barn out back, an old four-wheeler inside. You know the place?"

"We were there Saturday. Everything was locked—the doors, the windows, the barn."

I pulled away from Alex and buried my face in my hands. "Henry was there. He was in there all along. I knew it. And now he's gone."

* * *

Carpenter and Monroe stared at me, dumbfounded. Then Carpenter slapped his palms on the table, jumped up, and leaned toward me.

"What the hell were you doing?"

"What the hell do you think we were doing?" Alex said. "We were looking for Eddie Marsh. Nobody else was making any progress."

"Well, you almost found him," Carpenter said. "Except that he apparently saw or heard you snooping around, and our first chance at making any fucking progress in this case is out the fucking window."

Alex stood and jabbed a finger in Carpenter's direction. "And whatever the status of this case may be, you'll stop your fucking yelling and cursing at my friend."

Monroe put a hand on Carpenter's arm.

"Stop," I said. "Don't blame Alex. She didn't want to go up there. It's my fault."

"Everyone calm down," Monroe said. "Let's talk about where we are."

Carpenter slammed back into his seat and looked up at the ceiling. Alex sat down, folded her arms, and glared at him.

"I think we have to assume it was Eddie Marsh at Erwin's cabin," Monroe said, "and that Henry was there at some point. Eddie gets spooked by Elizabeth and Alex poking around, then the cleaning lady. So, sometime between yesterday and this afternoon, he clears out."

"And takes Henry with him," I said.

Monroe glanced at Carpenter. Carpenter frowned and studied his fingernails.

"It's been a month, Elizabeth. There's been no ransom demand, no indication that Eddie intends to let Henry go. He took Henry to get back at you."

I didn't understand. "Henry's boots were there. Henry was there."

"He was there at some point. Maybe even yesterday. But if Eddie's on the run, it's unlikely he would take Henry with him."

"What are you saying?"

Monroe rubbed his face wearily. "We have an APB out on Eddie. And we have cadaver dogs at the Erwin place and the surrounding area."

Alex turned to me and pried my fingers loose from the arms of my chair. I didn't realize I was gripping them so tightly.

"He's saying, honey, that Eddie would have no reason to keep Henry alive."

She gently pulled me to my feet. "Let's go home now. We need to let Paul know."

Monroe and Carpenter stood.

"We'll find Eddie," Carpenter said.

I stopped at the door, my back to them.

"Focus on finding Henry," I said. "He's alive."

CHAPTER

41

Paul

EDDIE MARSH. I didn't say anything for a few moments.

"Paul?"

Elizabeth was on the phone and I'd just heard the whole story. Before she began, she'd asked me if I remembered Eddie Marsh from the case she'd worked on years ago for the firm's client Allen Haas. "Of course," I said. "I remember him."

Here's what else I remember. That was the case that turned Elizabeth into a trial lawyer. Before she worked on it, she was ambivalent about her career, even questioning once in a while whether she'd made a mistake going to law school. I thought her doubts and hesitation probably contributed to her drinking—looking for the courage to get up the next morning and face another day at the firm.

Then came the Haas case. She'd quit drinking shortly before she got the assignment. And she was into it. She got off on it. Every time they crushed someone in a deposition or the judge ruled in their favor on a motion, she came home pumped. Sticking it to

Clint Scruggs and Eddie Marsh was her favorite pastime, and when the verdict came down she was euphoric.

"You need to be careful," I told her. "These are dangerous people."

She'd given me a smug little smile. "I'm a careful person. I'm just doing my job."

Doing her job with more swagger in her step from then on, more confidence every time she won a case, never any question that she would make partner. And no question that the lawyers in her firm thought she was a badass who wore the pants in our family.

"Paul?"

I'd been holding it together for Nick. He was upstairs doing his homework. Jimena had rummaged through the casseroles in our freezer and put one in the oven a few minutes before I got home from school. King ranch chicken, beef stroganoff, baked ziti, lasagna, shepherd's pie. I was so sick of casseroles. The night before, I'd loaded my plate and taken a bite and swore I could almost see Henry sitting across from me at the table, saying, "That's disgusting."

Like he'd said to Elizabeth earlier in the summer. She'd been home from Alaska only a few days, and decided to try a new recipe for dinner, something French like veal stew with vegetables and cream sauce, I think. She spent hours that Saturday afternoon shopping, chopping vegetables, making a huge mess in the kitchen, and had high expectations when we sat down together in the dining room, no less. I thought it was okay, and Nick said he liked it, but Henry took two bites, put down his spoon, and didn't just *say*, oh no, he *announced* to the table, "*This*—is disgusting." Nick's eyes got big and we all looked at Elizabeth, who put her head down in her hands. I was just about to send Henry to his room when Elizabeth looked up, the fatigue of trial still on her face, tears running down her cheeks, laughing and gasping for breath. In a few seconds, the boys and I were doing the same. "Oh, Henry," Elizabeth finally said. "We can always count on you. It is disgusting. That recipe's going in the trash."

Remembering that moment was like a knife in the chest, but since Henry disappeared there were a thousand knives every day. Now this one. Elizabeth on the phone. Telling me about Eddie Marsh. About the little hiking boots.

"Paul?"

"Wow." My hands were trembling. "All those times you saw the guy following you, and you didn't recognize him?"

"No, of course I didn't recognize him. If I'd recognized him, I would have told Monroe and Carpenter immediately."

"Well, I mean, how could you not recognize him? You saw the guy hundreds of times."

"That was more than ten years ago, Paul. He's been in prison and gained a huge amount of weight. He doesn't look anything like he looked back then."

"So how did they identify him?"

There was silence on the other end. Then, "We had a meeting with Brad Riegle. At the police station. He happened to come through Estes Park on his way home from vacation. Something he said made me think of Eddie."

Brad Riegle. She forgot to mention that detail earlier.

"Wow. Fortunate again to have Brad Riegle on the scene."

"Oh, for God's sake, Paul. We finally have a lead, and you want to be nasty about this? Blame me for not recognizing Eddie Marsh, insinuate that there's something wrong with meeting with Riegle? Focus on what's important. Focus on finding Henry."

"I'm not the one who's lost focus, Elizabeth. I'm the one who's always known what's important. You're the one willing to sacrifice your children for your career. Now look where it's gotten us."

I heard her gasp. And I knew I was going to regret what I said next, but it was like I was out of my mind and I couldn't stop myself. I jumped out of my chair and paced around the family room.

"You were hot shit, weren't you, Elizabeth. A big verdict that made the papers and Clint Scruggs and Eddie Marsh ending up behind bars. But that was just the beginning. You enjoyed destroying people's careers and lives—making them out to be frauds or cowards or, the greatest sin in your eyes, just not very fucking smart. It was only a matter of time until it caught up with you somehow."

I was shaking and out of breath. I sat down on the coffee table, stared into the fireplace, and thought of all the other things I wanted to say, things that had been accumulating for years, the school plays and soccer games she'd missed, all the times she'd called me last minute to cover an appointment, the promises to be home by dinner then by bedtime then by midnight at the latest, all of them gone unfulfilled. The weeks, months away from home and never the slightest worry from me that she might be unfaithful, or any pressure put on her that our marriage might be in trouble. I slumped over, head in one hand, phone in the other, suddenly nothing but tired. Just totally, absolutely tired.

"You bastard," she said. "You son of a bitch. I will never forgive you for this."

"Yeah, well," I said in a low voice. "I'll never forgive you."

She hung up. I tossed the phone on the sofa, looked up at the framed family portrait hanging above the fireplace. A professional photographer had taken it on a beach in Florida—one of those casual scenes where we're all wearing white T-shirts and jeans, and we're barefoot. Henry was about three when it was taken, Nick seven. We're laughing and holding hands and the sun is setting behind us. And I saw again what I'd seen so many times before. At that moment in time, captured in the photograph, Henry looked just like Elizabeth.

"Dad?"

I turned to Nick, standing in the archway that led from the family room to the hall. He still had on his school uniform, and it appeared to have had a hard day. Tears were rolling down his cheeks.

"What is it, buddy?"

He wiped his nose, snot smearing down his forearm. I motioned him over, but he shook his head.

"Why are you yelling at Mom?"

CHAPTER

42

Nick

I HAD A TERRIBLE day.

The first reason it was terrible was Kelly Waters's birthday. Kelly is the most popular girl in fifth grade and the meanest. Which is why I don't understand why she's so popular, but I guess it's because all the girls are afraid of her.

Here's the kind of stuff Kelly does. At recess the first day of school, some of us boys were playing dodgeball. Andrew Davis can throw really hard, and he threw the ball at me but it missed and went out of bounds, and I ran to get it. It rolled up to where a group of girls was sitting around Kelly and she was crying, and they were all like acting upset and giving Kelly hugs. Marci Melo picked up the ball and handed it to me and said, "Don't you want to know why Kelly is crying?"

I didn't really care, I just wanted to play dodgeball, but I said, "Yeah, I guess?"

"She's upset about Henry. She's afraid he's never coming home."

That made me so mad. Kelly didn't give a crap about Henry, she doesn't even know Henry other than she knows he's my little brother. I threw the ball at Kelly's stupid head and said, "Don't you ever say anything about Henry again." She ducked and the ball didn't hit her, but she hates me now as much as I hate her.

So that day it was her birthday. Her mom brought muffins and fruit and juice boxes to class in the morning. And I'm thinking, *Muffins and fruit? Whatever happened to cupcakes?* But the girls were all like, "These are so delicious," and "I can only eat half, I'm so full." And Kelly's like, "I told my mom not to bring cupcakes. They are so fattening." And the girls were like, "Oh, I know, they're so fattening." Then Kelly looked at me and said, "If you eat cupcakes, you'll get a fat ass like Nick English."

And the girls were sort of giggling, and Kelly gives me this nasty little smile. So I take a bite of muffin and spit it out and say, "If you eat turd muffins, you get a turd face like Kelly Waters." Kelly turned red and I was feeling pretty good, but then I stabbed the straw into my juice box and I must have squeezed before the straw got to my mouth because grape juice squirted all over my shirt. The white one.

The second reason it was a terrible day was I had to have my meeting with Miss Cindy. Miss Cindy came twice a week and would come get me in the cafeteria, and I had to take my lunch and go eat it in an office with her. I mean, she's nice and everything, but I hated how everyone knew that I was talking to Miss Cindy and how everyone watched me walking out of the cafeteria with her in my white shirt with the grape juice stain. Not only that, I didn't get to go back for second helpings, and that day was corn dogs, which I had been looking forward to for quite a while.

Miss Cindy always smiled and watched me eat for a minute then she'd ask how I'm doing. I mean, how am I doing? Seriously? Really crappy, that's how I'm doing. I have grape juice all over my shirt and a fat ass and about an hour after this lunch is over, I'll be hungry. And oh yeah, my brother Henry is probably dead and it's probably my fault. Even if it isn't, everyone probably thinks it is.

I shrugged. "I'm okay."

Miss Cindy opened a drawer and pulled out a pad of drawing paper and some colored markers. *Geez.* It was her latest brilliant idea. "Draw what you're feeling, Nick. Art can help you express what's deep inside, so we can talk about it." I mean, that's not what art is for. Art is supposed to be fun. Sometimes even funny. Like the time Henry brought home a little clay model of the Transco Tower he'd made in kindergarten and gave it to my mom to take to her office. It looked just like a penis. Seriously, like if you were trying to make a penis out of clay, you'd want to end up with Henry's Transco Tower. I couldn't wait until Mom got home so Henry could give it to her. I thought she'd fall over laughing, but she smiled and said it was a very good likeness of the Transco Tower, and I said, "But what does it really remind you of," and she said, "The Transco Tower," and I said, "No, really," and she looked at me like she didn't understand the question. Which was kind of disappointing. Not only that, she actually took it to her office and put it on her desk. It was a couple of days later that she said the Transco Tower was quite a conversation starter, and then I knew that she knew what I was talking about. So I'm thinking I like art, but if I have to keep drawing these stupid pictures, I may not like it anymore.

"Do you think you can draw something today, Nick?"

I folded my arms. "Do you think I could have another corn dog?"

Miss Cindy looked like she was thinking hard for a minute. "I think that can be arranged."

She picked up my empty tray. "I'll get that corn dog while you draw."

I was okay with drawing something if it would get me another corn dog. I tore off a sheet of paper and picked up a marker. I'm a pretty good drawer, actually, so once I got started it felt kind of good, and I drew all over the page and used all the colors in the box of markers. I don't know how long it was, but when I finished I looked up and Miss Cindy was watching me. She sat down at the table next to me and moved the picture a little bit and handed me the tray. With two corn dogs and another carton of milk!

"Is this your house?" Miss Cindy said.

I nodded.

"It looks like a beautiful place. I like all the trees and the porches."

I nodded again.

"Tell me about the people looking out the windows."

I pointed at the first floor. "This is Mom and Dad." I pointed to two windows upstairs. "This is Henry in his room, and this is me in my room."

"And what is this on all the windows?"

"Burglar bars."

"Interesting. Does your house have burglar bars on the windows?"

"No. But when Henry comes home, I'm going to tell Mom and Dad that we need to get some. To keep us all safe."

"Do you not feel safe at your house?"

I chewed on the last bite of corn dog and swallowed, but I guess it was too big of a bite because it kind of got stuck in my throat. I took a drink of milk and then another one, and it finally went down.

"I feel pretty safe. I mean, not like I used to, I guess."

"How did you used to feel?"

"I don't know. I just never thought about being afraid."

I actually used to think it was kind of silly that Mom made us come up with safe words, and we had to talk about not getting into a car with strangers and that Mom and Dad would never send anyone we didn't know to pick us up, and even if it was a policeman or someone we did know, Mom and Dad would tell them the safe word so we would know it was okay. That whole family meeting to talk about safe words and emergencies was kind of boring, so when Mom asked me what my safe word would be, I said, "Strawberry pie." And Henry laughed because the weekend before, my mom had a dinner party and dessert was strawberry pie. And the grownups were in the dining room, everyone but my mom drinking wine, and I sat in the kitchen eating strawberry pie until I'd eaten maybe half a pie. And sometime in the night, I woke up not feeling very good and I didn't quite make it to the toilet, and when we got up the next morning there was strawberry pie all over the white tile in the bathroom and Henry screamed when he got up and said, "Somebody was *killed* in the bathroom."

So I said strawberry pie and then Henry said his safe word was buttfart and Mom kind of rolled her eyes and said, "Of course." That was pretty much the end of that family meeting.

I looked at our house with the burglar bars and thought about strawberry pie and buttfart, and all of a sudden I was so mad at Henry, I picked up my drawing and tore it into little pieces. Then I put my head in my arms on the table and for like the millionth time since Henry disappeared I started to cry, which every time I did I swore I would never cry again my whole entire life. Miss Cindy put her hand on my back and patted me a little bit and asked me if I wanted to talk about it. I shook my head and pounded my fist on the table and cried until I thought I might throw up the corn dogs. Miss Cindy kept a box of tissues on her table, and she handed me some. I blew my nose and wiped my eyes.

"Can you tell me anything about what just happened, Nick?"

I heaved a couple of deep breaths and it was kind of hard to talk, but I finally got it out.

"I'm really mad at Henry."

"Okay. Do you know why you're mad at him?"

"He didn't use his safe word. Why didn't he use his safe word? Mom told him and Dad told him, and there's no way he was going to forget that his safe word was buttfart. So he should have said, 'What's the safe word?' but he didn't, because if he did, he wouldn't have gotten in the truck and he would have run to me and I would have protected him." Then I guess I was kind of crying and yelling at the same time because Miss Cindy put her arm around me and I just wanted my mom and I put my head in Miss Cindy's lap and cried over and over again, "Why, Henry? Why?"

So I'd had a terrible day. I was upstairs doing my homework when Dad came home, copying the week's spelling list and using the words in a sentence. I hated spelling. I didn't think I would ever for the rest of my whole entire life have to use the word spatula in a sentence. I'd decided to just skip that word when I heard Dad yelling.

I went to the top of the stairs and heard him say, "Elizabeth" and "your children" and "hot shit" and I knew he was yelling at Mom and not only yelling at Mom but calling her bad words. He never does that. I went down the stairs and my socks on the wood floor must not have made any noise because he didn't hear me coming and he kept yelling and then he said, real quiet, "Yeah, well, I'll never forgive you." If he'd heard me coming and knew about my terrible day, I don't think he would have said that, but he did say it and it was ugly and mean like it wasn't even Dad, and it made me cry again which, actually, I had kind of felt like doing ever since my meeting with Miss Cindy.

"Dad?"

"What is it, buddy?"

"Why are you yelling at Mom?"

I thought maybe he'd say he didn't mean it, that grownups sometimes have little disagreements but it's nothing to worry about, or something like that. But he didn't. He put his head in his hands and rubbed his face, then scratched his head really hard and fast until his hair was sticking up in all crazy directions and said, "It's a pretty rough time for Mom and me."

Which made me feel for the second time that day like I was going to be sick and Dad would be cleaning up corn dog puke from the family room floor. I picked up his phone from where he'd thrown it on the sofa and called Mom's number. She didn't answer, so I hung up and dialed again.

"Hello?" It was Aunt Alex. I told her it was me and she put Mom on. Mom's voice was kind of shaky and snotty-sounding.

"Hi, Nick. How's my sweet boy today?"

"Mommy?" Which I don't know why I called her that, because I haven't called her Mommy since I was little. Just Mom.

"Mommy?"

"What is it, honey?"

"I need you to come home."

CHAPTER

43

Alexis

WHAT A MESS. What an unholy, fucking mess.

Elizabeth was curled up on the sofa in a fetal position. Poor little Nicky was falling apart, and Paul was losing it. Elizabeth told me what he'd said. I wanted to strangle him. That wasn't Paul, not really, it was the circumstances. But Jesus, no matter how angry he was, there was no excuse for sticking it to Elizabeth like that. Looking to do maximum damage, my friend? Done.

Eddie Marsh was gone, and Henry likely was dead. After the meeting in Detective Carpenter's office, my gut was telling me Elizabeth should go home. After those telephone calls, I was even more determined. She was getting out of Estes Park if I had to throw her in the back of the Jeep and drive her all the way to Houston.

I went to the kitchen and made a cup of chamomile tea. I took it to the living room and set it on the coffee table, inches away from Elizabeth on the sofa. I held the cup out to her, but she didn't acknowledge me, just stared vacantly at the floor.

"Drink this, honey."

Her eyes moved to the cup, then back to the floor.

"Drink it."

She finally pushed herself up and took the cup from me, wrapping her fingers around it and taking tiny sips. Like someone who'd been ill for a very long time.

"I know what you're going to say."

"It has to be said. More importantly, it has to be done."

"When will we leave?"

"Tomorrow afternoon? Assuming we can get a flight."

She shook her head. "Not tomorrow. The day after."

"Don't do that, honey. Why put it off one more day?"

She took a sip. "I have to go back to Sky Pond."

I groaned. "Elizabeth." I stopped when her eyes filled with tears.

"I have to. I have to say goodbye."

That's when it hit me. A wave of grief, for the loss of Henry, for the suffering of this family that had become my family, pain so raw that I wanted to scream. I beat my fists on my thighs, doubled over and put my face in my hands. Elizabeth pulled me to her and held me so tight I could feel my body trembling against hers.

"I'm sorry," I said.

"Don't be. If you didn't feel this way for Henry, I'd be pissed that I'd picked the wrong godmother."

She got up and went to the fireplace, stacked logs on the grate, struck a long match, and lit the firestarter underneath. She watched the flames take hold, then turned, her back to the fire.

"You don't have to go with me," she said. "I can make the hike alone."

"Like that's happening. No way."

"You said the altitude bothers you."

"That was weeks ago. And it was pretty much bullshit when I said it then."

She gave me a half smile. "You brought hiking boots, didn't you?"

"No. I thought I would wear heels. I want my calves to look good when I'm out on the trail."

I pushed up from the couch and headed to the kitchen.

"Do we have any food around here? If I'm going on a fucking ten-mile hike tomorrow, I have to eat."

"It's only nine miles or so," Elizabeth called after me.

"Great. That makes all the difference in the world."

* * *

"This is reedickallus."

"What?" I said. We were a couple of miles up the trail, stopped for a rest. Elizabeth took a long drink of water, pulled a bag of trail mix from her backpack, and handed it to me.

"When we started this hike in August, Henry said, 'Are you crazy? This is reedickallus.'"

"He was right," I said, handing the bag back to her. "There's a lot of sense in that little body of his."

Elizabeth tossed a handful of trail mix into her mouth, chewed, and swallowed.

"Yeah. Maybe it will help keep him alive." She wiped her hands on her jeans, slung her backpack over her shoulders, and slid down from the boulder we were sitting on. "Ready?"

"Give me one more minute."

She squinted up at me. "You should try to quit smoking."

"I can quit smoking anytime I want."

"Then why don't you?"

"Because I don't want to." I carefully worked my way down from the boulder. It was a sunny day but cold up in the mountains, probably ten degrees or more colder than Estes Park. My nose was running, my legs were aching, and I was silently reciting every curse word I knew to describe my hiking experience that morning.

Elizabeth watched me, shaking her head. "Even in hiking boots, you walk like a beauty queen."

"Now that," I said, "is reedickallus."

We stopped briefly again at Timberline Falls, then pushed on. Up a cliff, no less, past yet another lake, before we finally made it to Sky Pond. We dropped our gear and lay on a flat rock by the water. I reached down to unlace my boots, then thought better of it when I realized what a pain it would be to put them back on. I closed my eyes and dozed for a few minutes. When I opened them again, Elizabeth was standing at the edge of the pond, looking out over its wind-chopped surface. I sat up.

"He was dancing. Slowly, like this." She raised her arms and moved her hips from side to side, dipped the toe of one boot into the water, then the other. "And singing. 'I . . . just want . . . to . . . fly.'" She dropped her arms and stood perfectly still. "He'd stripped down to nothing but his neon-yellow shorts that hung below his belly button to his knees. I wove a crown of shrub branches and set it on his head. His perfect, little buzz-cut head." She wrapped her arms around her waist and hugged herself. "He was so beautiful. So free. It was breathtaking."

I went to stand beside her. She looked at me for a moment, then back out across the water.

Her hair whipped in a gust of wind, and she hugged herself tighter.

"I keep thinking that he's somewhere near, that he can hear me. Is that crazy?"

"Maybe he can hear you. Tell him what you want him to know."

She was silent for a while.

"Do you want some privacy?" I said.

"No." She closed her eyes, took a deep breath and let it out. "Henry. There are no words for how much I love you. Being your mom, and Nick's mom, is the best thing I've ever done. I want you to know that I have to go home for a while. Nick misses you, and he needs me. So I'm saying goodbye. Not goodbye forever. Just for now. I'll see you one day soon."

That was all she said. We stood there together, tears rolling down our cheeks, as clouds blew in and blocked the sun, and the temperature dropped even more. I finally took her hand and pushed up the sleeve of her sweatshirt, held her wrist to my lips, and kissed her Henry tattoo.

"I think he heard that. Now let's go home."

* * *

We stopped in town for dinner, stuffed ourselves on fish tacos and queso, then drove in the dark back to the cabin. I dropped into a chair on the front porch, unlaced my boots, and lit a cigarette. Elizabeth unlocked the door and turned on the lights, then came to sit beside me. Light spilled out onto the porch through the open curtains.

"What time is our flight tomorrow?" she said.

"Five PM. Very civilized."

"Yes. Plenty of time to pack and close up the house. Does Monroe know we're leaving?"

"I haven't told him. I suppose we should let him know."

"Do you want to call him?"

"I can. Unless you'd rather do it."

She looked at me. I looked at my cigarette and took another drag.

"What?" I said.

"Nothing."

I crushed the stub in the ashtray, then slowly got to my feet. "Oh Jesus. I won't be able to walk tomorrow." I moved toward the door.

"You still have Monroe's number, I assume?"

"Yes indeed. On speed dial." I went inside to make the call.

C H A P T E R

44

Elizabeth

THE HIKE WAS beautiful, the aspen trees shimmering yellow-gold and orange. I was drained, not only from the physical exertion but also from the stress of reliving the day Henry was taken, then saying goodbye. Feeling guilty about leaving Estes Park and leaving him. Assuming, of course, that he was still somewhere nearby. I leaned back in the rocking chair and closed my eyes to wait for Alex to return with a report about her conversation with Monroe.

"Hey! Hey!" I heard Alex shouting inside, then a pop that sounded like gunfire.

My eyes flew open and I jumped up, for some strange reason the thought running through my mind that a bear had gotten into the house and Alex had shot it with the rifle she kept by her bed. I threw open the front door, then stopped, confused. For a moment, I didn't understand what I was seeing. Alex on the floor, at the far corner of the room near the hall. Someone coming toward me, grinning, his presence such a shock that at first I didn't know who he was.

"Hello, Elizabeth. It's nice to meet in person again."

Eddie Marsh. With the Remington pointed at me.

I screamed Alex's name and lunged in her direction. Eddie raised the rifle and met me with a blow to the head. Then everything went black.

* * *

I don't know how long I was unconscious. I think it was the throbbing in my head that finally woke me. I tried to rub my forehead, but couldn't move my right hand. My left hand wouldn't move, either. I opened my eyes a crack and saw that I was tied to a dining room chair. Duct-taped, in fact, bound to the arms and legs of the chair by tape wound up my forearms and around my calves from my ankles to my knees. My head slumped to my chest and I lost consciousness again.

I woke to sounds of *clink, scrape, clink. Clink, scrape, clink.* Eddie had positioned the chair I was tied to in front of the sofa, where he sat facing me. Eating a large bowl of ice cream.

"This is delicious," he said. "Salted caramel. I've never heard of salted caramel ice cream. It must have hit the stores while I was in prison. They tend not to serve such delicacies to federal inmates."

"You . . ." My jaw hurt, my tongue felt thick, and I was slurring the words. "You look. . . . You look like you've had your fair share of ice cream since I saw you lass, lass, lass time."

His face clouded. He scraped his spoon across the empty bowl, then licked it. He set the bowl on the coffee table, tossed the spoon into it, and wiped his hands on his thighs. He wore the mustard-yellow and orange plaid shirt I'd first seen him in, dirty jeans, but no stocking cap. He was balding on top, the rest of his hair a wiry, greasy gray.

"That is a very hurtful thing to say, Elizabeth. Very hurtful. But completely in character coming from you."

I looked at Alex, still lying on the floor. I could see the blood from across the room. She wasn't moving.

"Is she dead?"

Eddie peered at me with an exaggerated quizzical expression. "I'm not sure. Let me check."

He got up from the sofa and went to Alex. He stood over her for a moment, then bent down for a closer look. He straightened and kicked her in the ribs.

"Unh." Alex didn't move, but I heard her grunt.

"Nope, she's not dead. But that's a nasty chest wound. She'll probably die."

Eddie kicked her again. "Unh."

"Stop!" I yelled. "Stop!"

Eddie's eyes widened, and he gave a loud, exasperated sigh. "You're the one who wanted to know if she's dead."

He came back and plopped down on the sofa. "If she doesn't die after a while, I'll shoot her again." He tapped the rifle that lay on the side table near him.

"You shouldn't leave guns just lying around the house, Elizabeth. They can end up in the wrong hands."

"You should call an ambulance. It will go better for you if she lives."

"Oh, I don't think so. That would not be wise. Much more prudent for me to be long gone before they find you."

Before they find you. He was planning to kill us both. I fought hard not to scream, not to let Eddie see me panic.

"Where's Henry?" I said.

"Oh, Henry. Henry, Henry, Henry. We'll talk about Henry in a bit. But first, let's talk about you. I want to hear all about how your life has been the past ten years."

I licked my lips and tasted blood.

"There's not much to tell. Just work. Raising a family. Thass about it."

"Oh, come, Elizabeth. Don't be modest. It's unbecoming."

"You find modesty unbecoming?"

"Only because it's not in your nature. It strikes such a false note when you attempt it."

I tried to move. My back ached, like every other part of my body.

"You look uncomfortable, Elizabeth. Are you uncomfortable?"

"A little."

"See? There you go again. The false modesty, the studied understatement. I bet you hurt like hell. You look terrible."

He laced his fingers behind his head and settled into the cushions. "Back to the subject at hand. You've had, in fact, quite a successful career. Where do we even begin?" He looked up at the ceiling, then back at me. "Oh, yes. It really begins, doesn't it, with the case of *Allen Haas v. Transamerica Investment Corporation, Clinton Scruggs and Edward Marsh*. That's the case that launched your career in earnest."

"It was a good case," I said. "A great opportunity for a young lawyer."

"Embarking on the pursuit of truth and justice."

"Something like that."

Eddie snorted. "It wasn't anything like that, Elizabeth, and you know it. Allen Haas is about as far from truth and justice as you can get. He made his fortune cheating customers, colluding with competitors, bribing politicians. Clint and I were just spreading the wealth around."

"Thass one way to look at theft and fraud."

"Thass one way to look at theft and fraud," Eddie mimicked. "Come on, Elizabeth. Admit it. The real expert on theft and fraud was Allen Haas. That and whores—oh my God, the whores. Blow jobs in the back of limousines. Parties in hotel rooms with the girls and his guests and his son-in-law. His son-in-law! How perverted is that?"

"I suppose you were there?"

"Of course, I was there. And Clint, and whoever else Haas was trying to impress at the time."

"I didn't know anything about that. I was just doing what I was asked to do and learning to be a trial lawyer."

"Doing what you were asked to do. Learning to be a trial lawyer. In your prim little Brooks Brothers suits with the silk bow ties and black patent heels. All the while Haas was looking for any opportunity to take off your pantyhose. Bob Simon had his hands full with that guy."

I cringed at the memory—not only of the suits and ties, but of Allen Haas knocking on my hotel room door late at night when we were in trial in Dallas. More than once. I never answered the door, never responded to the drunken calls to let him in. And I never said a word about it to him or to Bob Simon. I knew that if I complained, my job was the only thing that would suffer.

"So. You got a boost to your career and I got federal prison."

"You seem to have forgotten that it was the federal prosecutors who sent you to prison, not me."

"In large part because of your good work."

My cell phone was ringing. I looked at my backpack, still where I had dropped it inside the front door. The phone rang eight or nine times, then stopped.

Eddie wagged a finger at me. "You won't be taking any calls this evening, Elizabeth." He pushed himself up off the couch and stretched, scratched the exposed belly that hung over his belt only a few inches from me. I recoiled, a tiny movement, but he saw it. Anger flashed across his face. He picked up the ice cream bowl, and I thought for a moment that he might hurl it across the room or hit me with it. But he carried it to the kitchen, then came back with a glass in one hand and a bottle of Jack Daniels in the other. He sat down again, and poured himself a drink.

"I took the liberty of bringing a beverage." He took a sip, savoring it, closed his eyes and sighed. "You cannot imagine how good this tastes." He opened his eyes. "But wait—I'm wrong about that. You're a whiskey aficionado as well. A bit too much of one in your early years as a lawyer, as I recall from research Clint and I did on your trial team."

"You seem to know a lot about me," I said. "Why are you even interested? Why me? I was the most junior lawyer on Haas's team. I was a nobody compared to Bob Simon and the other partners on the case."

He shook his head and took another drink.

"I don't know, Elizabeth. I have asked myself that very question. Why, in all those long, boring hours, days, weeks, years in prison, did I see your face so often? Why do I hate you so much?"

"Because I'm a woman. You think I'm weak, and cowards prey on the weak. How did it make you feel when you grabbed a six-year-old? Big? Powerful for the first time in your life?"

Anger flashed across his face again, then he composed himself. "I told you, we're not going to talk about Henry right now." He emptied his glass and poured another.

"It's not because you're a woman, Elizabeth. I'm very enlightened when it comes to gender equality. No, I think what has bothered me all these years is that you were so . . . sanctimonious. So satisfied every time the knife sank a little deeper into Clint and me. The raised eyebrows, the curled lip, the amused wink at your friend over there whenever she came to watch the trial. That victorious little sneer you threw my way when the jury came back with the verdict. I saw that sneer over and over again in my mind, and thought, *What does she know about anything? What does she know about what it takes to survive? What a lawyer sometimes is forced to do?*"

"I was green," I said. "I have since learned to keep my emotions more in check."

"Good for you. I, however, am quite the opposite. I've decided that the older I get, the more I'm going to let my emotions show. Put my feelings out there for the world to see. It's much healthier."

He stood and bent over me, his face close to mine. He had the skunky smell of someone who hadn't showered in a while and that, combined with whiskey, stale breath, and ice cream almost made me gag.

"Do you know what I'm feeling right now, Elizabeth?"

"No, I don't, Eddie."

"I'm feeling angry. Very, very angry."

He closed his fists and hit me in the left jaw, then as my head whipped from the blow, hit me on the right. Stars burst in my brain, cascading in sprays of light and color. I watched as each array brought a fresh wave of pain. I caught a faint sound, fading in and out as if carried on a breeze. Singing. Henry singing. I told the stars to stop. I wanted to hear Henry sing. There were more pops of light, then they were gone. The song went with them.

I opened my eyes. Eddie was sitting on the sofa again, rubbing his knuckles.

"See," he said. "I feel much better now."

There was something I wanted to ask Eddie, but for a moment I couldn't remember what it was. Then it came to me. My face ached with every syllable. "You're angry at me. Why not kill me? Why take Henry?"

He sighed and looked at his watch.

"Wow. It's getting late. Where did the time go?" He took a shot of whiskey, from the bottle this time. "I suppose we can talk about Henry now."

He leaned forward, rested his elbows on his knees.

"The only thing I had planned when I got out of prison was to see you. For what purpose, I wasn't sure. Then I read about your Alaska case. The fifty-million-dollar verdict, the quotes from you—that it was a difficult, technical case, and you were gratified that the jury hung in there for weeks and ultimately made the right decision. And I realized, Elizabeth English hasn't learned a thing. Ten years later, and she's still as smug and sanctimonious as I remembered."

"So you wanted to teach me a lesson."

"I suppose, of some sort. I wanted to do something. I just wasn't sure what."

"How did you find us? In Estes Park?"

He examined his hands, sucked a drop of blood from one of his knuckles.

"Ouch," he said. "That stings." He peered up at me, apparently inspecting the damage he'd done, then chuckled.

"How did I find you here? Once again, that's your fault, Elizabeth. You talked about this place—that your father had built it and you'd spent summers here growing up."

"I don't remember . . . I didn't discuss it with you."

"Of course you didn't discuss it with me. You were chatting with someone during a break in a deposition—a legal assistant, maybe? Chatting, chatting, chatting like I wasn't even in the room, about escaping the Houston heat, the cool nights in the mountains. As if going to their summer place in Colorado was just what everyone did."

He jumped up and I winced, afraid that he would hit me again. He went to the fireplace, picked up an iron poker, and paced back and forth.

"I'm sure this comes as a surprise to you, Elizabeth, but most people don't grow up with happy kids and moms and dads piling into the family station wagon for a summer in the mountains. They grow up in shitty two-bedroom houses with vinyl siding and no air conditioning, sweating their little asses off and unable to sleep in the summer heat."

He pointed the poker at me, and I thought I was in for a diatribe about his miserable childhood or whatever it was he intended to blame for the despicable human being he'd become. But he stopped.

"I digress." He came back to the sofa, bringing the poker with him.

"So. It was easy to conclude that your return to Houston from the Alaska trial would be followed shortly by a vacation in Estes Park before the kiddos went back to school. And after ten years in prison, I decided that I deserved a vacation myself. What better way to spend it than in the mountains with the family English? I rented a cabin and looked you up in the property records and waited for you to arrive."

"You were here? From the day we got here?"

He grinned. "From the very first day. I was at the big slide, the go-karts, the miniature golf. The movies, the pizza place, the hikes—not that I did any hiking myself, of course. I don't hike." He grinned wider. "The cozy evenings around the fireplace, roasting marshmallows for s'mores. You really should close the curtains. You don't know who's out there looking in."

It was hard to comprehend. And sickening. That Eddie Marsh had watched our family in our most intimate, joyful moments. I tried to think back on those days together, whether I might have seen him in the crowds. My mind was foggy, but I didn't think so. No. I had been focused on Nick and Henry.

"You still haven't answered my question," I said. "Why Henry? Why not me?"

He tapped the poker on the floor, a thoughtful expression on his face. *Tap, tap*, pause. *Tap, tap*, pause. I shrank back in the chair, expecting the poker to come swinging unannounced in my direction.

"Henry was an opportunity," he finally said. "I was parked close to the trailhead. It was raining and dark, and I was coming to the realization that you and Paul are really very irresponsible parents. Up on that trail in a storm, anything could have happened. I was relieved when Nick and Henry ran into the parking lot and took cover under the Jeep. I kept thinking that you and Paul would arrive shortly afterward, but the minutes ticked by and ticked by and then here comes Henry again, waving a flashlight and running to the toilet. He opened the door slowly and peeked inside—I think he was afraid of what might be in there. Poor little boy. No parents in sight to take him to the bathroom. He was very, very brave. He went in alone."

I gasped, sobs rising in my throat.

"Henry in there all by himself. I got out of my truck and opened the door to the toilet—that's another of your failings as a parent, Elizabeth. You should tell your sons to lock the bathroom door. So there he was, his little legs hanging off the seat, shorts down around his hiking boots. Singing. To keep himself company, I suppose."

Eddie folded his hands over the handle of the poker, rested his chin on top, and watched me.

"He looked relieved at first when I opened the door. I'm sure he thought it was Nick or one of his missing-in-action parents. But no. It was me. He was a little shocked, a little terrified, I suppose. I told him not to be scared. That his dad and mom had sent me to get him. And then—you'd be proud of him, Elizabeth. He did something that restored my faith in you as a mother. Not completely, understand, but a bit."

Eddie stopped, looking at me expectantly.

"Aren't you going to ask me what he did?"

I didn't know if I could bear to hear it. "What? What did he do?"

Eddie leaned toward me, paused for dramatic effect, then spoke in a loud whisper. "He said . . . 'What's the safe word?'"

Eddie reared back and laughed, then wiped his eyes. "Oh, God, it was comical. I said, 'The safe word? I forgot the safe word. Tell me what it is again?' And Henry said, 'No, I can't tell you, and if you don't know the safe word, I'm not going anywhere.'" Eddie laughed again. "I thought, you plucky little bastard. The safe word." He shook his head. "The safe word."

He pushed up from the sofa with the poker and tapped across the room. He stood over Alex for a moment, then jabbed her with it. There was no response.

"She's not quite dead yet. Still cooking." He walked back toward me.

"The problem with a safe word, Elizabeth, is that it creates a dilemma for the individual who doesn't know it. Do I try to guess what it is? Do I turn around and leave? I really had no time to decide."

"What did you do, you son of a bitch?"

"I just whacked him up one side of the head." He shifted the poker to his left hand and demonstrated with his right. "Bam! Knocked him out cold. Then I picked him up and carried him to the truck, his little pecker flapping in the wind. I threw him in and away we went."

For the first time in my life, I wanted to kill someone. I wanted a gun in my hands, and if I'd had one, I would have pulled the trigger. No hesitation. I knew I would never get the opportunity because Eddie was going to kill me, but I wanted him dead, hoped that Paul or Monroe or Carpenter would hunt him down and cut him to pieces.

"Oh," he said, as if he'd just thought of something else. "I almost forgot. Nick—under the Jeep. I had a moment's hesitation. What to do about Nick? But then I thought, there's really no time, so I just drove away. And you know the best part about that?"

I didn't answer.

"Elizabeth?"

He stood over me with the poker, swung it over his head and brought it down on my left wrist. The pain from the blow and bones cracking knocked the wind out of me, and I went under again. I woke to Eddie pulling me up by my hair and slapping me gently on both cheeks.

"Let's have some audience participation here, Elizabeth. It helps with the story."

My head dropped when he let go of my hair. He pulled me by the hair again, and this time I was able to hold it up, bobbing from side to side.

"So. Where was I? Oh, yes. Nick. Under the Jeep. I drove away. Do you know the best part about that, Elizabeth?"

This was my cue. "What's . . . What's the best part?"

"Nick will live with the guilt of that moment for the rest of his life."

He sat on the sofa with a satisfied smile, savoring the moment. "Nick will never forgive himself. He'll believe it was his fault. It will eat him up and eat him up. And finally, it will kill him."

I didn't say anything in response. Because on that point, only on that one, Eddie was right.

"Could I have a drink of water?" I finally said.

"Are you thirsty?"

"Yes."

"How about a drink of Jack?"

"I don't drink alcohol."

"There you go, all sanctimonious again. Lying, sanctimonious bitch. You drink alcohol."

He picked up the bottle of Jack Daniels, stood over me, and held it to my lips. I clamped my mouth shut and shook my head again.

"Now, what happened before when you refused to cooperate, Elizabeth? I would hate to break your teeth with the poker. Your parents spent a significant amount on orthodontia in your childhood, it appears."

I opened my mouth slightly. He tipped my head back and poured whiskey down my throat until I choked. He let go and pulled the bottle away. I bent forward, coughed and retched, the whiskey rising, and it was all I could do not to vomit. I took several deep breaths through my nose, then sat up straight.

"The Alaska plates? Stolen?"

"Of course they were stolen. But that's of no consequence. They were sent to me, Elizabeth. Like a burning bush, or a rainbow, a sign, telling me what I needed to do."

"I don't know what you're talking about."

"I was sitting in a shitty little diner in Tulsa, having a shitty dinner, looking out the window at the shitty motel across the street. And I saw them. Alaska plates on a car parked outside Room 6. The day after I'd read about your victory. Who would have believed that? Alaska plates in Tulsa. So I went back late that night and took them."

"Alaska plates in Tulsa aren't that rare," I said. "Or in Houston. People in the oil business move around."

Eddie sighed. "You're so shallow, Elizabeth. You have so little imagination."

"The poncho. Dolphie the dolphin. You did those."

Eddie slapped his thigh. "Brilliant, weren't they? Especially the dolphin. I was sorry I couldn't stick around to watch you find the dolphin grave, but oh God, I can imagine how upset you were. Priceless."

"Did Henry tell you where to find the spare key?"

"In the fake rock?" Eddie shook his head. "I wasn't sure I could find it. Henry showed me where it was."

For a moment, I couldn't breathe. I stared at him, my mouth open.

"Is something wrong, Elizabeth?"

"Henry. . . . Henry showed you? Henry was here?"

"Waa, waa, waa." Eddie pursed his lips and rubbed his eyes, a grotesque imitation of an upset child. "He was so sad. He kept asking if he could stay, and I told him no, his mommy and daddy were gone and there was nobody here to take care of him. He was happy when I let him take Dolphie, but then all sad again when we had to take him away and bury him. I told him Dolphie was dead and he kept bawling and saying, 'He's not dead, he's not dead.'"

The whiskey rose in my throat again, and this time there was no holding it back. I leaned over and vomited between my knees. Eddie jumped up and moved to the far end of the sofa.

"Gross, Elizabeth. What a mess. You almost got some on my shoes."

I spat several times, then sat up.

"Do not expect to share my Jack Daniels after that."

I struggled against the duct tape. "Fuck your Jack Daniels. And fuck you."

Eddie clucked his tongue. "Such language. Now I know where Henry got his foul mouth."

"Where is he? Did you hurt him?"

"Hurt him? Hurt him? You mean did I torture him or molest him like some people would do to a child found alone in a public bathroom? No. You were very fortunate in the selection of Henry's kidnapper. I am not a monster."

"Then where is he?"

"God, Elizabeth, you're so impatient. We'll get to that, but I do want you to know that I treated him well. I had to lock him in the closet sometimes when I went to town, use a little duct tape or rope when necessary. He was a bit of a fighter at first, but we eventually got along fine. I told him every day that you and his father were happy he was gone, and that no one was looking for him because they hoped he would never come back. That he was lucky not to have you as a mother anymore because you're a bad person. And that if he tried to get away I would kill you, which I probably would do anyway because you're such a bad person. Sometimes he would cry, but I let him eat all the Froot Loops and Lucky Charms he wanted and watch TV all day."

"Henry would never believe that. I looked for him every day. I looked for you. I *saw* you. Outside Lester's General Store."

"I know. I saw *you*. Driving down the highway, then pulling over to turn around. You really should get that taillight on the Jeep fixed. You're more clever than that. So clever—tell me how you found Erwin's cabin. I thought, surely she won't find me here, but by God you did."

"It was a hunch. Henry was there, wasn't he?"

"A hunch. Oh yes, he was there. Listening to you rattling the windows and doors, wanting his mommy when he heard you and your friend talking. I know you saw the No Trespassing signs. Do you not have any respect for property rights and the privacy of others? I would have expected better from an officer of the court, but obviously you don't think the rules apply to you."

Eddie looked at his watch. "We're running out of time." He stood, then paced around the room. Behind the sofa, behind my chair, over to Alex, the span of the fireplace then back again.

"I had just stocked up on cereal again. I knew I had to make some decisions soon, but I wasn't quite ready. I needed another week, maybe two. But no, there goes Elizabeth, setting in motion the chain of events that led to where we find ourselves today. This is where we end up when you act rashly on a hunch."

He paced and paced.

"I might have thought of a solution that we all could have lived with. But I didn't have time. Because of you, I didn't have time."

He passed behind the sofa again, picked up the rifle from the side table. He waved it at me, then resumed his pacing.

"I didn't have time."

"You said . . . You said you didn't hurt him."

He stopped by the fireplace and turned to face me. "I didn't hurt him. I mean, okay, I killed him. But until then, until yesterday morning, all those weeks I didn't hurt him."

"No," I whispered. "No no no no no."

"I felt kind of bad about it. But what else could I do on short notice? I told him we were going to see you, that we were going up a mountain trail and you were going to meet us there for a picnic. We went up the mountain and stood at the edge of a cliff looking out over the town. Henry said, 'Where's my mommy?' I told him you'd decided not to come after all, that you didn't want to have a picnic with Henry. And you know what that little bastard said?"

Eddie giggled. "He said, 'You're a dirty rotten liar. I never believed anything you said, you fucking fucker.'" He giggled again. "See what I mean about the language? That's unacceptable, Elizabeth. What six-year-old says that kind of thing?"

I struggled to get the words out. "What . . . did . . . you . . . do?"

"Do? What did I do? I pushed that foul-mouthed little bastard off the cliff. That's what I did."

"No." It wasn't a whisper this time. It was a scream. And once I started to scream, I couldn't stop. I screamed and screamed and screamed. Eddie tucked the rifle under one arm and put his hands over his ears. He paced while I screamed, muttering, "Shut up, shut up, shut up, shut up." He finally paused beside me, held the rifle to my head and yelled.

"Shut up, Elizabeth, shut up, Elizabeth, shut up, shut up, shut up."

That's when the front window exploded.

C H A P T E R

45

Monroe

I WAS LONESOME THAT night. Missing my Maggie and, truth be told, thinking about Alexis LaDay going back to Houston one day soon and wishing she would stay. Which was crazy, I knew. I cracked open a beer and went out on the porch. I leaned against the porch rail, listened to the river and the wind whistling down the canyon, a sound that didn't do much to cheer me up. I pulled out my cell phone and called my daughter.

"Hey, Dad."

"Hey, pumpkin. What are you up to?"

"Trying to get your ornery grandson to take a bath. He prefers running up and down the hall buck naked."

"How's the baby?"

"She's great. Sitting in the tub with a flotilla of ships and ducks. Which is why I can't go capture her brother."

I heard the noises in the background. The baby splashing and babbling, Petey's whoops as he ran past the bathroom door.

"I won't keep you, then."

"Dad?"

"Yeah?"

"You okay? You sound kind of down."

"No, no. Everything's fine. Great, in fact. I'm sitting out on the porch looking at the stars."

"You really should get a dog."

"Yeah. I might just do that."

More shouts from Petey and squeals from the baby.

"Oh, for God's sake."

"What is it?" I said.

"Petey just pooped in the hall. Squatted down and dropped a turd right outside the bathroom door."

I had to laugh. "Sounds like something his mother would have done at that age."

"Oh no, don't lay this off on me." She yelled away from the phone. "Petey, get in here right now!"

"I'll let you go. You have your hands full."

"Okay. I'll call you later. Or maybe tomorrow." She paused. "Dad?"

"Yeah?"

"Get a dog."

I hung up the phone and finished my beer, then went inside. I heated up leftover stew and sat down to eat in front of the TV, scrolling through the channels to see if anything was worth watching. I'd finished the stew and was about to turn the TV off when my phone rang. I pulled it out of my shirt pocket, expecting that it was my daughter again. My stomach did a little jump when I saw who the caller was. Alexis. I flipped open the phone.

"Hello?"

No response.

"Hello?"

I heard static. Indistinguishable voices in the background. Then the call ended.

I waited a few minutes for Alex to call back. She didn't. I pulled up her number and dialed. I don't know why I was so damn nervous.

The call went straight to voice mail. That Georgia drawl, honey sweet but very professional. "This is Alexis LaDay. I'm not available to take your call. Please leave a message."

I cleared my throat. "Uh . . . Alexis . . . Alex. This is Monroe. I saw that you called. If you need to reach me, please call again." I recited the first few digits of my phone number, then cut myself off. "Oh, yeah. I guess you have that number. Call me if I can be of assistance."

I waited another minute or two, then carried my dishes to the kitchen. I washed the bowl and spoon in the sink and stored what was left of the stew in the refrigerator. I lit the burner under the coffee pot and brought the remains of the morning's brew to a boil. I drank it leaning against the counter, cup in one hand, phone in the other.

Okay, I thought. *She called me by mistake. If she really wanted to talk, she would have called after she got my message.* I drank a little more coffee and poured the rest down the drain, took a deep breath and dialed Alex's number again. Straight to voice mail. I listened to her greeting, then hung up without leaving another message.

I went to the living room and pushed back in my easy chair. I shuffled through the stack of reading materials on the table beside me, magazines and travel brochures, a book on Lewis and Clark that I'd checked out of the library a while ago. I looked at the return date and saw that it was seriously overdue. I made a mental note to start reading it tomorrow, then settled on a *New York Times* crossword puzzle. A Saturday puzzle. The harder the better.

I scratched at the puzzle. The minutes ticked by. Still no call from Alex. I put down my pen, stumped for the moment, and rubbed my eyes. I took out my phone, put it back in my pocket, then pulled it out again and called Elizabeth.

Her voice mail picked up after eight or nine rings.

"Elizabeth, this is Monroe. I thought I would check in with you about what your plans are, whether you're thinking you'll go back to Houston. And to be sure I have all your contact information. I don't have your office and home numbers. Just your cell. So, if you have a minute, please call me."

I went back to the crossword puzzle but couldn't concentrate. I tossed it aside, grabbed my keys and jacket, and headed out the door for a drive.

* * *

I've spent a lot of hours in my Bronco over the years, driving with no particular destination in mind, watching the road and clearing my head. I didn't have any particular destination in mind that evening, either, but I guess it's no surprise that I ended up on Devil's Gulch Road. I slowed as I passed the English place. The gate was closed, lights on at the house. I thought about calling Elizabeth again, maybe Alex, then thought better of it. If they wanted to talk to me, they'd call. I picked up a little speed, then tapped on the brakes.

A truck was parked on the other side of the road. Dark-colored, no lights, facing my direction. I passed it at a crawl. No one in it, apparently. I went a couple hundred yards farther, then killed the lights on the Bronco and made a U-turn, pulled off the road, and came to a stop behind the truck. I found my flashlight under the seat, shut the door quietly behind me, and took a look around.

I went to the driver's door first and knocked on the window to identify myself if there happened to be someone inside. No response. I shined the flashlight into the cab. It was littered with candy wrappers, a half-eaten burger, empty soda cans, and an open box of Froot Loops whose contents were scattered across the seat. A bed roll and duffle bag were dumped on the floor on the passenger side. I tried the driver's door. It was locked. I stepped to the back of the truck, aimed the flashlight at the license plate, and my heart began to beat a little faster. Not Alaska plates. Oklahoma.

I pulled out my phone and found Carpenter's cell number. It appeared, however, that no one was answering their damn phone that evening. I hung up and dialed the Estes Park police station. I told the dispatcher who I was and asked him to run the plates for me, then call me back. I went to the Bronco, strapped on the pistol and holster I kept in the glove compartment, and unlocked my rifle from the rack. I put my phone on silent and walked down the road to the Englishes' drive.

The gate was locked. I propped the rifle on the other side of the fence, climbed up and over. My boots would make too much noise walking on the gravel driveway, so I skirted wide to the west side of the property, making my way past trees and boulders and grateful for the moonlight. I was halfway to the house when my phone buzzed.

"Yeah?" I said quietly.

"Officer Torres, Estes Park police. I have the information on those plates, Monroe."

"Go ahead."

"The truck is registered to a Leona Marsh of Tulsa. You need the address?"

"No."

I had that address, courtesy of the warden at the Texarkana unit. Eddie Marsh's mother.

"Officer Torres?"

"Yes?"

"Can you call me back in exactly three minutes? I may need your assistance with something else."

"Sure thing."

I put the phone in my pocket, held the rifle by my side, and stepped closer to the house, close enough that I could see into the living room but hopefully not be seen by those inside.

Someone, a woman, was seated in a chair. I couldn't tell at first whether it was Alex or Elizabeth—she was bent forward, head between her knees. She finally raised her head. Elizabeth. When she struggled to get up, I saw that she was bound to the chair. She turned her head and said something. I took a few more steps and saw him. Eddie Marsh. Sitting at the far end of the sofa. Alex was nowhere in sight.

I walked away from the house as my phone began to buzz. I parked myself behind a boulder and answered.

"Monroe."

"Officer Torres here."

"Officer, I need you to connect me with Detective Carpenter."

"Detective Carpenter is off duty, sir. Can someone else help you?"

I'd met Officer Torres once or twice. He was new to the force, and I was probably old enough to be his father.

"No, Officer Torres. No one else can help me. This is an emergency. Find Carpenter now and put him on the goddamn phone."

I waited for what seemed like an eternity, then Carpenter came on the line.

"This better be good, Monroe. The kids are having dinner with their grandparents and the wife and I are enjoying a little alone time, if you know what I mean."

"Eddie Marsh has Elizabeth. I don't know where Alex is, but it looks like this situation may blow any minute."

"Shit. Where?"

"At the English place."

"I'm on my way."

"Bring backup. And an ambulance. But come quiet, no sirens, no lights. Stop before you get to the gate and call me."

"Got it." He hung up.

I picked up my rifle and inched back toward the house. Eddie was pacing now, circling the room, flapping his arms and talking. He paused at the fireplace, then resumed the pacing, went around the back of the sofa and picked up something from the table. Elizabeth's Remington. He waved it at Elizabeth, then moved away from her. I stepped closer to the house, almost to the front porch. Elizabeth began to scream. She screamed and screamed, like someone possessed, like she couldn't stop if she wanted to. I kept my eyes on Eddie. He put his hands over his ears, still holding the gun, lips moving and shaking his head. I raised my rifle when he came in Elizabeth's direction. I heard him yell over her screams, "Shut up, Elizabeth, shut up, Elizabeth, shut up, shut up, shut up." He held the barrel to her forehead.

I fired.

* * *

The front window exploded in a shower of glass shards. Eddie Marsh went down.

I jumped up onto the porch and kicked open the front door, rifle pointed to the floor at Eddie. Elizabeth looked up at me, then at him. He'd beat her up pretty bad. Her face was cut, swollen and bruised, and white underneath like she was going into shock.

Eddie was lying on his back in a pool of blood and vomit. I squatted beside him, felt for a pulse. Faint but still there.

"Alex," Elizabeth said. "Help Alex. There." She nodded at the corner of the room, and I saw Alex for the first time, crumpled on the floor, halfway into the hall.

"Oh, Jesus," I said, rushing to her and falling to my knees. There was blood everywhere, a gaping wound under her shoulder. I pulled off my jacket and folded it on her chest, pushing down with one hand while I called Carpenter with the other.

"We're almost there," he said.

"Come hard. Marsh is down and Alex is dying. The gate's locked, but if you hit it full speed, it'll give."

A few seconds later I heard the sirens, a crash of wood and iron at the gate, tires spitting gravel as they came up the drive.

"Here," I yelled as Carpenter burst through the door, two uniforms behind him, then seconds later paramedics with a gurney. One of the medics paused at the sight of Eddie, but I yelled, "No! That son of a bitch can wait." I stepped back and let them work, putting compression on Alex's wound, inserting an IV, then carefully lifting her onto the gurney and rolling her out the door. I followed them to the ambulance, watched as it sped down the drive and turned onto Devil's Gulch Road. I heard the siren of a second ambulance on its way for Eddie as I walked back into the house.

The two uniforms were tending to him. Carpenter wielded a pair of scissors, carefully cutting away the duct tape binding Elizabeth.

"Eddie puke on himself when he got shot?" Carpenter said.

"No," Elizabeth said. "Sorry. That was me."

"No reason to be sorry."

"Monroe," she said when she saw me come in. "We have to find Henry. He's been alive the whole time. Eddie pushed him off a cliff. He could still be alive."

Carpenter pulled at the duct tape around her left hand. She howled.

"Oh, man," Carpenter said. "That wrist is broken."

"Eddie's good with a poker," she said. "When his opponent can't fight back." Freed now from the chair, she stood, left arm dangling awkwardly, unsteady for a moment on her feet. She stepped over to Eddie before any of us could stop her and kicked him in the ribs.

"You piece of shit!" she screamed. "Where's Henry?" She kicked him again. "Where's Henry?"

"What the hell?" This from one of the second set of paramedics, who had just arrived.

Carpenter grabbed Elizabeth from behind, trying to avoid her left hand. She kicked and struggled as he pulled her away from Eddie.

"Elizabeth," I said. "If he dies, he can't tell us where Henry is."

She stopped kicking but Carpenter still held her around the waist. We all watched the medics work on Eddie, hoist him onto a gurney, and push him out the door.

"Let's go," I said to Elizabeth. "We'll ride with Carpenter."

"Where?"

"To the hospital. To get that wrist treated."

"No. We have to look for Henry."

I grabbed her good arm. "Get in the damn car. You can fill us in on the way."

I led her to Carpenter's car, helped her in the back then climbed in beside her. Carpenter drove, the squad cars following.

"Pretty fortunate you showing up like that, Monroe," Carpenter said.

"Yeah. Alex accidentally dialed my number. When I couldn't roust either her or Elizabeth, I drove by for a look."

"It wasn't an accident," Elizabeth said. "She was calling you. Eddie must have shot her just as she dialed your number."

"Why was she calling me?"

"To say goodbye."

All of a sudden, I didn't think I'd be able to get any words out in response. I swallowed hard a couple of times, and we rode in silence for a while. We were halfway to the medical center when Torres's voice came over the radio.

"Detective Carpenter, I have an update for you on the shooting victim." Elizabeth and I leaned forward to hear the report.

"Go ahead."

"Alexis LaDay has been life flighted to Denver. Surgical team standing by."

Carpenter didn't ask about her condition. We knew.

"Any report on Eddie Marsh?"

"Eddie Marsh did not survive. He died in the ambulance."

"Oh, God," Elizabeth said. She slumped back in her seat, pressed her swollen cheek against the cold glass, and gazed out the window.

"I'm glad he's dead. But how will we find Henry in time?"

Carpenter met my eyes in the rearview mirror, and I knew his opinion was the same as mine. There was no way in hell we would find Henry English in time.

* * *

Carpenter and I stayed with Elizabeth in the emergency room while she waited for the x-ray results. She sat on the edge of the examining table, left arm temporarily immobilized, an IV drip in her right, and gave us the whole account of Eddie ambushing Alex and the things he'd said to Elizabeth.

"This story of throwing Henry off a cliff could be bullshit," Carpenter said. "But let's assume it's true. We have to start somewhere. The cadaver dogs got nothing at the Erwin place."

Elizabeth swayed. I jumped up and grabbed her.

"Here," I said. "Lie back."

I eased her down on the table and covered her with a blanket. She was shaking.

I pushed the call button and when the nurse appeared, asked for more heated blankets. Elizabeth stared at the ceiling, silent tears sliding down her temples. The nurse came back with blankets and tucked them around her.

"You let me know if you need anything else," she said, patting Elizabeth. The door slowly swished closed behind her.

"Eddie said he and Henry stood at the edge of the cliff and looked out over the town. There are hundreds of places on lots of different trails that match that description," I said.

"He didn't hike there," Elizabeth said.

"What?"

"He didn't hike there. He said he never hiked. I believe that. He was in terrible shape. And lazy."

"So it had to be somewhere accessible by truck," Carpenter said. "But remote enough that he could take Henry there without being seen." He stopped and looked at me.

"The four-wheeler," I said. "At Erwin's place. There was mud on the tires."

Elizabeth struggled with the blankets and pushed up onto her right elbow.

"That's it," she said. "He took Henry somewhere on the four-wheeler. That narrows it down, doesn't it? ATVs aren't allowed in Rocky Mountain National Park. He didn't take Henry to the park."

Carpenter and I exchanged another glance. If Eddie took Henry somewhere on Erwin's four-wheeler, there still were any number of places he could have gone. Even if Henry had survived the fall, his injuries and the elements would finish him off. And an equally likely scenario was that Eddie killed Henry at Erwin's place, then tossed the body somewhere we'd never find it.

"Yeah," I said. "That narrows it down." I turned to Carpenter. "How about you take me to get my Bronco, then we'll meet at your office to map out the search. We can send teams out at first light."

"Good," Carpenter said. "I'll call in a tow for Eddie's truck and have someone go through it. See if there's anything that might tell us where he took Henry."

Elizabeth kicked at the blankets.

"I'm going with you," she said. "Get the nurse. Tell her to take this thing out of my arm."

I pressed the call button. There was a knock at the door shortly as the nurse pushed it open.

"May I help you?"

"Just wanted to let you know Detective Carpenter and I are leaving now. We want you to keep good watch over Mrs. English."

Elizabeth kicked at the blankets again. "Fuck you, Monroe. Fuck you."

The nurse's eyes widened. "I'll take good care of her."

I nodded to Elizabeth. "We'll be in touch." Carpenter and I left in a hurry.

* * *

I rubbed my eyes and took another drink of lukewarm coffee. It was almost three in the morning. Carpenter and I had been poring over motor vehicle use maps for the Canyon Lakes Ranger District and trail maps for Rocky, discussing where we would send the search teams to look first. The more we discussed the possibilities, the more hopeless it seemed.

Carpenter looked up from the maps, said, "What the hell."

It was Elizabeth. Arm still in the temporary sling, looking even worse than when we'd last seen her.

"It was taking too long," she said. "And in case you've ever wondered, it is possible to get a cab in Estes Park in the middle of the night."

I pulled out a chair. She sat down and bent over the maps.

"He could have driven his truck into the park," I said. "But I don't think he would risk it. Too much of a chance that he'd be recognized."

"There are ATV trails all over the area south of Erwin's cabin," Carpenter said. "Lots of places he could have dumped the body if he killed Henry at the cabin. I think we should concentrate on that area."

Elizabeth looked up in shock.

"Sorry," Carpenter said. "You wanted in on this."

"I think he did exactly what he said he'd done," she said.

"Why would he make up that story about a picnic and take Henry up in the mountains to throw him off a cliff? Why not just kill him in the woods somewhere and hide the body where we'd never find it?" Carpenter said.

"I don't know—maybe he hadn't made up his mind he was going to kill Henry. Or he did it that way for dramatic effect when he told me."

"Seems like a chickenshit way to kill someone."

"That's probably the best explanation for it."

She turned back to the map. Pointed. "Here. Pole Hill Road."

It was east of Estes Park in Roosevelt National Forest.

"It has cliffs accessible by four-wheeler and a view of the town," she said. "He could go up there in the early morning on a weekday without anyone seeing him."

We contacted the Larimer County Sheriff's office and the search and rescue groups that had looked for Henry before. Their personnel started arriving before dawn. Hernandez came in to touch base in case we decided to resume the search in the park.

"Jesus," Hernandez said when he saw me. "You look like you had a rough night."

I glanced down at the dried blood on my shirt and jeans.

"Not as rough as Alex's," I said.

By six AM we had dispatched teams with four-wheelers and dogs on the ground to Pole Hill Road and locations south of the Erwin place. Helicopters were on the way. Elizabeth slumped back from the conference table, put her feet up on a chair, and closed her eyes. I didn't know how she was still conscious.

"You want a cot?" Carpenter said. "I can have one set up for you."

"No," she said. "I can't sleep."

"I'd be grateful if you could find us some breakfast," I said. "Eggs, bacon, maybe biscuits. It's gonna be a long day."

"Right you are."

Elizabeth closed her eyes, and despite what she'd said, dozed off for a little while. She woke to Torres pulling Styrofoam containers out of a bag and the smell of fresh coffee. I stood and stretched, then set food out for Elizabeth.

"How you doing?" I said.

"Fine." She sat up straight, wincing, adjusted the sling. "I thought of another possibility."

"What's that?"

"What if Eddie took Henry up in the mountains intending to kill him, but couldn't do it? And just left him there to find his way back? That's possible, isn't it?"

She looked up at me.

"Sure," I said. "It's possible."

She nodded. "I think so." Then she picked up a fork and started on her eggs.

I sat down again to eat with her, and Carpenter came into the room.

"We got an update on Alex," he said. "She made it through surgery. She lost a lot of blood, but she's hanging on."

"Thank God," Elizabeth said.

I put down my fork and wiped my mouth with my napkin.

"Excuse me a minute." I went to the men's room, leaned against the sink, and took a few deep breaths. I turned on the faucet, splashed cold water on my face, then turned on the hot and washed my hands. I went back to the conference room, wiping my face with a paper towel.

"You okay?" Carpenter said.

"Yeah." I dug into the eggs and bacon.

We finished breakfast then went to the communications room and listened to periodic reports from the teams throughout the morning.

The day dragged on with no news. Except for trips to the ladies' room, Elizabeth refused to budge. Carpenter and I took turns pacing the hall, with occasional excursions outside for fresh air, watching the daylight hours tick away and the temperature fall. The weather report was for storms overnight, with possible sleet and snow at higher elevations. I stood in the parking lot looking at the sun dropping in the sky, my heart sinking a little more with each passing minute.

"Monroe," Carpenter yelled as he emerged from the doorway, Elizabeth close behind him. "My car. We've got something."

I broke into a run. "Where?"

"The canyon below Pole Hill Road."

I helped Elizabeth into the back seat and buckled her in, then sat up front with Carpenter. He hit his lights, and we headed east on Highway 36 across Lake Estes. The radio squawked, and Torres put the helicopter pilot through, shouting to be heard above the noise of the chopper.

"We went over this area half a dozen times," the pilot said. "Nothing. Then one of our crew thought he saw a flash of yellow. We've made a couple more passes but haven't been able to find it again."

"Keep looking," I said. "Henry English was wearing neon-yellow shorts when he disappeared."

Carpenter sped up the highway, braked, and turned left. It was a mile or so up a gravel road to the entrance for Pole Hill.

"I told Torres to have a couple of the four-wheeler crews meet us at the parking area," Carpenter said.

They were waiting for us. We hopped on, Elizabeth wedged between me and the driver of one of the vehicles.

"Go slow," I said. "Mrs. English is injured."

"No," she told the driver. "You get us there as fast as you can."

It was a short, wild ride to where the rest of the ground search team were clustered at the side of the road, radios in hand and overlooking a steep drop to the canyon. The helicopter passed below.

"We see it," the pilot said. He did a short circle, then came back and hovered. "We're over the target. We're sending a man down."

We watched the rescuer descend slowly, dangling from the end of a cable as they winched him through the air, until he disappeared below tree cover. Agonizing minutes went by with no communication from the pilot.

"Why is this taking so long?" Elizabeth said.

"Goddamn it," Carpenter said into his radio. "Has he found anything?"

"It's a child," the pilot said. "A boy. We're assuming it's Henry English."

Assuming it's Henry English. Elizabeth's fingernails dug into my arm. My stomach roiled as we waited for the condition of the body.

Our radios squawked again.

"We're sending down a stretcher," the pilot said. "He's unconscious, got a broken arm and a broken leg and God knows what other injuries. But Henry English is alive."

Elizabeth turned to me, eyes brimming and locked on mine. Then her head drooped and her knees buckled. I caught her before she hit the ground.

CHAPTER

46

Paul

I BOOKED A LATE afternoon flight to Denver. Elizabeth had called in the middle of the night. She was beaten up, Eddie Marsh was dead. Alex might not make it. And the search was back on for Henry.

I rousted Nick out of bed, put toast and cereal on the table when I heard him in the shower. He came downstairs dressed in his school uniform but barefoot, hair still wet. I poured us glasses of orange juice and sat across from him. Never exactly chipper that early in the morning, he looked more tired than usual. He hunched over his cereal bowl, elbows on the table, head resting on his left hand, spoon in the right. He slurped a mouthful of cereal and, milk running down his chin, said, "When is Mom coming home?"

I picked up a napkin, leaned across the table, and wiped his face. He grabbed the napkin from my hand.

"Geez, Dad. I'm not a baby."

"I know, buddy." I took a couple of drinks of orange juice. "So, there's been a change of plans."

He looked at me, eyes immediately tearing up.

"What do you mean a change of plans?"

I took a deep breath, thought, *Shit, how do you talk to a ten-year-old about this?*

"I don't want you to be scared. Everything's going to be okay. Mom had an accident and broke her wrist, but she's fine."

He put down his spoon. "Does she have a cast on it?"

"I think so."

"So she can't come home today? It may be tomorrow?"

"Actually, I'm going out there. This afternoon."

He looked at me for a minute, mouth open, then sat up straight and folded his arms. "I'm going with you."

"I think it will be better if you stay here. I'll pack your clothes and stuff, and you can stay with Aunt Kathleen. That way you won't miss any school or soccer."

"I don't care if I miss school or soccer. I'm going with you."

I pushed back from the table, went to the sink, and rinsed my glass. I stood looking out the window at the backyard. The water in the pool was algae-green, the bottom covered with bamboo leaves. I couldn't remember the last time I'd cleaned it. The hummingbirds had gone south, their sugar-crusted feeders still half-full of cloudy syrup. Rivulets of mud from the last rain had dried and hardened on the patio. It was the first of October, and temperatures in Houston were expected to hit the low nineties.

"It's a little more complicated than that," I said.

"Of course it is. You never tell me anything."

I turned to face him. "They caught the man who took Henry."

He suddenly looked sick.

"Is he in jail?"

"He's dead. Ranger Monroe shot him."

"Where's Henry?"

"They're looking for him."

"He wasn't with the man?"

"No. But they have some clues about where to find him."

Nick's mouth began to tremble.

"Is he dead?"

"We don't know. We hope they'll find him alive."

Nick burst into tears. I went to him, lifted him out of his chair, then sat down and pulled him into my lap. We sat like that for a while, then he spoke, his voice muffled in my chest.

"I'm going with you, Dad. You can't stop me."

"Okay, buddy. We'll go together."

* * *

I let Nick's school know he would be gone for a few days, then sent emails to my professors saying the same. We packed our bags, locked up the house, and headed for the airport.

Tension fairly radiated from Nick's body. Everything upset him—the long security lines, the rude TSA agents, the lukewarm burger he ate while we waited at the gate. His eyes welled up when he dripped ketchup on his shirt, and he finally lost it when he couldn't get his suitcase into the overhead bin. I shoved it in, then sat beside him and took his hand. He rested his head on my shoulder and as soon as we'd taken off, was asleep. I woke him on the final approach into Denver.

When the plane touched down, I turned on my phone. Elizabeth had called. I listened to her voice mail.

"Paul, call me the minute you land." She was crying. "They found Henry. He's alive."

Heart thumping, I punched her number. She picked up on the second ring.

"They found him?"

"Yes." She could hardly talk.

My hands started to tremble. For a moment I thought I might pass out. I leaned forward, rested my elbows on my knees, and forced myself to breathe.

"Where is he?"

"Denver General. Monroe and I are almost there."

"What's his condition?"

"I don't know all of it. Broken leg, broken arm, some internal injuries."

"Jesus."

"I need to hang up. We're at the hospital."

"Okay. We'll pick up the rental car and meet you there."

"Is Nick with you?"

"Yeah. No way he was staying home."

"Good. Call me when you get to the hospital, and I'll tell you where to meet us."

I put my phone in my pocket, took a deep breath, and looked up. The plane was almost empty. I turned to Nick. He was staring at me wide-eyed, terrified. I rubbed his head.

"They found him," I said. "Let's go see your little brother."

* * *

Elizabeth was in the surgery waiting area. She stood and waved when she saw us. Her left arm was in a sling and holy shit, her face was bad. Black eyes, cuts, swollen lips. I thought Nick might lose it again, but he held her tight for a minute, then leaned back.

"Sit down, Mom. Dad and I are here to take care of you and Henry."

She squeezed him again. "I'm so glad you're here."

"How is he?" I said.

"They have to remove his spleen and do some repair work on his arm. Sew up a couple of deep cuts. He had pine needles and rock fragments stuck in his hands. They think somehow he was able to break his fall and that's what saved him."

I had to sit down.

"I knew it," Nick said. "I knew he'd be okay."

It wasn't until then that I realized the small crowd milling around Elizabeth were with her. Detective Carpenter and a dozen or so people who shook our hands and introduced themselves as part of the search and rescue team, their names and faces all a blur.

"Where's Monroe?" I said.

"In the ICU with Alex."

"Oh, Jesus. I forgot about Alex. She's here?"

Elizabeth nodded. "They think she's out of the woods."

It was after midnight when the surgeon came out. He looked at our group, Nick asleep with his head in Elizabeth's lap, most of the others slouched in their chairs and dozing awkwardly, and said, "Mom and Dad?"

I stood. Elizabeth gingerly slid out from under Nick and did the same. The doctor shook our hands.

"He's out of surgery and doing fine." He explained the procedures they'd done, and that Henry would need to be in the hospital for a while before we moved him to Houston.

"He'll need physical therapy and time, of course. But he should come out of this with no permanent disabilities. It's incredible, really, after all he's been through. He's one tough little guy."

"Is he awake?" Elizabeth said.

"Just starting to wake up and complaining that he's thirsty. They'll come get you in a few minutes."

He held out his hand. "I'm very happy for your family."

We thanked him and watched as he walked down the hall and disappeared around a corner. I turned to Elizabeth and we looked at each other silently. I reached for her and she came to me. We put our arms around each other and rocked slowly side to side.

* * *

It was another thirty minutes or so until the nurse came out to get us. We left Nick sleeping in the waiting room under the watchful eye of Detective Carpenter and followed the nurse into the recovery room. She led us to the only occupied bed. And there he was.

Henry. Head wrapped in gauze, right arm and left leg in casts, perched in the center of a sea of bed and blankets. I'd forgotten how small he was. He was propped up, sucking apple juice from a straw, still groggy. The nurse holding the cup handed it to Elizabeth and stepped aside. Elizabeth bent and pressed her lips to

Henry's cheek and whispered something. She offered him the straw, and he took a long slurp. He paused, the straw dangling from a corner of his mouth, and looking a little puzzled, squinted up at Elizabeth. Then he gave her a gap-toothed grin.

"Hi, Mommy. This juice is really good."

C H A P T E R

47

Nick, Epilogue

HENRY WAS IN the hospital in Denver for two weeks. Mom stayed with him, but Dad and I had to go home after a few days. I tried to get Mom to let me stay longer but she said, "No, school is important." I knew she'd say that.

At least I got to hang out with Henry some in his hospital room. He slept a lot, but I turned on the TV real quiet and watched a lot of stuff that I don't get to watch at home. Like Jerry Springer, which Mom was not happy about when she came back from a meeting with the doctors and caught me with it on.

Ranger Monroe was hanging around a lot. He spent a lot of time with Aunt Alex, and I got to see her, too. The first time he came into Henry's room, I was there. He went over to Henry's bed and shook his hand, the one not in the cast. Ranger Monroe didn't say anything for a while, he just looked at Henry and then he kind of swallowed a few times and said, "Henry English, I am glad to make your acquaintance."

When Henry finally came home, it was on a *private jet*. One of the dads in Henry's class is president of an oil company, and he sent the jet to pick up Henry and Mom. How cool is that. Dad and I went to the airport, and the plane was in this private hangar. They rolled Henry off in a wheelchair and Mom came out, then the pilots, and I got to go inside the jet and take a look around. It was awesome. It had big leather seats and tables, and trays of sandwiches and drinks and a big bowl with like fifteen different kinds of candy bars and gum. One of the pilots got a bag and dumped the whole bowl into it and told me to take it home and share with Henry. And Mom saw it and didn't even say anything!

There was a big surprise when they got home. The neighbors and a bunch of kids and parents and teachers from school decorated our yard with balloons and signs that said, "Welcome Home Henry." They brought a bunch of food, and I was hoping that we'd have a big party. But Dad said no, it would be better to give Henry some quiet time at home, so they just brought all the stuff over then left.

Henry didn't have to go back to school until January. Mom had tutors for him that whole school year and he ended up not having to repeat first grade. I mean, he was reading chapter books in kindergarten, so he was already ahead of a lot of kids. And I looked at his homework and it's not like there's anything very hard about first grade.

It was awesome when Henry came back to school. We had an assembly to welcome him back, and he got to sit up on the stage in his wheelchair, which he still used sometimes when he got tired. And I got to sit up there with him. At the end of the assembly, he pushed up out of his wheelchair and balanced on his right leg, not the one he'd broken but the other one, and he pumped his fist in the air. And everybody stood up and clapped and cheered.

So it was awesome to have Henry back, but things were still kind of hard. Like when he couldn't play baseball in the spring, he was really sad. But everyone says he'll be able to play next year, and I told him he'll probably hit three home runs in his first game. And like the time we were sitting at breakfast eating scrambled eggs and wheat toast and I asked Mom if we could get Froot Loops and Lucky Charms the next time at the grocery store because those are Henry's favorites and I thought maybe she'd say yes. And Henry started to cry and said he hates Froot Loops and Lucky Charms. Mom sat him in her lap and rocked him and I said, "Okay, we don't have to get Froot Loops and Lucky Charms."

I saw Miss Cindy for the rest of the school year, but only once a week. Henry still talks to someone like Miss Cindy, but not at school. Even Mom and Dad are getting some counseling.

It's been almost a year since that hike to Sky Pond. We came back to Estes Park this summer, but we haven't done any hiking. Dad said maybe we should skip Colorado this year and Mom said he was right, but Henry said he wanted to come. I think they were kind of afraid when we opened the door to the cabin for the first time and went in. But Henry looked around, then he went to his room and when he came out he was holding something behind his back and I was pretty sure I knew what it was, but I didn't say anything. He came up close to me, yelled, "Prepare to die," then he pulled out his Nerf gun and shot me like five times. And I went to get my Nerf gun, and after that being in Colorado was okay.

But the coolest thing was the main reason we came to Estes Park. Aunt Alex and Ranger Monroe got married! Only Ranger Monroe's not a ranger anymore. I'm not sure why, but Mom said it was something like mutual agreement between him and his boss. But it's cool because he's running for sheriff in the fall, and everyone says he'll win.

Aunt Alex only came back to Houston to quit her job and sell her house and put all her furniture in storage. She moved in with Ranger Monroe, and they're building a house up on a mountain that should be ready before winter. We went over to Ranger Monroe's house one night, and we sat out on the porch while him and Aunt Alex finished cooking dinner. We could hear a lot of laughing from the kitchen and what I'm pretty sure was a lot of kissing, and Henry started acting like he was kissing me on the lips and I was trying to push him away until Mom told him to stop. On the way home after dinner, Mom said, "It's a little cramped in that cabin," and Dad said, "Yeah, well, they don't need a lot of space right now."

The wedding was at our house in Estes Park. Mom worked like crazy with Aunt Alex and the caterers. They set up a big tent in the yard, and tables with flowers. Aunt Alex's mom and dad came from Georgia, and her two brothers and their wives and little kids. Ranger Monroe's daughter was there with her family, and a bunch of other people like park rangers and Detective Carpenter. There was a big party after the wedding, with a band that went really late and most of the grownups except Mom had a lot to drink and everyone was dancing and having a great time.

But the best part of it was the wedding ceremony, even though the church part is not usually my favorite part. It wasn't really a church, because it was outside, but it was set up kind of like a church, with the preacher standing under an arch of flowers. Aunt Alex was beautiful, and Ranger Monroe looked really cool in a tux and cowboy boots, and after they kissed and were pronounced husband and wife, Aunt Alex lifted up her dress and showed off her cowboy boots, too, and everybody laughed and clapped.

It was a small wedding party, just two people standing up with Aunt Alex and Ranger Monroe.

Mom was matron of honor.

Henry was best man.

ACKNOWLEDGMENTS

Thank you to my editor, Marcia Markland, who found this book and brought it to life. You saw how to make it better and I'm so grateful for your insight and sage advice.

Thank you to the talented, hard-working and dedicated people at Crooked Lane Books: Thaisheemarie Fantauzzi Pérez, Rebecca Nelson, Julia Abbott, and everyone on the art, production and design, and marketing teams.

Thank you to my family, my friends, and my neighbors for your love and the joy you bring me.

Gabe and Zach, without you there would have been no Nick and Henry.

And last, thank you to my husband David, for being my first and constant reader, and for your unwavering support and encouragement.